ENTWINED

KNIGHTS OF 2 BRETHREN

Books by Jody Hedlund

Knights of Brethren Series
Enamored
Entwined
Ensnared
Enriched
Enflamed
Entrusted

The Fairest Maidens Series
Beholden
Beguiled
Besotted

The Lost Princesses Series
Always: Prequel Novella
Evermore
Foremost
Hereafter

Noble Knights Series
The Vow: Prequel Novella
An Uncertain Choice
A Daring Sacrifice
For Love & Honor
A Loyal Heart
A Worthy Rebel

Waters of Time Series
Come Back to Me
Never Leave Me
Stay With Me

The Colorado Cowboys
A Cowboy for Keeps
The Heart of a Cowboy

To Tame a Cowboy
Falling for the Cowgirl
The Last Chance Cowboy

The Bride Ships Series
A Reluctant Bride
The Runaway Bride
A Bride of Convenience
Almost a Bride

The Orphan Train Series
An Awakened Heart: A Novella
With You Always
Together Forever
Searching for You

The Beacons of Hope Series
Out of the Storm: A Novella
Love Unexpected
Hearts Made Whole
Undaunted Hope
Forever Safe
Never Forget

The Hearts of Faith Collection
The Preacher's Bride
The Doctor's Lady
Rebellious Heart

The Michigan Brides Collection
Unending Devotion
A Noble Groom
Captured by Love

Historical
Luther and Katharina
Newton & Polly

KNIGHTS OF 2 BRETHREN

JODY HEDLUND

NORTHERN LIGHTS PRESS

Entwined
Northern Lights Press
© 2021 Copyright
Jody Hedlund
Jody Hedlund Print Edition

ISBN 978-1-7337534-9-4

www.jodyhedlund.com

Scripture quotations are taken from the King James Version of the Bible.

This is a work of historical reconstruction; the appearances of certain historical figures are accordingly inevitable. All other characters are products of the author's imagination. Any resemblance to actual events or locales or persons, living or dead, is entirely coincidental.

Cover Design by Roseanna White Designs
Cover images from Shutterstock
Interior Map Design by Jenna Hedlund

TUNDRA SEA
N
W
E
S
St. Olaf's
Abbey
Frozen
Wilds
The Hundreds
Finnmark
Golden
Plateau
NORVEGIA
SNOWDEN
MOUNTAIN
RANGE
SWAINE
DARK SEA
HARDANGER FOREST
Romsdal
ATLAS RIVER
BLOOD RIVER
Moors of
Many Lakes
Wahlburg
Castle
Valley of
Red Dragons
Richlande
Lowlands
Vordinberg
Bay of
Fire
Ostby
Sound
Cimbrian
Strait
WHITE SEA
UTHELANDE
Cimbrian Peninsula
THE WEND

Chapter

1

∽

ANSGAR

"THE KING IS NOT HIMSELF." I HUNCHED OVER THE TABLE AND kept my voice low. "He has an ailing that goes beyond his injuries."

My five closest companions from the Knights of Brethren were huddled around the table with me, their expressions somber, the overcast morning adding to the gravity.

I glanced over my shoulder toward the door of the antechamber. We oft congregated in the small, private room to discuss matters of the kingdom's safety. However, for a reason I couldn't explain, the meeting place off the great hall no longer felt secure, as if somehow the door and walls were listening to our conversations and conveying them to the entire world.

"He deteriorates more every day," I said. "In fact, the deterioration is happening much too swiftly. We need to determine why."

The king had sustained multiple injuries in the battle a month ago against Swaine, but his chain mail had prevented the assassin's knife from penetrating his innards. While he'd suffered lacerations and severe bruising, which had made movement difficult in the early days of his recuperation, his wounds were healing.

Why, then, was he growing weaker, especially in his mental capacity?

The question taunted me and was clamoring louder with each passing day.

Kristoffer rubbed his smoothly shaven chin, the only one of our group without facial scruff. "'Tis possible his humors are out of balance—too much black bile, leading to this melancholic state." As the most learned among our Knights of Brethren, I could always count on Kristoffer to keep us well informed.

For all his education, Kristoffer couldn't compare to Maxim, the wisest and most intelligent man I'd ever met. If only he were with us. He would diagnose the king's illness and devise a solution all in one breath.

As it was, I hadn't heard from Maxim since we'd parted ways on the bank of the Atlas River during our hasty retreat from the Valley of Red Dragons after the fighting. He'd put his own life at risk by riding to the frontline to inform me of the plot to kill the king. In addition to learning about the king's danger, Maxim had discovered Princess Elinor was in peril and had subsequently taken her into hiding.

At least, that's what I wanted to believe, although I had no proof of where he'd gone or why. I couldn't yet accept the current theory making its way through court that Maxim had kidnapped the princess. Not after the honor and self-sacrifice he'd displayed.

The fact that King Ulrik adamantly blamed Maxim only confirmed the decline of his faculties. The intelligent and kindhearted king who'd earned the name Ulrik the Good had never assumed the worst about people. Previously, he'd waited to form judgment until he had solid evidence.

He'd also accused Maxim of orchestrating the murder attempt against him. Such an allegation was false, even ludicrous. I'd been there in the middle of the combat. I'd witnessed everything, including the desperation in Maxim's expression as he'd warned me of the impending danger.

The truth was, without Maxim's intervention, the king would have suffered more than surface wounds. He would have died. Maxim was a hero, not a criminal.

My efforts at reasoning with the king and relaying facts from that day had only been met with sullen resistance instead of sound judgment. And for the first time since coming to court as one of his elite knights, I'd grown hesitant in speaking to him with my usual frankness.

"Could someone be poisoning him?" I asked, although I didn't know how such a thing was possible since I was testing his food and drink.

"If poison, he would likely already be dead." To my right, Sigfrid fiddled with the fletching of an arrow on the table in front of him. "Perhaps the physicians missed an internal injury."

To my left, Torvald gripped the hilt of his sword, his jaw tight and his lips pressed in a thin line. Across the table Espen and Gunnar sat on either side of Kristoffer, all of us attired simply in dark-brown tunics and hose, leather belts, and calf-length leather boots.

We made up six of the ten Knights of Brethren, the brave group chosen to guard the king in battle and serve as his bodyguards during times of peace. As the Grand

Marshal, the leader of the Brethren, I was cognizant that we shouldn't be meeting without the entire group of ten. But I no longer trusted all the knights, especially now that we'd gained new members.

"Whatever is wrong with the king"—I dropped my voice to a whisper—"we must uncover it."

Gunnar drummed his thumbs on the table. "Perhaps we ought to collaborate with the Noble Council and inform them of our concern." With his older brother on the council, Gunnar had connections to the group of noblemen closest to the king. In addition, Gunnar had an easy way about him that many people liked, making him a natural liaison.

At the slap of passing footsteps outside the chamber, Kristoffer paused before responding. "Do we know if we can trust everyone on the council?"

Torvald gave a curt shake of his head. "We cannot trust anyone at this point."

"I say we come up with a test," Gunnar interjected. "And let's flush out who's faithful to the king and who's not."

"What kind of test do you propose?" I asked.

Gunnar shrugged.

Kristoffer glanced around the table at the others, giving them a chance to voice their thoughts before making another suggestion. "One of us could feign interest in plotting against the king, drop crumbs of malcontent. Those who are already conniving against him will most certainly attempt to gain another ally."

"You're suggesting that one of us spy?" Gunnar's eyes lit with the prospect of being that spy. But such a role would be dangerous, and only someone with a façade of stone, like Torvald, could pull it off.

As if sensing the direction of my thoughts, Torvald sat straighter. "I'll do it."

Before I could respond, the chamber door swung open. At the sight of the king, we pushed back from our chairs and stood.

"Your Majesty." I bowed my head in his direction, but not before I caught sight of others behind the king, including the remaining four Knights of Brethren and Rasmus.

"And what exactly are you men doing in the meeting chamber by yourselves?" The king's voice rose with uncharacteristic anger. A bulky, muscular man, the king had always been imposing, but now, slouched and shuffling, he appeared to have aged well beyond his fifty years. His tunic was stained, his doublet unbuttoned, and his light-brown hair was disheveled as if he hadn't been properly groomed.

The king couldn't have known we were having a private discussion unless someone had informed him, likely in an effort to undermine my authority. The king knew I was a man of integrity, and the best way to manage this situation was to speak honestly. "We believe that your life continues to be in danger, Your Majesty, quite possibly from someone within the ranks of your trusted staff. Thus, we were discussing how we might eliminate the threat."

The room was shadowed, lit by a single candle on the table. The wind rattled the shutters that were battened to keep out the cold draft that had blown in as October turned into November. 'Twould not be long now, ere southern Norvegia was blanketed in snow.

In the dim lighting, the king's face appeared thinner, more haggard, and paler.

I loathed that the king was suffering. And I blamed myself. I was tasked with not only leading the other knights, but with keeping the king safe, guarding his life above my own, and sacrificing myself for him.

Somehow, despite my most rigorous efforts, I'd failed. I'd failed during the battle to see the danger among our own ranks. And I was clearly failing again to protect him from the threat within the royal residence.

Familiar frustration wound through me. I hated failure, and lately it was following me like a hound sniffing its prey.

The king wobbled and pressed a hand to his forehead, as though dizzy. Or truly unwell, as I suspected.

I hastened to the king's side, but one of the new knights reached him first. Gotfred. The dark-haired, dark-eyed knight was tall, well built, and seemed to have the fortitude required of the Brethren. Even so, knights were selected to be part of the Brethren based on valor in battle, and Gotfred hadn't fought in the recent confrontation with Swaine. I doubted he had any fighting experience other than upholding peace among his clansmen.

The young knight had obviously been chosen because he was Rasmus's nephew. As one of the seven Royal Sages, Rasmus had earned his position from years of education and demanding work. I couldn't deny he was wise. But he was also crafty. And if Maxim had been correct, Rasmus was behind the threat against the king in the recent battle.

Though I'd protested Gotfred's selection a fortnight ago, the king had gone forward with the decision anyway, disregarding my opinions on the matter as if I'd never spoken.

At that point, I should have realized something wasn't right with the king, but I'd never questioned the king's decisions, having grown to respect and trust him deeply. I'd assumed the pain of his injuries was affecting his ability to reason. But now, after repeated uncharacteristic behavior, I had to finally admit something more was going on.

Gotfred gently tucked the king's hand through his arm as if he were a son and had every right to assist the king so personally. "Your Majesty, would you like to sit?"

"No." The king glanced around, his eyes filling with confusion as though he didn't know where he was or what was happening.

Rasmus stepped to his other side. In his black scholarly robe and long black cap that hung down into a tasseled tip, the Royal Sage's dark eyes were always shadowed, as if the shutters to his soul were closed tightly. Since the king's return from battle, Rasmus had hovered near the king, like a worried parent with a sick child.

I had the sudden urge to secret the king away from Vordinberg and away from the danger, perhaps to one of his summer estates along the northern coast. Or perhaps I could hide him in an abbey until he was well. Would doing so help him? Or would failure trail after me?

More likely, I'd be accused of kidnapping the same way Maxim had.

Rasmus swept his gaze over the six of us before focusing on me. "We believe the king's life continues to be in danger too, possibly from someone within the ranks of his trusted staff."

I didn't look away. Rasmus was using my words from moments ago against me, twisting them to turn me into a suspect. He was wise enough to know my loyalty to the king was genuine. He couldn't believe I was capable of treachery, could he?

"Yes," the king spoke, his eyes clearing of confusion. "Someone is plotting against me, someone I trust. And I believe we are getting closer to uncovering who." The king narrowed his eyes upon me with his last statement.

My chest pinched. Surely the king didn't mean me. Not after how faithfully I'd served him over the past four years. I'd devoted myself to him and the other knights wholeheartedly, leaving no room in my life for anything else. I'd given myself to the task without reservation.

His Royal Majesty had always praised me for my loyalty. How could he turn against me now?

He glared at me a moment longer, then turned his attention to Rasmus. "You were right as usual, Rasmus. Unfortunately, I do not know whom I can trust anymore."

The Royal Sage was the one the king shouldn't be trusting. But how could I say so when I still had no proof of Rasmus's involvement in the assassination attempt? Not when he'd shifted the blame of every problem to Maxim. The real question was, why was Rasmus undermining me and the other knights who were most loyal to the king? Did he hope the king would eliminate us? And if so, why?

"Your Majesty." I had to try once again to help the king see reason. "I have done everything in my power to remain steadfast to you. I have always spoken the truth and nothing less. And I shall remain honest with you now and forevermore."

Rasmus waved a hand at me as though to silence me. "Sneaking around behind the king's back in clandestine meetings is hardly honest."

"We seek only the king's highest good, Your

Excellency." Even as I spoke, doubt remained etched on the faces of the Knights of Brethren standing behind the king and Rasmus. Perhaps our meeting did seem suspect. If everyone else chose not to believe us, I would have to labor all the harder to prove we were faithful.

Gotfred, still at the king's side, regarded us with contempt. "We can escort Sir Ansgar and his compatriots from the royal residence, Your Majesty."

"No." My spine grew rigid at the prospect of leaving the king defenseless. I couldn't let Rasmus cast me out. At the moment, nothing was more important than staying close to the king and exposing the real threat. "The king knows we are more than trustworthy, that we would die for him. He has naught to fear from us." As I spoke, I locked eyes with the king, once again hoping he'd see the earnestness of my declaration.

He wavered, the same confusion as earlier flitting across his features. "You're a good man, Ansgar Nordheim." He spoke and then spun back toward the door. Without another word, he exited.

The others filed out after him, but Gotfred and Rasmus lingered behind, watching the group of us warily. "Should we rid the castle of the lot of them, Uncle?"

The title of address was informal, and I expected Rasmus to rebuke Gotfred and demand the respect due his position. But the Royal Sage's expression remained as impassive as always. If the offense bothered him, he didn't show it. He inclined his head toward me and spoke softly, without a trace of emotion. "Henceforth, if you have concerns about the king, you must come to me in order that we might work together."

Work together? What did he mean? Was this an underhanded means of threatening me to cooperate with him? Since he hadn't been able to eliminate the king at the battle, was he hoping now to make the king his pawn, to control him and rule through him?

I stifled a shudder at the prospect. I didn't want to imagine Norvegia under the control of a man like Rasmus. But from what I could see, his influence was growing as the king's seemed to decrease.

I bowed my head, neither accepting nor declining Rasmus's invitation. My gut told me I would do best to steer far away from Rasmus. But at the same time, if I angered him, I feared he would make sure I never had access to the king again.

As he turned to go, his expression gave nothing away. I could only watch him depart with a strange feeling of being trapped. Gotfred followed Rasmus. Once they were gone, Gunnar opened his mouth, likely ready to spew his dislike for Rasmus and Gotfred. But I cut him off with a curt shake of my head.

We could no longer gather here in the castle. Instead, we needed to have our discussions elsewhere to evade Rasmus and his spies. In the meantime, we would have to pretend to comply with Rasmus.

While I didn't speak the words of instruction aloud, the expressions of my closest companions told me they understood my directive.

As we exited the chamber, one of the castle stewards approached and handed me a small piece of parchment rolled up and tied with twine. "A message, sire."

When the steward strode away with no interest in what was inside, I guessed he—or perhaps Rasmus—had already read it.

"Who delivered it?" I called.

"A street urchin," he replied over his shoulder.

Which meant the writer of the message wanted to remain anonymous. I untied the note and read it aloud. "'I am a secret admirer and would like to meet you. Please come to the Dragon Tavern at high noon.'"

Gunnar and Espen both whistled, grins lighting up their faces. The two had no trouble with the ladies. With how handsome and charming they were, maidens flocked to them.

Torvald, Kristoffer, and Sigfrid were popular among the ladies too, mainly because of their status as firstborn sons and the accompanying wealth and titles. The three had recently participated in Princess Elinor's weeklong courtship in which twelve of the most eligible firstborn noblemen of marriageable age competed with one another to become the next king.

Princess Elinor hadn't ended up choosing any of the men and had invoked the Sword of the Magi for help in finding her husband. The engraving on the sword indicated that the man who wielded the sword would be worthy of being king. So far, none of the noblemen who'd come from all over the kingdom had been able to loosen the ancient relic from the cedar box that held it.

Recently, we'd learned the law was being changed so that any man, whether noble or common, could attempt to pull the sword free, marry Princess Elinor, and become the next king.

A commoner marry royalty? A commoner become the next king? The idea was preposterous. But already the chieftains—including my oldest brother—and the Royal Sages had agreed to amend the law. A majority vote from the Noble Council would make it official. The council had yet to gather, but with the king supporting the change, everyone believed it would happen soon, likely within the next month.

"Are you going to meet your secret admirer?" Gunnar asked, his grin still wide. "If not, I shall go in your stead."

I was tempted to hand Gunnar the note and give him leave to seek out the maiden for me, but I hesitated. Why would a maiden want to meet at the Dragon Tavern? Taverns weren't places women frequented. Why not pick the Stavekirche or city center or even the waterfront?

"Probably a rich young noblewoman trysting without her father's knowledge, hoping to win your heart," Gunnar teased, shaking his head and sending his overlong dark-brown hair off his forehead.

"Soon enough we'll be able to marry those *rich young noblewomen*." Espen clamped my shoulder. Like me, Espen was one of the few Knights of Brethren who wasn't nobly born and instead belonged to the northern clans.

"Even if the law is changed," I said, "the nobility will still guard their status. No baron or earl will give his daughter to a commoner. Tell me I am wrong about the matter."

"You are not wrong," Kristoffer answered. "Though I would gladly give you each my daughters if I had them, most of the nobility will attempt to keep the current boundaries in place."

I nodded. "Laws may change, but traditions will remain the same."

"You are too serious, my friend." Gunnar laughed. "At the very least, go and have fun. You deserve it."

Gunnar was never one to pass up an opportunity to make merry or meet with maidens. He spent most of his free time doing that very thing. But he knew how I felt, that I had no wish to be in a relationship and give a woman false hope of a future together, not when I intended to serve the king for as long as I had life and breath.

But this time, with this note, I sensed something deeper was happening. I couldn't yet put the clues together, but I needed to explore further.

"If you have a mind to meet your admirer," Gunnar said, "I shall go with you. No doubt she'll have a lady companion needing attention."

I couldn't afford to draw suspicion, not when I was already suspect and would likely be followed. Taking Gunnar would add credibility to my journey. "Very well. You may join me."

Torvald's stoic expression registered surprise. He had the same viewpoint I did about getting into relationships. The two of us had oft remained at the castle while the other knights frequented taverns and public houses for the pleasure of mingling with maidens. Torvald and I had played many games of chess while the others were out.

I needed to provide an excuse for why I was reconsidering my position, hopefully one Torvald would be able to see through. I tossed out the first I could find. "If my days are numbered as one of the king's knights, I might have need of a wife soon. I may as well begin the process of meeting maidens." If the doors and walls truly had ears, then my explanation would hopefully sound reasonable enough.

I just prayed I wasn't walking into a trap.

Chapter 2

Ansgar

WHAT IF I'D BEEN A FOOL TO ANSWER THE MESSAGE?

I flexed my fingers around my reins, loosening my grip as if that would ease the tension radiating through me. The narrow street was moderately busy at midday, with tradesmen selling their wares and townspeople coming and going among the businesses. Now with the colder weather, fewer shops had stalls outside, which made the progress down from the castle into town easier and less time-consuming.

Most buildings were constructed of sturdy Norwegian timber that could withstand the cold and wet winters. They were brightly painted, a tradition that helped imbue color and cheer through the long winter months. The paint also added an extra layer of protection against the elements, preventing the wood from easily rotting.

Ahead, amidst the signs jutting out above the establishments, a picture of a dragon marked the spot of the Dragon Tavern. Though the sun was hidden behind the clouds, I guessed high noon had just passed, that

Gunnar and I were only a little late.

We'd changed out of our Brethren attire and donned plain garments and simple cloaks to draw less attention. Even so, upon our muscular steeds, people stopped to stare, and I tugged my hood farther over my face, hoping to stay anonymous. Once word spread that I was visiting in the area, men, women, and children alike would crowd around, hoping for a glimpse or a word.

Upon reaching the tavern, I halted, my attention returning to the sign. The dragon was red. Did that mean something?

Red dragon. Red draco. As we dismounted, my thoughts veered in a direction I'd steadfastly refused to venture for the past month. A direction that involved images of a beautiful maiden and her red draco.

Lis.

As Gunnar gave our horses over to the care of our squire, I pictured Lis standing in the stern of the longboat, her reddish-gold hair blowing in the wind, her face pointed to the sky. She'd commanded the red draco during our retreat from the battle. Of course, I hadn't let on to Lis or anyone that I knew of her unique ability. I might not have noticed if Maxim hadn't hinted that I'd be glad for Lis's assistance.

The moment we arrived back in Vordinberg and disembarked, I'd lost track of Lis in my haste to deliver the king to the royal residence and his physicians. By the time I returned to the waterfront, she'd gone, and no one had any knowledge of her whereabouts.

I'd searched only a little before deciding my motives in finding her were too mixed. I'd tried to convince myself I only wanted to thank her. But I hadn't been able to deny my desire to look upon her one last time.

Her absence had been for the best. Seeing her again would have incited longings I didn't want to have, ones that were incompatible for a knight who never planned to take a wife.

Besides, it wasn't as if we'd become friends during the voyage to the capital city. Instead, we'd mostly kept to our respective ends of the vessel.

Lis had shown no interest in me. In fact, she'd seemed as intent in keeping her distance from me and the other men as I was in keeping my distance from women. Her attitude, so unlike most ladies at court, intrigued me. I wasn't used to being ignored or rebuffed or contradicted. Lis did all three, and I liked her better for it.

"Ready?" Standing beside me, Gunnar peered up at the sign too, his thumbs looped through his belt. "Or are we planning to stare at the sign the rest of the afternoon?"

With a grunt, I brushed past him up the short flight of stairs. I pushed open the door to a dimly lit dining room and the waft of spicy mead and fried fish greeted me. A few older patrons populated the tables. And from what I could see at first glance, the proprietor's wife was the only woman present. In the process of wiping a table, she planted a hand on her ample hip and sized us up.

I surveyed the room again, counting people and weapons along with locating an alternative exit. Taking an assessment of my surroundings had become second nature to me over the past few years of guarding the king. With the uncertainty regarding this meeting, I wanted to be prepared for anything, even a trap.

As I scanned each face, strange disappointment settled over me. Lis wasn't in sight. If not Lis, then who was my secret admirer?

"How can I be helping you, love?" The proprietor's wife returned to her scrubbing.

Gunnar stepped into the tavern behind me, and now, at the sight of both of us, the chatter dwindled to silence. Even with our simple attire, we were imposing figures. Although I was slightly taller than Gunnar, we were more muscular than ordinary men as a result of the drills and training we did daily to keep ourselves strong and fit.

"You hoping to meet with a secret admirer?" The woman tossed me another glance.

I guessed this woman was playing a part in the arranged meeting. "Do you know where she is?"

"A halfpence might help me remember."

I nodded at Gunnar, who opened his leather pouch, pulled out a coin, and flipped it onto the table in front of the proprietor's wife.

She picked it up and tucked it into her apron pocket. At the same time, she extricated a piece of parchment similar to the one I already had. "Here you are, love."

Gunnar crossed to the woman and retrieved the note. As he passed it to me, I could see the warning in his eyes. Whoever wanted to meet with me was going to great lengths to keep the exchange private. Now I needed to do the same.

Was it possible Maxim had come back to Vordinberg? Was this his doing? I prayed it was so and that he could help me bring a swift end to the growing trouble.

Quickly I unfolded and read the message: "Come alone to the lover's place that is dry but wet, quiet but loud, lonely but intimate."

Lover's place? Why would Maxim suggest such a location? Unless he intended to deceive anyone who might be spying on me. It would certainly continue the charade that I was meeting with a secret admirer.

I pulled out the nearest bench and lowered myself. As Gunnar took the seat across from me, I passed him the note.

He read it several times through.

"What do you think it means?" I whispered as the attention shifted away from us and conversations resumed.

"There are several places lovers go," he whispered in return.

Of course Gunnar would know the details about the places couples visited for time alone. Maybe most men knew. But I'd never frequented any such rendezvous spots.

The proprietor, a plump man with a long beard, approached our table carrying two mugs filled to the brim. As he plunked them down, mead sloshed over.

"Many thanks, my good man." Gunnar placed several more coins on the table.

The man didn't step back but instead looked directly at me. "The rumors are growing, sire. Some be saying the king is no longer in his right mind."

Did this man recognize me?

"We be praying you can keep 'im safe." He watched my face as though expecting me to admit to my connection with the king.

I lifted my mug and took a sip of mead.

"What think you, Sir Ansgar?" he persisted.

Inwardly I sighed. How long had my anonymity lasted? Maybe I'd only been fooling myself all along that I could ride through town without people guessing my identity. And how would I possibly leave this establishment undetected and convene with Maxim or whomever else was orchestrating the meeting?

Maybe instead of avoiding my biggest supporters, I'd simply have to use my popularity to my advantage and enlist the aid of this proprietor and other townspeople in making my escape.

An hour later, I directed an old cart and mule into the hills northeast of town. Wearing a merchant's cap, I pretended to be the proprietor in one of his worn cloaks, stuffed with a pillow to add to my girth. With the empty casks rattling in the wagon bed, I was on a mission to deliver them to a local farmer who brewed mead. With the disguise and help of the proprietor and his wife, I'd easily escaped out the back door of the tavern and traversed through town without anyone being the wiser for my deception—at least I hoped I had.

Now I paused and gauged the last of the distance until I reached the path leading to Lover's Lane. Many leaves had fallen, but those remaining were swirling around me, the wind causing them to rain down. I prayed I was in the right place and hadn't wasted the past hour of travel.

Gunnar had decided this out-of-the-way place fit the description of the riddle best. It was a dry path that ended in wet spray from the waterfall, a quiet route that resulted in loud rushing water and a lonely place outside of town, but it contained an intimate cave for a rendezvous.

Gunnar intended to tarry at the tavern until my return. If anyone came inside to spy on our doings, Gunnar would loudly complain that I was taking too long and ask the proprietor to ascend to the room I'd supposedly taken and tell me to hurry.

The false story embarrassed me. I didn't want rumors circulating that I was becoming a womanizer. I took pride in my example to other men on remaining above reproach when it came to temptation and lust. However, in this instance, I'd known no other way to sneak to Lover's Lane without anyone following me.

I breathed in the dampness of soil and decaying leaves and took note of the thickening evergreens and the rocky incline ahead. I'd reached the point where I would have to leave the mule and cart behind.

I hid them among the brush as Gunnar had instructed and shed my disguise. Then I wound my way up an overgrown path leading to the waterfall, taking in every detail. From what I could tell, only one person had ascended the trail ahead of me today.

Even so, I slowed my steps and withdrew my knife.

As I drew near the waterfall, the mist filled the air and the rushing water grew louder. I kept low in the brush beyond the riverbank, staying out of sight just in case someone was waiting to ambush me. When I reached the rocky path that led to the cavern behind the waterfall, I paused and examined a wet footprint.

It was too small to belong to a man of Maxim's size. Was it Lis's? Or had I wasted time in pursuing an amorous noblewoman who truly wished for a tryst?

I glanced back the way I'd come, the landscape eerily still, as though every creature had already gone into hibernation for the winter. I could only pray I was alone, that no one had followed me from the city.

Ducking my head under a rocky ledge, I followed a winding path until at last I stood behind the waterfall. The water seemed in a hurry, pouring over the ledge into the river below with a speed that never let up.

However, the spray was too wet, the noise level too loud, and the place too open. I honed in on the passageway that led deeper into the hill, away from the waterfall. It was narrow and dark. Did I dare traverse it without light?

What choice did I have?

With my knife at the ready, I crept forward. Thankfully, my eyes adjusted as the way grew murkier. When an expelled breath came from my immediate left, I feigned ignorance. Yet the moment I was one step beyond the person, I grabbed her and pressed my knife to her throat.

"What are you doing here?" I said in a low voice, searching the rest of the cavern for anyone else. As far as I could tell, this maiden was alone.

Teeth clamped down on my arm where my cloak fell away. Pain sparked hot.

Was she biting me? My surprise overshadowed the pain. And I knew with certainty that this was no enamored admirer. It had to be Lis.

Chapter
3

Lis

As Sir Ansgar removed his knife blade from my throat, I removed my teeth from his arm, and not a second sooner.

I wasn't letting down my guard with this man. Even if he'd proven himself to be valiant and noble during the time I'd watched him on the day-long journey to Vordinberg, he was still a stranger. Of course, I'd learned a great deal about him as I wandered about Vordinberg that day after the battle a month ago. Everyone everywhere talked about Sir Ansgar as if he was a hero. And women, young and old alike, swooned over him, gushing about his handsomeness and strength as if he were God's greatest creation of all time.

I couldn't deny he was easy to look upon. His clipped hair was light brown like toasted grain. His features were strong and chiseled, with a square jaw, broad cheeks, and a perfectly proportioned nose and forehead. His shoulders were thick, and his body sculpted with muscles. For a man of only twenty and four years, he carried himself with a commanding presence, one that demanded respect from his subordinates and yet was devoid of haughtiness.

As if all that hadn't been enough to set him apart, his eyes were his best feature. The brown was rich and deep, seeming to see everything all at once with the keenness of a good leader. And yet, at times they turned a golden brown, one that was almost mesmerizing and could draw a maiden in and make her feel as though she were drowning in sweet, thick honey.

Not that I'd felt that way. Well, maybe I had initially. And maybe that's why I'd remained in Vordinberg for a short while last month, because I'd wanted the chance to look into his eyes a final time before leaving.

Once I'd learned he had the same effect on all women, I tucked my tail between my legs and left the city, chagrined at how easily I'd fallen prey to his magnetism. I blamed my fascination on the fact that I was overly naïve for a woman of nineteen years.

I'd lived in isolation on our farm, and my father had been the one to travel into the closest village whenever we needed supplies we couldn't grow or make on our own. I'd stayed behind with my mother, especially in her later years when she'd become bedridden. She'd been a kind and sweet soul, teaching me to face adversity without complaint.

Only in the past two years as Father's health declined had I gone to the village to do the trading, a strange restlessness for more pushing me. Even there, the eligible young men hadn't struck my fancy the way

Sir Ansgar had. Almost from the moment of first seeing him upon the shores of the Atlas River, I'd been unable to ignore his compelling presence.

Now, here he was again. He'd come.

I'd hoped he would understand my clues and realize I was the one seeking him out for urgent matters. But if he believed I was a secret admirer, then I needed to correct him straightaway.

The darkness obscured his face, but enough light remained that I could see his outline. I grabbed the torch I'd prepared ahead of time and thrust it in the embers I'd brought from my campfire the previous night. The torch flamed to life, and I held it up so he could identify me.

The light also shone upon him, giving me full view of his face. He was more handsome than I'd remembered. Even though I'd tried not to think about him, he'd infiltrated my dreams these past weeks regardless.

He took me in, his gaze sweeping over my face, cloak, and down my peasant skirt. Had he expected a beautiful noblewoman to be waiting for him, ready to throw her arms around him and shower him with praise and affection?

Then he would surely be disappointed in seeing a plain farmer's daughter such as myself, especially when he learned I would offer him naught but a warning.

"'Tis I, Lis." For some reason, I wanted to comb the stray wisps of my hair back into my loose braid, and I wished I'd taken time to brush the dried bits of leaves from my skirt and cloak. "I accompanied the king's army during the retreat from the Valley of Red

Dragons nigh four weeks past."

His gaze drifted over my face again, lingering on my cheek line, down to my chin, and back up to my other cheek. "Yes, I remember and suspected the message was from you."

"Then you'll know I didn't summon you here as a secret admirer."

"And you'll know I didn't come seeking admiration."

"Good."

"Good." His eyes connected with mine.

The brown swirled with flecks of amber, flecks that sparked something inside me and made my insides hot and flustered.

This man. He was powerful. If I wasn't careful, I'd easily give him more sway over me than I wanted him to have. Maybe I already had. Maybe this craving for him had been secretly growing since I'd met him, influencing me to seek him out rather than someone else.

"I came to give you news," I said.

He sheathed his knife. "Very well. I give you leave to speak it."

Something about his request was dismissive, almost as though he was eager to hear what I had to say so he could be on his way. I straightened my shoulders. "I shall give you the news once you've proven worthy to hear it."

He paused, his eyes rounding just slightly, telling me my statement had been wholly unexpected. "Exactly what must I do to prove I'm worthy?" Once again, he regarded me in that molten way, one that left me strangely breathless.

He already was worthy. I'd seen enough on the day of battle to know it. Although the Norvegian forces had begun their retreat by the time I arrived, I'd still witnessed the fearless way he led his men, the bravery in the face of incredible odds, and the calmness of spirit in the midst of chaos. He'd operated without any thought of saving himself, with only one goal: protect the king.

Nevertheless, I didn't want him to think he could so easily capture my attention and then dismiss me at will. I threw out the first challenge that came to mind. "You must hunt and kill game before I do."

He gave me another once-over. "You're prepared to hunt?"

"I am." Would he discount me because I was a woman? Maybe among nobility in the capital, women were good for little but filling their roles as wives and mothers. But in the world where I'd been raised, women were essential for survival, aiding in planting crops, caring for livestock, fighting against predators, preserving food, and much more.

As an only child, I'd also learned to do the labor of a son.

"You're the firstborn child of Princess Blanche, sister of King Ulrik." Maxim's words from the day of the battle reverberated in the chambers of my mind. I couldn't be the firstborn of Princess Blanche. And Princess Elinor couldn't be my younger sister. Such prospects were inconceivable.

Why, then, had Maxim's declaration crowded my mind, giving rise to unnerving questions? Like, why was I an only child? Why had my parents waited until they were old to have a child?

I hadn't wanted to ask such questions of Father any more than I'd wanted to ask them of myself. But regardless of my efforts to ignore the questions, they'd persisted.

Sir Ansgar glanced around the cavern. "Have you a weapon?"

"My knife."

"Is that all?"

"'Tis all I need."

One of his brows rose. "Then you have no intention of summoning your draco?"

"'Tis not my draco." From my youngest days, Father and Mother had given me strict guidelines with Red. I'd already broken the rules not to be seen with Red and never, ever to communicate with him around others. But I'd had no choice while aboard the ship with the retreating Norvegian army. Not if I'd wanted to help save the king.

Sir Ansgar pulled himself up to his full height, nearly a foot taller than me and at least two of my widths. "I'll agree to your bargain if you agree to mine."

"No." I knew without him saying what his bargain would entail. He'd want to know more about Red.

"If you won't agree, then we have no deal."

"Then go."

"Very well." Without another glance, he spun and began to stride back through the passageway.

Would he really leave? Or was he simply manipulating me into accepting his bargain?

I watched his retreating back, straight and proud and solid. I waited for his steps to waver. But he continued without a break in his stride, leaving the cavern.

He'd come back. He wouldn't have risked so much to visit me only to leave without the information he sought. I waited a moment longer and then started after him.

As I passed the rushing waterfall and exited, I glimpsed him already well down the trail. My heart gave a thud.

I was manipulating him into accepting my bargain. Why should he not attempt the same with me? I need not tell him everything about Red. Nothing that might put me in danger. Only enough to satisfy his curiosity.

"Wait," I called.

He halted but didn't turn.

"What is your bargain?"

Slowly, he pivoted. The peasant cloak with its bulky hood cast shadows across his face, making the layer of facial hair on his jaw and cheeks darker. "Whoever loses the hunt shall dress and roast the game."

"And . . .?"

"And while we share a meal, we may ask each other three questions and only three."

Share a meal with this glorious specimen of a man? The prospect sent a tingle of pleasure dancing along my nerve endings. I would relish spending time with him. But why would he want to drag out his time with me?

"What if I do not wish to answer all three questions?"

"You must do so truthfully."

"And you vow to do the same?"

"I vow it."

I hesitated. I'd already learned bits and pieces about Sir Ansgar—about how his father, a clan chieftain, had died in a terrible logging accident, how his oldest brother had succeeded his father as chieftain, how Sir Ansgar maintained close ties to his kin and was known for his love and loyalty to his family.

Even if he hadn't already been so well respected, I sensed I could trust this man who'd pledged his life so fully to the king. His devotion was pure and true. Even the king had concluded the same and made him the youngest Grand Marshal to ever oversee the Knights of Brethren.

Sir Ansgar waited, his gaze unswerving upon me. His countenance held no ulterior motivation, giving me no reason to fear he meant for our meal to turn into anything more than a sharing of food and information.

"Yes."

He arched a brow.

"I accept your bargain." The words came out stiffly.

"Then let us begin the hunt."

I started forward. "We must stay within the vicinity of the riverbanks one hundred paces or less from the waterfall."

His keen eyes swept over the brush as though measuring distance. "We have scared all the game away."

"Not all."

"Not all?" Sir Ansgar unsheathed his knife and made his way to the water's edge. "What is left?"

I paused, unable to keep from looking at his rugged profile and unable to keep my heart from speeding in an erratic tempo. How was it possible for any one man to be so handsome?

He slowed his steps and raised his knife. "'Twould

seem you have an inclination toward cooking."

"Because I am a woman?"

"Because you appear content to stare at me rather than join in the hunt."

I rapidly bent and scoured the tall grass, pretending to search for prey. "I was analyzing your capability." My excuse was weak, but I had to defend myself somehow.

"And do I measure up?"

I didn't dare gaze at him again. He measured up and went way beyond. But I only shook my head with what I hoped was a look of exasperation. "Only time will tell."

"Time has a way of revealing the truth."

"Perhaps." I wasn't accustomed to giving in. My mother and father had indulged my every whim while I was growing up. I could admit that as an only child, I'd become rather strong-willed. Even so, they'd been good parents, and I owed them much for their love and care. Now that Mother was gone, Father needed me more than ever—all the more reason to put Maxim's words about my royal heritage far from my mind. I was content with my life on the farm, wasn't I? I had no wish to upset the path set out for me.

I treaded lightly to the river's edge and studied the tracks in the mud. From the corner of my eye, I could see Sir Ansgar do likewise. I'd seen several hare nibbling on the clover earlier and suspected a burrow was nearby.

Carefully, I plucked away the dry grass and fallen leaves, following prints and droppings to a hole burrowed in a tangle of brush. Testing the wind so the hare wouldn't catch my scent, I knelt a safe distance from the dark opening, my knife poised to thrust.

From my spot, I couldn't see Sir Ansgar. Even if I'd been able to watch him, I didn't dare take my attention from the burrow. I watched intently for long minutes, having learned patience and persistence over many years of hunting with Father.

The cascading of the waterfall and the rustling of the river drowned out my noise and Ansgar's, although the hare had the capability of hearing well beyond that of a human or even a dog.

Of course, no creature could match that of the red draco in the ability to hear. I needed only to whisper, and Red would detect the sound from over a league away. Usually, though, he stayed closer than that. Our bond was too strong for him to wander far. In fact, I sensed he was in the hills nearby doing his own hunting.

Whether I wanted it or not, Red was my bodyguard. Though Father had spoken against my venturing again to the capital, in the end he'd sighed and lifted his hands in a gesture of surrender. With Red watching over me, Father knew he had nothing to worry about.

Even if Red hadn't been protecting me, I still would have come. The recent news of the king beginning to lose his mind was too great a problem to ignore, especially when I might possibly have the answer to that problem. I couldn't hide away in my secure home while the king faced grave danger.

A movement in my periphery distracted me. I glanced aside to see Sir Ansgar standing several paces away, holding a hare by its back legs. "I do hope your cooking skills are better than your hunting skills."

I stood, irritation rising within me. How had he

managed to seize his prey so rapidly? I took in the clean cut at the rabbit's throat. One thrust. "You are lucky, sire. 'Tis all."

Beneath his hood, his eyes took on a twinkle. "I have no need of luck."

"Nor have I."

"Perhaps you simply need more practice?"

"I need no more practice than you."

His lips curved up into a smile, one that caused my stomach to flip upside down.

"Come," he said. "I'm growing hungrier with each passing moment."

I didn't find humor in the situation. I'd wanted to prove myself to this fierce warrior, and all I'd done was puff up his head. But a bargain was a bargain, and I wouldn't go back on my word now. I'd dress and roast the hare for him. But I wouldn't do so happily.

I began to cross toward him. Before I could take the hare from his grip, he started ahead of me up the path toward the waterfall. With his long stride, he disappeared behind the rushing wall before I managed to climb halfway.

Hastening my steps, I followed him into the cavern, knowing he was wise to move into the hiding place to cook the hare to hide the smoke from anyone passing by. Even so, my pace slowed the closer I drew to the inner cavern. As thrilled as I was at the prospect of spending more time with Sir Ansgar, I was suddenly nervous. What must he think of me? A poor peasant maiden? Compared to the beautiful noblewomen he supped with every day, I would be a sorry companion for a meal.

And why, exactly, did I care what he thought? It

shouldn't matter.

As I reached the far cave, Sir Ansgar was already in the process of dressing the hare, tossing entrails into a small fire he'd started from the flame of the torch I'd left behind.

I knelt beside him and reached for the hare. "Allow me."

He shifted it away from me. "I don't mind."

"As part of our bargain, the duty belongs to me."

"It does. But I would do it to repay you for your news."

"And how do you know my news is worth repaying?"

"You went to great lengths to insure secrecy."

I sat back on my heels.

He resumed skinning the animal. He'd shed his cloak and rolled up his shirtsleeves, revealing his thickly corded arms. For a moment, I was mesmerized by the way the firelight glistened over him, lighting his features, making each line in his face distinct. He had a tiny scar above one eyebrow, a groove in his forehead from worry, and laugh lines at the corners of his eyes. His skin was sun bronzed and his hair streaked with lighter strands.

"Do I finally pass your test?" His gaze flicked my way before returning to the hare, which he dressed with a proficiency that told me he'd done it many times in his life.

"Test, sire?"

"You're scrutinizing me."

He'd caught me at it again. Though I was tempted to blush, I'd never done so in my life and wouldn't start now. "I'm wondering why a man such as yourself is here in a cave with me when you could have commanded any one of your knights to do the deed in your stead."

He paused in his work but didn't look at me. "I wanted to see you again."

He wanted to see me? My pulse spurted with strange warmth. "Why?"

Chapter 4

ANSGAR

"I WANTED TO SEE YOU AGAIN." HAD THOSE WORDS REALLY JUST slipped from my mouth? What was wrong with me? Why was I reacting this way around Lis?

I ducked my head, embarrassed by the confession. I hadn't needed to share a meal with her. Nor did I need to learn more about her with the three-question game.

But somehow, I'd found myself doing everything within my limited womanizing capability to entice her to stay and spend a little time with me. I wanted to know more about her, where she was from, and what motivated her.

Though time was short, taking an extra hour wouldn't endanger me any more than coming here already had. If anyone was watching the Dragon Tavern, they'd probably assume I was enjoying myself to the fullest. They might grow impatient, but they'd wait.

"Why did you want to see me again?" she persisted.

I liked how blunt and honest she was. But I had no wish to answer this particular question, so I used diversion. "I'll answer only if you tell me why you wanted to see me."

"To give you the news."

"You could have picked any one of my knights to tell in my stead." I used her own reasoning against her.

She fell silent, as she did whenever she didn't have a ready response. She was quick-witted, but she also chose her words carefully. Both were skills I admired.

I would have to go first. What could I say that was honest but wouldn't frighten her? I tossed around several answers before landing on the least threatening. "You intrigue me."

"How so?"

"You're different than other women."

"Should I take that as a compliment?"

"Yes." I finished the last scrape of my knife against the hare and focused on my efforts to skewer the carcass on a long stick for roasting.

"I would guess you're also different than most men," she said after a moment. "But I'm afraid I cannot begin to compare you to others, as I've had limited interaction with men like yourself."

"Why the limits? Have you lived in a convent?"

She released a soft laugh, the first one I'd heard from her.

My gaze slid to her regardless of my efforts to keep from staring at her kneeling only an arm's length away. I was struck, as with the first time I'd seen her, with just how beautiful she was. Not in the usual way with elaborate hairstyles and elegant clothing and fine jewelry.

Instead, her beauty was natural with her flushed cheeks, wind-tossed hair, and the vitality radiating from her. Nothing in her expression was flirtatious or calculating or ambitious. She had no desire to please me, garner my attention, or seduce me into her arms. Rather, her face contained an innocence and honesty I found refreshing.

"Do I pass your test, sire?" Her voice hinted at humor, and her lips quirked up into a smile, one that turned the green of her eyes as bright as the first leaves of spring.

I couldn't make myself avert my gaze. She was an enchantress. And she was drawing me under her spell with each passing second.

Of course, I didn't believe in enchantresses and spells. But something about this maiden seemed to be weaving through my blood, so that the more I was with her, the more I wanted to be with her, not less.

"Well?" Her smile widened.

My breath snagged at such unfettered beauty. "Well what?"

"Do I pass your test?" Her question mocked mine from moments ago.

"You have no need of a test." Had I really spoken such words? I wanted to hit myself across the head. Instead, I tore my attention away from her and focused on roasting the hare.

"No need of a test? Am I to assume I surpass all the other maidens who chase after you and throw themselves at your feet?"

"There are no maidens throwing themselves at my feet." I held the hare into the flames.

"Of course there are. I have heard nothing but your accolades from every woman, single and married alike. They adore you and worship the ground you walk upon."

My companions never failed to point out such women, but I had no patience for their flirtations. The attention annoyed me, although I always remained as respectful and considerate as I could. My father's example and teaching had held me in good stead . . . until now. He'd never prepared me for how to act with a spirited maiden like Lis.

I twisted the stick so the rabbit would cook evenly. Even though I didn't know exactly where this conversation was headed, I was enjoying it more than I should. 'Twas a game of cat and mouse, one I intended to win. "If you've heard about my accolades, then 'tis clear you have been inquiring after me."

"Oh, there's no need to inquire." Her tone turned scoffing. "Women share freely even when I have no wish to hear it."

I held back a grin. She was good at this game. "And what information have you been so brutally subjected to hearing?"

"'Tis entirely brutal. I'm glad you can acknowledge it." She settled against the cave wall, her posture relaxed.

I allowed the tension I'd been holding to subside. Had I been afraid she'd bolt at the least mishap? Perhaps. Did I want this conversation to keep on going? Most definitely. "Tell me the most brutal thing you've been subjected to hearing on my account. I would surely like the chance to apologize."

Her eyes crinkled with amusement. She was bridling her mirth the same as I. "'Tis excruciating to hear women speak of how handsome they think you are."

For some reason, women favored my appearance, although I couldn't fathom why since my fellow Knights of Brethren were equally endowed. "'Tis an exaggeration, as you can see."

"Very much an exaggeration." Her tone took on a

sarcastic edge. "I cannot abide looking at you." She stared directly at me, surveying first my hair, then my forehead, shifting her gaze down to my nose, mouth, chin, and back to my mouth.

The touch of her gaze sparked heat deep within me, a heat that began to seep into my blood. I had to be careful, had to stop this interaction. But the words poured out past the crumbling walls of my resistance. "I sincerely apologize for causing you such agony."

This time she let out a long, hearty laugh. I couldn't contain a laugh of my own. And with it came a liberation of something I'd tried hard to keep locked away. Desire. It pulsed through me, uncaged and growing stronger with each passing moment.

I wanted this woman. In a way I hadn't wanted a woman in a very long time. If ever.

As if sensing the shift in my humor, her laugh faded and her eyes widened before she dropped her gaze. Likely my desire was evident in every line of my face, all too easy for her to read. And though she played a good game of cat and mouse, she was as innocent as she appeared.

She picked up a twig from the kindling left by a previous visitor and began to peel the bark.

I focused on the hare, the roasted scent beginning to permeate the cavern. For as many maidens as had thrown themselves at my feet—at least according to Lis—I wasn't accomplished in the art of courtly romance.

Of course, I'd observed other knights woo and win women. If Gunnar had been with Lis, he would have figured out a way to smooth over this awkward moment. He likely would have professed his desire in some flowery manner. He always did. And women always loved it. He enjoyed the attention for a short while before moving on, never making promises and never getting serious.

But I couldn't toy with a maiden and then walk away. And the truth was, I would have to walk eventually. There was no place my desires could go but away.

While no written laws prevented Knights of Brethren from marrying, the unspoken standard was that upon marriage, the knight would resign from the honored position. Even if not married, some would need to return to their estates, especially firstborn heirs who would take over the leadership of their lands and oversee the people who lived there.

Other knights who had no family responsibilities awaiting them stayed longer, until advantageous marriages were made or the king bequeathed land or an estate upon them as a gift for service.

As a third-born son of a chieftain, the most I could hope for if I returned to my clan was being given an overseer position in the lumber business that had been in my family for decades. Such work might once have been enough. But it wasn't anymore. Not since my father's death.

Shortly after his funeral, Ice Men from the Snowden Mountains attacked farms and towns in the moors and plateau area. The king had asked for each chieftain to provide a contingent to help defend the land. I wasted no time in meeting with my brother, who'd taken over the clan, and I offered to lead my clansmen.

During the months of defending the land from the Ice Men, I had made a name for myself, proven my value, and helped orchestrate an end to the invasions. The other warriors I fought alongside looked to me as a leader and hero. But it wasn't until I saved King Ulrik from an attack that I won royal favor.

The king bestowed upon me the high honor of returning with him to Vordinberg, not only to be a part of his Knights of Brethren but to serve as Grand Marshal. When I accepted the position, I privately vowed I would spend my life in the king's service. The king needed me more than my family did. Besides, my brothers understood that serving the king gave me renewed purpose and brought them honor.

My resolve left no room in my life for a woman and most certainly not a wife and children. If I felt anything for Lis, it would stay here in this cavern and would never leave it.

Besides, she'd singled me out to give me news of some kind. I couldn't forget the true nature of our meeting.

I lowered the hare deeper into the embers to hasten its cooking. "Would you like to go first with asking a question or shall I?"

She looked up from peeling the twig. "What happened with your father?"

I stiffened. How did she know about my father? Was everything about my life common knowledge?

She met my gaze directly, unabashedly. "The rumors abound. Some say you had an argument that led to his death. Others claim you tried to save him but failed. All agree you loved him and that his passing impacted you profoundly."

My mind slipped back to that fateful day when I'd been in the western woods with my father and a team of our woodcutters. With the spring thaw, we'd felled and dragged more than a hundred trees to the riverbank. After the holding area was full, all we had to do was release them into the swollen river. They'd float down to the mills, where my brothers and other men were waiting to pull them up onto the banks.

After a week away, the woodcutters were as ready as I was to let the logs loose and start following them downriver, breaking up jams and keeping them moving. They wanted to get home to their families. I wanted to get home to Britt. She was my friend from childhood, a woodcutter's daughter. On the day our expedition was readying to depart, she'd taken me by surprise, kissing me good-bye in public in front of many people.

I hadn't known what to do in response to her kiss, hadn't really kissed her back. But after a week of thinking about it, I was ready to try it again.

"When we get home, you'll need to be honest with Britt," my father said as we made our way to the river's edge. He'd obviously sensed my eagerness to be on my way home and guessed the reason why. "She put her claim on you with her kiss, a claim she doesn't have a right to."

Had she put her claim on me?

"The women like you, Ansgar. Many would claim you if they could." He squeezed my shoulder in a friendly way, one that told me he was beginning to think of me as an equal.

I'd inherited Father's tall frame and thick muscles. We shared the same brown-blond hair and brown eyes. But his features were more rugged and weathered than mine. While I maintained a scruffy layer of facial hair, his beard was long and braided in the custom of our clan. I imagined after forty more years of travailing in the wilderness, I'd be just as worn.

As much as I respected my father, I aimed to have another kiss from Britt, this time one that satisfied my newly awakened cravings. "She's a fine maiden. What harm can come from a few kisses?"

"You know I've been in contact with Osvald Borsheim." Father paused beside the holding area and ran a gloved hand over the stack of tree trunks piled in a pyramid. "A union with Borsheim's daughter is inevitable."

As another chieftain in the mountainous region near the Golden Plateau, Borsheim shared the river we needed for our lumber operations. Marriage to his daughter would solidify our two families working together to protect the river.

"Asmund shall marry her." Older than me by a year, Asmund was still unattached. He was next in line for a match, especially now that our oldest brother Aksel had just wedded a wealthy chieftain's daughter, adding a large dowry to the family fortune.

Father continued toward the river, the rushing water glistening in the morning sunshine. "Borsheim has asked for you."

"Tell him Asmund is next in line."

"His daughter wants *you*."

I tried to picture Borsheim's daughter from the last gathering of clans but couldn't. Truthfully, it didn't matter what she looked like. I would marry any woman my father wanted me to.

"If only Asmund put forth more effort. Instead, he is always worming his way out of doing his duty."

Father reached the bank and hopped up on the logs, climbing his way easily to the pinnacle, just as he had a hundred times during my childhood. "I've offered him Asmund, and his daughter refuses any man but you."

I shielded my eyes from the bright rays and peered up at my father. From his perch on the top log, he looked like the king of the forest. Surely Borsheim was a strong leader too. "Borsheim can tell his daughter she'll have Asmund or no one."

"Or I can tell you that you'll have Borsheim's daughter or no one." My father's voice turned firm, a tone warning me I would do best to hold my tongue.

My chest tightened. All I wanted to do was go home and kiss Britt. But my father was telling me I couldn't, that I was all but pledged in marriage to Borsheim's daughter. I kicked at the nearest log, needing to vent my swelling frustration.

The log rolled forward. A rumble resounded from within the pile. A log from farther up tumbled down and then another. One fell over the makeshift fence that served to hold the logs back from the river. The rest crashed into the barrier and came to a stop.

I watched anxiously for several heartbeats, and as nothing more happened, I released a breath of relief. But before I could move or speak or throw out a warning, the fence cracked. The splitting of the wood rent the air, followed by the rumbling of logs as they rolled down the remainder of the bank and into the river.

At the top of the pile, my father threw out both arms to stabilize his balance. But as the logs tumbled faster, his feet were swept out from underneath him. He fell to his back and the momentum carried him toward the river.

I started to throw myself toward the stream of timber picking up speed, but strong arms yanked me back. Panic pushed up into my throat. The logs were moving too fast now. If I waded into the plummeting mass, I'd be crushed in an instant.

Even so, I jerked myself free of whoever was holding me back. Maybe I wouldn't be able to help my father as he fell with the logs, but I could pull him free once he was in the water. As he dropped into the swiftly moving current, the pile continued to pour down into the water, pushing him under.

I grabbed a pike pole from the shore and hopped onto the closest floating log. The spikes on the bottoms of my boots held me firmly, and I moved from one to the next in the sea of tree trunks that now stretched from shore to shore.

"Father!" Frantically, I scanned the river and the logs for any sign of him.

Chapter 5

Lis

In the firelight, shadows flitted over Sir Ansgar's face. My question about his father was bringing back painful memories.

I'd assumed he would ask me challenging questions and so had wanted to ask him one first. But now I wished I could take it back. "Forgive me. You need not answer—"

"I hold myself responsible for my father's death." His tone was low and harsh. "The rumors are true. My arguing led to the accident. I attempted to rescue him, but by the time I pulled him from the river, he was dead."

"Say no more, sire. I shouldn't have pried."

He rotated the rabbit, his jaw flexing with tension. "I will never forgive myself for putting him in such danger."

"Is that why you strive to keep the king from danger? To make atonement?" As soon as the question was out, I wanted to bite my tongue. I was doing it again. Pushing him to talk about matters that were too private. Why couldn't I be satisfied with asking him about his favorite food or best childhood memory or even about what life was like at court?

"Is this your second question?" He stared straight ahead, his face hard like flint.

"Yes, but I retract it. Again, I was too hasty—"

"I'll never make atonement, but I shall live the rest of my days trying to keep the king safer than I kept my father."

Juice from the hare dripped down into the flames and sizzled.

"Your final question?"

I had to go with something more lighthearted, or he would surely loathe the sight of me for the rest of our brief time together. "Have you ever loved a woman?" Inwardly I groaned. Of all the questions I could have asked, why this one?

His gaze snapped to me. The intensity of his eyes fanned the flutters in my belly.

I busied myself again, needlessly peeling the strips of remaining bark from the twig. "If that is too personal, then you may tell me if you've ever been betrothed."

"I *may* tell you?" Mirth crept into his voice, chasing away the heaviness of moments ago.

"With all the women who adore you, surely you have loved at least one."

He withdrew the rabbit, lowered it to a stone at the side of the fire pit, then proceeded to slice off a piece of meat with his knife. He blew on it for several seconds before he took a small bite.

He chewed it slowly and swallowed. All the while I

stared at him, wishing I could cross to him, take his cheeks in my hands, and tell him what a good man he was so that he'd believe it.

"Give me your knife." He extended his hand.

I hesitated.

"For the hare. Unless you want to hold the hot morsel in your fingers."

I unsheathed my knife and gave it to him. He sliced off a chunk, stuck the tip of my knife into it, and handed it back. As I blew on my piece, the scent of tender meat made my stomach gurgle. I hadn't eaten much since leaving home two days ago. I'd been in too much of a hurry. And nervous. Though I hadn't wanted to admit it, my stomach had been in knots at the thought of meeting with Sir Ansgar.

"I have never loved a woman." His admission was soft.

It sent a strange shimmer of anticipation through me. "There has been at least one you have cared about."

He hesitated as if thinking back on the past, then shook his head. "I might have learned to care about one, the maiden my father and I were arguing about the day of his death. But since then, I've decided I'll not let thoughts of a woman distract me from my duties."

Who was this maiden? Not someone he'd loved, but obviously someone he'd cared about. "Was she your betrothed?"

"I've already answered three questions."

"'Tis the latter part of the third."

"I thought my reply was optional, based upon my willingness to answer the first part."

"Then you were betrothed?"

A grin played at the corners of his lips. He liked our banter as much as I did, and I took pleasure in that thought. "No, but she claimed me with a kiss."

"Claimed you with a kiss?" I couldn't keep my voice from rising, surely not with jealousy.

"Yes, she kissed me in front of half the town."

"If she claimed and kissed you, then she must be waiting for you to return and marry her."

"When I left, I made sure she knew I wouldn't be coming back."

"I see."

He twisted the meat on the end of his knife, then bit off a hunk.

"And did you like her kiss?" My curiosity of this man was getting the best of me. But I'd never sat with any man before, and my social skills were severely lacking. Even with that knowledge, I didn't retract my question.

One of his brows rose. "And why would you want to know if I liked the kiss?"

I shrugged. "From your hesitation in answering, am I to presume you did not like it?"

"As a matter of fact, I liked it very much and anticipated kissing her again at some point."

"But you never did."

He fell silent, staring into the flames, likely reliving the past.

I took another bite. And waited. Why did I care if he'd kissed this maiden twice? My attention drifted to his mouth. It was strong and certain, and I had no doubt that kissing him would be the experience of a lifetime.

He glanced my direction and caught me staring at his mouth.

Oh heaven's above. I shifted my attention to the piece of hare on the tip of my knife.

"My first question. Have you ever loved a man or been betrothed?"

"Such an original question, sire."

"If you can ask, then am I not allowed the same liberty?"

"Of course. I simply assumed you would have more creativity than to parrot back my questions."

"I do so only because they are so profound."

I fought back a smile. This bantering was the most fun I could remember having with anyone in quite some time. I could do this with him all day.

"Love, betrothal, kisses?" he persisted. "What say you?"

"None." Heat crept into my cheeks. Maybe 'twas possible for me to blush after all. "I told you the truth. I've had limited interaction with men."

"Oh yes, because you've spent your life in a convent."

My smile broke free. "No. Though I may come across as angelic, I live on a farm in the foothills of the Snowden Mountain Range less than two days' ride from Vordinberg. It is a remote place in the hills, and we don't see people oft."

"Surely now that you're grown, your parents have a plan for your betrothal."

"Father has never spoken of it."

"What a shame." His tone was mirthful. "You will deprive some lucky fellow of your sharp tongue."

"And my brilliant wit."

"All the more reason to persuade your father to begin the matchmaking process."

Even though I had felt longings over the past year for love and a family of my own, I could never leave my father. He needed me too much, could never manage the farm without my assistance. Even these few days of my departure were a hardship for him. If ever I were to marry, I would have to find a man who was willing to live a simple life on a simple farm.

"You don't intend to get married either." His statement was quiet.

"I don't have my heart set on it."

He nodded before he took another bite.

"I see what you're doing." I needed to lighten the mood again. "You're plying more information from me without asking an actual question."

"Very well. Then tell me how you came to be at the battle with Swaine in the Valley of Red Dragons."

'Twas a much easier question to answer than those of love and marriage. I launched into the story of how Princess Elinor and her guard had arrived at my farm looking for a place to hide from pursuers, how Maxim had tracked her there, and then how I'd aided them in escaping so that together they could ride to the battlefront and warn the king of the impending treachery. Soon after, I'd overheard the trackers plotting to harm the princess, so I'd followed.

I waited for Sir Ansgar to use his third question to ask me about Red. Instead, he shifted the conversation to my knowledge of hunting, questioning me about my tactics and the various animals I'd caught.

"I would have captured a hare but a moment later than you," I insisted as I finished a second piece of the tender meat and licked the grease from my fingers.

"Perhaps."

"We shall do it again sometime. And I will prove I am just as proficient."

He didn't respond.

Disappointment pinched in my chest. There wouldn't be another time.

He wiped his knife on the ground before sheathing it.

I expelled the tightness. As much as I wanted to come to this cave and meet Sir Ansgar again, what good could come of it? We were two different people walking two entirely different paths. Our lives weren't entwined in any way.

I'd come to give him a message—more a warning of sorts. And now it was time to do so. "You've proven yourself worthy of my news."

"And you've proven yourself trustworthy to bear the news."

So, his three questions had been to test me? To allow him to determine whether or not I was a reliable source and not someone intending to trap him?

I might as well tell him what I knew now. I had no excuse to linger any longer with him, and the sooner I told him, the sooner I could return home. "I have heard rumors the king is not himself. Some believe he is growing deranged."

Sir Ansgar tossed the remains of the carcass into the flames. "And . . .?"

"If such rumors are true, I have reason to believe he is being poisoned with a tonic made from the hermit mushroom." The rare mushroom was known for altering a person's mind, giving hallucinations and confusing them.

Sir Ansgar rose, his expression grim. "Why have you reason to believe this?"

"The trackers spoke of using the tonic to control the princess, which is why Maxim took her into hiding."

"Now you think the king is under its influence?"

"Yes."

Sir Ansgar shook his head. "I have considered the possibility of poisoning, but I have been testing everything he eats and drinks after it's placed on the table before him."

"Perhaps whoever is giving it to him—"

"Rasmus."

I didn't know much about Rasmus, but 'twas possible the Royal Sage was behind it. "Is it possible Rasmus is giving him the tonic when you aren't there?"

"'Tis entirely possible, especially of late since the king has been shutting my closest companions and me out of his fellowship."

"You must search for the tonic and destroy it."

He nodded. "Once he stops ingesting it, how long before it's out of his system and he returns to his right mind?"

"I don't know." I wasn't an expert on herbal remedies and tonics. Though we grew many herbs on the farm, I hadn't taken an interest in them the way my mother always had.

Sir Ansgar finished stamping out the low embers left of the fire.

Had he expected more detailed news? Was he disappointed with what I'd shared? Surely he could see the risk I'd taken to deliver it to him.

"I must be on my way back." He pulled up his hood.

I did likewise, then extinguished the torch.

As darkness engulfed us, the faint light from beyond the waterfall ahead guided our steps. We traversed the passageway silently. I guessed he was lost in his thoughts about what a waste of time the trip had been for him. I hadn't offered him news he hadn't already considered. Even so, I'd completed what God had laid on my conscience, and I could rest in that.

Ansgar ducked out from underneath the waterfall first but then stopped so abruptly that I crashed into him. He slid a hand back onto my arm and steadied me. Rather than let me go, the pressure of his hold tightened, and he shifted me just slightly so I was more firmly behind him.

Before I could question him or complain, he spun me to him, wantonly, brazenly, almost seductively, wrapping his arms around my body and dipping in so his mouth hovered near my ear.

My breath stuck in my throat, and I couldn't speak past my surprise. A part of me knew that a hug or any other physical contact with this man was inappropriate. But another part of me tingled with anticipation.

"Someone is spying on me downriver." His whisper tickled my ear. "We must play the part of lovers, or he will suspect I have deeper motives in being here with you."

I rose onto my toes, wanting to look over his shoulder downriver, but Ansgar glided one hand up my arm and to my shoulder before drawing my face into the crook of his neck. The scruff of his jaw brushed against my face, the nearness making me weak so that I had no choice but to clasp his cloak.

"I regret I must ask you to engage in deception, but if we do not, we will surely face reprisals." The low whisper in my ear made me even weaker.

"What must we do?" I managed.

"Pretend to kiss me."

"How do I pretend such a thing?"

"Act like you want to be with me."

I started to pull away, my indignation growing. "Perhaps *you* should act as though you want to be with *me*."

He gave a soft growl of frustration, but for some reason it only stirred a strange longing inside me. In the next instant, before I could question him again, he dipped in and captured my mouth with his.

If I thought I'd gone weak before, I nearly crumpled to the ground as his lips pressed warmly and solidly against mine. For a second, I just closed my eyes and relished the sweet, tender pressure.

But I guessed if we wanted to be taken seriously, I needed to do more than stand there letting him touch his lips to mine. Besides, I couldn't deny that I was entirely taken with the idea of kissing Ansgar. What maiden wouldn't be?

I stretched my arms up, tossed back his hood, and let my hands roam up his neck and into his hair. I plunged my fingers in and then rose into the kiss, softening my lips and angling so I could feel him better.

Oh holy saints. He was delicious.

He moved into the kiss too, deepening it and, in the process, sweeping me totally away to a place I'd never known existed. I didn't want to leave the bliss of connecting with this man, but the kiss lasted only a moment longer before he broke it.

He didn't immediately pull away and instead pressed my cheek against his chest and rested his chin on my crown. His chest rose and fell rapidly, and his heartbeat thundered hard against his ribs.

Had he liked our kiss? Or had it only been pretense for him?

It hadn't been pretense for me. It still wasn't. I was relishing every second of this closeness, of being in his arms, of him holding me as though he cherished me.

"I'll see you to your horse," he whispered without letting go.

"I can see to myself."

"I realize that. But I want to ensure you are well on your way so the spy is left with no choice but to follow me and not you."

He was wise. And kind. I didn't want to bring more suspicion upon Father than I already had. Since the day Princess Elinor arrived at our farm, others had snooped around, perhaps looking for her again. And I feared that one of these times, someone would decide to punish us for helping the princess and Maxim.

As though sensing my acquiescence, he stepped away, releasing me slowly. His eyes didn't let me go, however. They held me captive within their hot, swirling depths, weakening my legs again.

I swayed, and he reached for my hand. Yet gloveless, his fingers were warm and tender. "Ready?" he whispered.

I wanted to shake my head no, that I'd never be ready to walk away from him. But I simply turned and tried to tug my hand free.

He didn't let go and instead strengthened his grip

before following on my heels.

Was this another way to pretend we were taken with each other, that our secret meeting was genuine?

My heart continued its erratic thudding as I led him several dozen paces away to where I'd secured my horse. Wordlessly, I unraveled the lead line, still clinging to his hand as I did so. Upon finishing, I faced him.

The tree cover was thick and the shadows of the gray day heavy. But with his hood still thrown back, I had a clear view of his countenance. His eyes were a warm liquid that had the power to turn me into liquid too. He studied my features, lifting a hand and brushing back a stray wisp of hair. The caress of his fingers upon my cheek made me tremble.

His gaze came to rest upon my mouth. Without giving warning or asking permission, he bent down and kissed me again, fusing his lips to mine for an exquisitely long second. I had the urge to rise to my toes and wrap my arms around his neck again.

But before I could press in closer, he released me. He took a step back, surveyed me one last time as though memorizing me, then spun and stalked away without looking back.

I watched until he disappeared. Even then, I couldn't make myself move. I stood frozen to the spot for long minutes. When finally Red's soft trill nudged me, I pressed my fingers to my lips and relived every beautiful moment of Ansgar's kiss. And I did so the whole way home.

Chapter
6

ANSGAR

I SHOULDN'T HAVE KISSED LIS. NOT ONCE. AND CERTAINLY NOT twice.

The great hall hummed with activity all around me, but I couldn't concentrate. Since returning the previous day from my meeting with Lis, I'd been distracted by thoughts of my time with her.

I'd assumed a little feigning would protect us both. But had such a display been necessary? Because the kisses had loosened the knot of self-control I'd tied tightly in place. Now that it was loose, I wasn't sure I could cinch it again.

I should have given her a lingering hug instead. That would have sufficed, would have proven to the spy downriver that Lis and I had met as lovers and for no other reason.

From my place at the king's table, I supped silently, my mood solemn. Around me, my companions, too, ate more quietly than usual. They cast each other glances, raising their brows, sensing my unrest, but I ignored them and focused on my trencher, though I didn't taste a bite of the meal.

What could come of kissing Lis? Save to stir up discontentment and make me wish for more than I could have. Because, as sure as spring flowers bloomed, my body and my desires were fully awakened—just like after Britt had kissed me those many years ago, except much more powerfully.

For a reason I couldn't explain, possessiveness toward Lis surged through me. I felt as though she was mine and belonged to no one else. I wanted—no, needed—to be with her again. But my feelings were entirely irrational. Lis didn't belong to me. I'd likely never see her again. In fact, I couldn't see her again, needed to put her far from my mind.

The king's laughter from down the table drew my attention. He was leaning toward Gotfred, beaming at the young knight. Standing behind the king, Rasmus watched passively, his expression as unreadable as always.

If only I could find something with which to indict Rasmus... but even with Lis's news about the hermit tonic, I hadn't been able to locate any evidence during my discreet search in the king's chambers last night. After sharing Lis's suspicion about the hermit tonic with my closest companions, they'd also done their share of investigating. But they had nothing to show for their efforts either.

Helplessness wound through me, the same I'd felt that day when I balanced upon the logs in the river and shouted my father's name, scanning the water, praying he'd surface so I could hoist him out of danger.

Lis had asked me if guarding the king was my attempt

to make atonement for losing my father. Although I'd never analyzed my motivations before, perhaps I was hoping to succeed in protecting the king where I'd once failed with my father. But I wasn't succeeding. I might have saved the king from outside forces in the recent battle—with Lis's help. But with each passing day, I was failing to keep the king safe from the forces within.

Across from me, Gunnar was scrutinizing me the most. Last night, after I returned to the inn and we started on our way back to the castle, I'd relayed to him a very abbreviated version of my time with Lis. Although I mentioned the spy at the end, I didn't tell him I had kissed Lis. Nor did I reveal her identity. She'd come to me in secrecy, and I intended to honor that.

Now, he sat up and snapped his fingers. "I've figured it out. You like the girl."

"I barely know her." I knew whom he was referencing without his spelling it out.

"You're thinking of her, and that's why you're full of such angst."

He was right. But I couldn't admit to it. I tore off a piece of lamb and dragged it through the greasy gravy.

At my silence, Gunnar's lips curled into a lopsided grin.

"A maiden who has turned Ansgar's head?" Espen whistled. "Perhaps we need to make a national holiday out of the occasion."

The others watched me with interest now too.

Gunnar's brow rose. "Methinks you're smitten."

"I have no need for a woman in my life."

"Such a denial is the clear sign you *are* smitten."

I heaved an exasperated sigh. Before I could defend myself further, the steward approached the king's place at the center of the table, a sense of urgency radiating from his face and quick steps. As he was one of the familiar royal servants, I didn't suspect he was a part of any plotting against the king. Nevertheless, I stiffened in preparation for the news he was delivering.

As he reached the table on the dais, he bowed.

In the middle of a loud conversation with Gotfred, the king paused, his countenance darkening with irritation.

From her spot at the side table with her ladies-in-waiting, Queen Inge fell to silence and watched the king warily.

Did I need to approach the queen with my concerns? Day by day, I'd witnessed the worry lines in her face grooving deeper whenever she looked at her husband, and I suspected I would find an ally in her. But in seeking her out, would I alienate both of us from the king all the more?

The steward lifted his head tentatively. "An important message, Your Majesty."

The king motioned at him impatiently. "Well, get on with it."

I stiffened. Had King Canute of Swaine decided to attack again? After his lack of success during the recent battle, he'd taken his army back to Swaine and hadn't regrouped. With winter soon upon us, I didn't think he'd attempt another confrontation, at least not until spring. I could only pray Canute had learned a Norvegian invasion wouldn't be as easy to accomplish as he'd assumed, especially since we had a draco on our side to fight his. Even so, I'd been on edge, awaiting news of another Swainian encounter.

Beside me, Torvald had grown rigid too, his hand upon the hilt of his sword.

"Speak!" the king shouted.

The steward's face was pale, and his gaze flitted to the door as if he'd rather run away than bear the tidings. "We received news that the Princess Elinor is . . . the princess has . . . the princess has married Maxim."

The king shot to his feet and shoved the steward away. "Liar!"

The steward stumbled and nearly toppled from the dais. "No, Your Majesty. 'Tis the truth. The word has spread all throughout the northern lands—"

"You pig!" The king's angry words echoed through the great hall. "You spout nothing but treason."

While I was concerned about the king, I was more interested in Rasmus's reaction to the news of his son marrying the princess. Would he be happy about it? Was that what he'd wanted? For his son to wed Princess Elinor so that he might have his own flesh and blood on the throne?

Rasmus's expression remained emotionless. If he was surprised by the news, he didn't show it.

"The messenger is there." The steward nodded in the direction of a side door, where a disheveled courier stood in the shadows.

I rose, ready to escort the steward and messenger away if need be . . . for their safety more than the king's.

The king stared at the courier and then the steward, confusion filling his eyes. "Why is the princess not here? She ought to be here. Go and fetch her this instant, and I will question her for myself."

The steward hesitated, then looked to Rasmus as though the Royal Sage would direct him.

The queen rose and skirted around the other ladies, who were now watching the king with pity. Everyone knew Princess Elinor was no longer in Vordinberg. Most people believed the rumor that Maxim had kidnapped her, although the few who truly knew Maxim understood he'd never be capable of such a thing.

"What are you waiting for?" The king's face turned red with sudden rage, and he shoved the steward again. "Go get the princess! Now!"

This time the steward couldn't gain his balance. He toppled from the dais and landed on his backside in the rushes on the floor. The queen halted halfway to the dais and stared at her husband as if she no longer recognized him.

"Princess Elinor would never betray me this way." With a stricken expression, the king dropped into his chair.

No one spoke or moved. I wanted to approach the king, to reason with him, even to shake him out of this mood. But Lis's revelation yesterday had confirmed that the king wasn't himself anymore because he was being drugged. No amount of talking or pleading with him would help.

The only thing to do was to find the source. But how?

Rasmus laid a steadying hand upon the king's arm. "'Twould appear the treachery is deeper than we thought possible, Your Majesty. The princess is clearly conspiring with Maxim to take the throne from you."

The king groaned, leaned forward, and covered his face with his hands.

"That's not true." I couldn't stand idly by any longer and allow Rasmus to perpetuate more lies. My honor demanded that I share what I knew. And I did know more now after speaking with Lis. "Maxim learned that the princess's life was in danger, and he took her away to keep her safe."

Rasmus eyed me levelly. "If that's all he was doing, then why would he marry her?"

"Perhaps she married him because she recognizes his worthiness to become the next king. Every soldier on the battlefield can attest to their bravery that day. Every citizen has heard about their valor, and they have become heroes." Although I hadn't supported changing the law to allow for the princess to marry a commoner, I could this once make an exception for Maxim.

The king looked up at me, his eyes clearing for just a moment. He started to nod but then paused and glanced at Rasmus.

"Your Highness," Rasmus said gently. "Maxim and Elinor hope to rally the kingdom to their side. All the more reason to squelch them before they can return to Vordinberg and demand the throne from you."

"Demand the throne?" The king's voice rose with indignation. "How dare they? How dare Elinor? After all I have done for her, and she will repay me this way?"

"Exactly." Rasmus met my gaze, his eyes challenging me to say more. "Perhaps it is time to appoint someone worthier."

"She is the only one with royal blood." The king waved his hands erratically toward the queen. "If only my wife had borne me a child, then I would have a loyal subject instead of an ingrate."

The queen's face blanched at the cruel accusation, and her shoulders slumped as if she no longer had the energy to fight against whatever ill had befallen the king.

"What shall we do, Rasmus?" The king's question echoed in the now-silent hall like the wail of a spoiled child.

"We shall do as we planned and allow the sword to

determine the man who is worthiest to be king. He shall become your heir with your approval. And with the approval of the clans, Sages, and council."

An uneasy murmur met Rasmus's statement. But the king didn't reject it.

I started toward the king, needing him to have a moment of clarity, to see the situation with the wisdom and logic he'd always displayed. "Please, Your Majesty. You know Princess Elinor is devoted to you and only seeks to please you. She would never attempt to take your throne."

"And how do you know so much about the princess?" Rasmus spoke in a low, even tone, one void of emotion. "Only someone who is working closely with Maxim and Princess Elinor would rise to their defense."

"I serve only the king. He has been and always will be my priority."

"Perhaps your secret meetings without the king have to do with conspiring with Maxim and the princess."

"They have to do with how we can protect the king from forces within that seek to weaken and control him." I wanted to tell Rasmus I knew all about the hermit tonic, but I couldn't risk him hiding it, making the task of finding it even more formidable.

"Forces within?" Rasmus raised an eyebrow. "Then you admit to knowing of forces within that are seeking to weaken His Majesty . . . so that Maxim and the princess can more easily return and take the throne, perhaps without opposition?"

"You are twisting my words, Your Excellency."

"Then tell us the truth, Sir Ansgar. Do you support Maxim and the princess? Or do you support the king?"

Rasmus was trapping me and pushing me into an

alliance with him whether I wanted it or not.

If I spoke in support of the king, I would condemn Maxim and the princess. With so many people respecting me and trusting my word, if I condemned the princess and her marriage to Maxim, I had the power to turn people against them, which I didn't want to do. Not when they hadn't done anything wrong. Not when they weren't conspiring against the king.

However, if I spoke in support of Maxim and the princess, I would alienate myself from the king. Rasmus had orchestrated the evidence against me so the king would believe I was no longer his loyal and faithful servant. Was there any way I could prove it to him?

"Your Majesty," I started.

"I'd like to hear where you stand, Sir Ansgar," Rasmus interrupted. "The king is also very interested in hearing where your loyalties lie."

The king was taking a sip from his goblet and seemed oblivious to the conversation, as if he no longer heard us or cared. His eyes were glazed again, and as he placed his goblet on the table, it would have tipped over if not for Gotfred catching it.

The poor king looked more and more like a madman. 'Twas no wonder Lis had heard the rumors. No doubt word would continue to spread about his madness, undermining the populace's faith in the kingdom and leaving Norvegia vulnerable to Canute.

This was my fault. The failure that had been chasing me seemed to catch up, stringing me in a noose and cutting off my air.

"Well, Sir Ansgar?" Rasmus asked. "Where are your loyalties?"

"My loyalties are first and foremost with the king—"

"Very well. Then you and your cohorts will take the lead in tracking down and arresting Maxim and the princess and bringing them to the capital to face charges of treason."

The queen had returned to her spot and now gasped.

Something in her protest unleashed my own. "I shall continue to serve the king, but I won't bring charges against the princess and Maxim, charges I cannot in good conscience make."

Rasmus didn't immediately respond except to bow his head as though suddenly burdened by my words.

"I am sorely tired." The king began to push up from his chair, wobbled, and sat back down heavily. As he rose again, Gotfred stood and steadied him. "I should like to go to bed now."

"Yes, Your Majesty." Rasmus bowed as if the king's strange behavior were perfectly normal. "Perhaps after you are rested, you can dispense your wisdom on what steps to take with Sir Ansgar."

What steps to take? Would Rasmus so twist this predicament that he would now level charges against me?

The king was already shuffling forward. "Do what you see is best, Rasmus. I leave the matter in your trustworthy hands."

Rasmus's hands weren't trustworthy. In fact, his scheming was far more complicated than I'd expected. Now the entire royal court had just heard the king give Rasmus license to do whatever he wanted.

If Rasmus had hoped to gain control, he was succeeding. He'd figured out a way to manipulate King Ulrik. And no doubt he wanted to do that with the future king.

Had he originally intended to do so through Maxim?

After having failed on that accord, was he recruiting Gotfred instead? The knight docilely led the king across the dais and assisted him down the steps as if he were an old man instead of the strong and vital king he'd been only weeks ago.

As soon as the king left via a side passageway followed by several guards, I pulled myself up, trying to prepare myself for whatever wrath Rasmus would unleash upon me.

He regarded me for a moment as if attempting to decide my fate, although I was beginning to think he'd planned every detail of this encounter well in advance. "Sir Ansgar, your inability to stand with the king against Maxim and the princess could be construed as treason."

Murmuring resounded around the room, especially from nearby where my friends stood. I knew they would fight to the death for me if necessary. But I wanted to prevent them from facing my disgrace. No matter what fate might befall me today, the king would still have these loyal five knights to watch over him.

"However," Rasmus said more forcefully, "because of your faithful service to the king heretofore, I shall not condemn you to death for your treachery."

I wanted to ask Rasmus if he really thought he could get away with condemning me to die. My knights, the commoners, even the nobility would never allow it. Perhaps his mentioning it was simply a way for him to make others believe he had the power over my life and death when he didn't.

"Instead," Rasmus continued, "I shall dismiss you from the king's service and send you home to your clan. You must remain there all the days of your life and never again return to Vordinberg. In the future, if you come inside the city, I permit anyone to capture you and bring me your head for a reward of fifty pieces of silver."

As Rasmus met my gaze, I realized this was what he'd wanted. To send me away so I could no longer interfere in his handling of the king. He couldn't publicly condemn me, but he could make me go far away where the people would eventually forget about me and where I wouldn't be able to meddle in the affairs of the kingdom.

Was this Rasmus's ultimate goal: to eliminate everyone who posed a threat to his authority, allowing him the freedom to do whatever he wanted?

"I hereby strip Sir Ansgar of his position as Grand Marshal and as a Knight of Brethren." Rasmus's voice carried through the great hall, now silent again. "You must remove yourself from Vordinberg before the break of day, or you will leave me no choice but to behead you myself."

Chapter 7

ANSGAR

"RASMUS DOESN'T HAVE THE POWER TO SEND YOU AWAY," Kristoffer said, his intelligent features forlorn in the moonlight, the same as the other knights.

"The king gave him permission." I slipped the knot on my pack on the back of my steed, tying all my possessions there. "The entire court was witness to it. Rasmus made sure of that."

"I think we should rush in together," Gunnar whispered earnestly. "We'll grab Rasmus and all the men colluding with him and lock them up until we can prove his wrongdoing."

I glanced around the deserted stables and bailey. I suspected Rasmus had eyes and ears everywhere. I shook my head and pressed a finger to my lips.

"We cannot stand back and allow him to dismiss you." Torvald, who rarely protested, had been pacing back and forth, clearly agitated. "Perhaps, Gunnar is right that we should fight."

I shook my head. "If we attempt an overthrow, no

doubt Rasmus will be expecting it. Then he'll use the aggression as further evidence we were conspiring against the king."

"As much as I would like to fight," Kristoffer said, "I agree that we would be walking into a trap if we did so."

I tugged at the stirrup and then the flank cinch. I'd delayed long enough. Dawn would light up the sky erelong, and I needed to be on my way so I didn't bring more trouble upon myself or my friends.

I turned and nodded farewell to the five who had become closer to me than even my own brothers. I regretted that we must part ways.

"If you won't fight," Gunnar said, "then let us go with you."

"You're needed here," I said again, as I had already many times. "The king needs you to guard him now more than ever."

With a glance to the sky and the fading stars, I hoisted myself into the saddle. I studied the inner bailey, taking in the stillness of the usually busy place. The dogs and chickens were still asleep. The windows of the barracks as well as the castle were dark. The various workshops built against the walls were now silent and still.

"Godspeed," one of the men whispered.

I nodded. "You must send me a message straightaway if the situation worsens."

"We will," Gunnar answered quickly.

Before I lost my ability to keep my emotions in check, I nudged my horse toward the gatehouse. The guard on night duty began to raise the portcullis.

I waited silently as the chains creaked and groaned under the weight of the heavy iron gate. When it was finally up, I started through, and the guard bowed his head as I passed by.

I didn't have to look back to know my friends were watching my departure. I could only pray they would take my instructions to heart and continue the search for the hermit tonic as well as any evidence that could implicate Rasmus.

With each stride my horse took away from the castle and the king, the weight of frustration grew heavier. All I'd wanted to do was serve the king and protect him. My every waking moment had revolved around that goal. And somehow, no matter how diligently I'd labored, I hadn't done enough. I'd fallen short, and now the king was in more peril than ever before.

One thing was certain. I couldn't return to my clan and do nothing about the problem. That wasn't an option. Over the past hours since Rasmus's dismissal, I'd decided my best plan of action was locating Maxim and gaining his help. I had the distinct feeling he was the only one wise enough to unravel Rasmus's schemes.

I needed Maxim. And I aimed to find him no matter how long it took.

As I reached the fork in the road a short distance from the castle, I stopped to deliver a missive to a trusted courier before I veered onto the high road leading away from town and up into the hills and moors to the north. The path followed the Blood River for many leagues, making travel level and smooth. After reaching the Golden Plateau, the terrain would be more strenuous to traverse. But the many forests and rivers of the western plateau were familiar to me.

The most difficult aspect of the coming days would be uncovering clues to find Maxim and the princess. I prayed the courier with my missive would eventually reach the couple and that they would reveal their location to me sooner rather than later. For the king's sake.

The thick mantle of bear fur covering my chain mail protected me from the freezing temperatures of the early morning hour. Only my fingers and toes and nose grew cold. After having grown up with frigid temperatures, I knew I had to stop every hour to move around and work warmth back into my hands and feet to keep them from freezing.

I'd learned much about survival from my father. I had no fear of the cold or snow or wild predators that grew ravenous in the winter. Even so, I traveled with caution, knowing ignorance was oft a man's worst enemy in the wilderness.

After several hours of riding, the sun came out, the bright rays angled to cause the remaining leaves in the trees to glisten with vibrant red and orange and yellow. As a hare dashed out of underbrush ahead, my thoughts returned to Lis as they frequently did. I pictured her intensity as she'd waited by the burrow to capture the first hare.

At the time, I'd almost dropped my prey so she'd have the chance to beat me. But I was too much a man of integrity to deceive her in any way, even in something so small. And as a man of honor, I shouldn't have resorted to pretense when leaving the cave.

Lying always exacted a price. And this time it had cost me peace. My soul was still in turmoil many hours after kissing her. I tried to keep from replaying each moment of the kisses, but all too oft my blood heated with the memories, especially the last kiss. If I was completely honest with myself, I hadn't given her that kiss to put on a show for the spy. I'd given it to her in a moment of weakness because I wanted to taste her again.

But she hadn't pushed me away. Rather, she welcomed me—at least it felt like she had.

I slowed my mount and followed the trail of the hare. The hour was too early to stop for a meal. But I could capture the hare and roast it later.

I reined in my horse and slid down. As I flexed my hands again and stomped my feet, my steed's ears flickered and he lifted his muzzle, sniffing the air. He gave a nervous whinny.

Someone or something was in the vicinity.

I scanned the area, taking in every shadow and movement. The leaves fluttering in the breeze, the rippling river, the migrating starlings taking flight from a tree.

Although I could spot nothing out of the ordinary, I couldn't ignore my horse's innate ability to pick up on the scent of danger.

Without waiting to discover what that danger might be, I mounted and urged my horse onward. At a shout, I glanced behind to find half a dozen riders charging out from the cover of the trees and galloping along the river path toward me. At the sight of two Knights of Brethren, one of them Sigfrid, along with a handful of squires, I let the tension ease from my shoulders.

Where had they come from and what did they want? Perhaps they already had news for me regarding the king.

My muscles tightened, and I tugged on the reins to slow my mount. Something must have happened. Had Rasmus been waiting for me to leave before doing his worst damage?

The other knight who rode with Sigfrid was Casper, one of the newest Brethren. Why was Sigfrid with him?

He knew Casper couldn't be trusted.

Sigfrid rode at the forefront, his bow in place over his shoulder. He was an expert archer, one of the best in the land. As he reached into his quiver at his belt, removed an arrow, and nocked it, his fluency never failed to impress me.

Less than a hundred paces away, he shifted his aim, pointed his arrow at me, and released it.

I reacted before I allowed myself time to think. I threw myself low against my mount and kicked him forward. In the next instant, the arrow whizzed past my head, barely missing my shoulder.

Again, I didn't give myself the opportunity to analyze what was happening. I simply responded with the quick instincts that had earned me the reputation as the top warrior in the land. I glanced at Sigfrid to see that he was fitting another arrow, his aim lower this time.

I knew Sigfrid's methods well enough to count out ten seconds before jerking my mount to the left, escaping the arrow by only inches. The problem was, Casper was also an expert archer, but I hadn't yet learned his strategy, and a moment later, the tip of an arrow pierced my cloak and mail into my lower back. It didn't go into my flesh far, but it was enough to cause pain.

"Come on." I leaned in and urged my horse to gallop more swiftly. But the path was growing rockier, and the climb was gradually uphill. I couldn't stay on my course, or I would have a difficult time outrunning them. I needed to get into the cover of the forest where I wouldn't be an easy target.

With another glance behind me, I dodged the next arrow, all the while guiding my horse into thicker brush. Before I could escape into the cover of the trees, another arrow, this one Sigfrid's, sliced into my shoulder. It went deeper, which not only showed the power and skill of his archery ability but also that he was gaining ground.

Only one thought flitted through my mind. I'd trusted him, counted him one of my closest friends, and he'd betrayed me.

I gritted my teeth against the pain that radiated from my shoulder all the way down my arm. Even though each slight movement jarred my wounds, I used every ounce of mental energy I had to focus on the landscape ahead. I picked out an obstacle course that would keep my pursuers from having a straight shot at me, and I wound in and out of the trees.

With the erratic nature of my riding, they didn't attempt any more shots, but every time I gauged their positions, I could see that they were drawing nearer. I realized why, when I reached down to pat my mount and encourage him to go faster and found the arrow embedded deep in his flank with blood oozing from the wound.

My heart sank. I loathed the prospect of an innocent creature such as this steed having to suffer. Even more, I knew he couldn't go on indefinitely. It was only a matter of time before he collapsed from weakness and pain.

I would have to engage in hand-to-hand combat with the two knights and their squires. But I needed to gain an advantage somehow. Perhaps if I found higher ground, I could force them to climb up to fight me. Was there any such place nearby? More importantly, would my mount survive to deliver me to it?

Beneath my thighs, I could feel his breathing becoming more strained. "I'm sorry," I whispered, my own breathing labored from the chase. Ahead, I glimpsed a rocky incline at least twenty hands high. If I could reach it and scale it before the knights caught up to me, I might have a chance of defeating them.

Nudging the horse in that direction, I rose to a crouch in the saddle. Only a few paces away, I stood, then leapt. I landed on top of the rock surface at the same moment one of my pursuers released another arrow. It grazed my leg but didn't puncture it. I caught my balance and spun, my sword out in one hand and my knife in the other.

Moments later, Sigfrid and the others circled around the rock. One tree hung overhead, casting shade. But otherwise, I had no other shelter. I lifted my sword, ready to fight the first man who dared to ascend the rock. If they decided to attack me at the same time, I would be sorely at a disadvantage, but I would do my best.

"You're the one who was giving Rasmus information about our plans." I threw the accusation toward Sigfrid even as I attempted to keep my eye on each of the men, alert to their positions and guessing who would be the first to climb up and fight me.

"I had no choice, Ansgar." His voice held enough regret for me to know he was telling the truth. "Rasmus threatened my kin with reprisals if we do not cooperate with him."

How deeply had Rasmus woven his influence and threats into the Noble Council? Did he have control of each councilman in some way? If so, was there any hope of keeping Rasmus from gaining complete power over the kingdom?

"Then Rasmus never had any intention of allowing me to return to my clan?" I was glad now I hadn't told my companions about my plan to find Maxim or of the missive I'd sent him.

"The people love you too much." Sigfrid ran a gloved finger along the feather fletching of an arrow. "Rasmus couldn't risk killing you directly. But if you were to die in an ambush by thieves on your way home? That would be tragic."

"And convenient. Do you really think everyone will believe such a tale?" I swung at the first squire to reach the top. I sliced him down in one swift blow, sending him toppling back over the edge.

Even though I could feel myself weakening from my injuries, I was determined to fight until the end. When the next two squires ascended together, I dodged their blows and parried in quick succession.

As I injured one and was gaining the upper hand with the other, I glimpsed Casper with an arrow trained upon me. Sigfrid was shaking his head at the man, but Casper stretched the bow back anyway.

The rules of warfare demanded a certain level of courtesy. Surely he would wait and fight me nobly and not attempt to kill me while I was engaged in defending myself from the squires. Such a killing wouldn't bring him any honor.

But in the next instant, as an arrow plunged into my leg, I realized Casper didn't care about honor. He only cared about following Rasmus's orders, likely so he wouldn't face the brunt of Rasmus's scheming against himself.

As the arrowhead struck deep, I couldn't move as quickly. A blade swiped against the exposed part of my neck, and in the next instant, the warmth of fresh blood pooled in my collarbone.

A sword slammed into me from behind at the same time as a blow to my shoulder dropped me to my knees. I tried to jump to my feet with my usual agility, but I couldn't get my wounded leg to move or support me. I made it only halfway up before another hit sent me back to my knees.

I slashed anyway, determined to fight until I no longer had breath. But I was growing fainter by the second. Dizziness swept in, and as I swung my sword, I wavered.

Before I could gather my wits, a sword crashed against mine with enough force to send my weapon flying from my grip. It hit the stone, bounced, and then flew over the edge.

I tried to switch my knife to my stronger hand, but my fingers were slick with blood. The knife slipped from my hand and landed near my opponent's feet. He kicked it, sending it out of my reach.

This was the end. Without a weapon to wield, I was at the mercy of Rasmus's murderous plans. I hung my head, ashamed I hadn't recognized Sigfrid's treachery sooner. Ashamed I would die in disgrace. And ashamed I hadn't found a way to save the king.

One of the squires yanked down my mail hood, revealing my neck. The other raised his sword above the bare flesh, the blade glinting in the sunlight. My blood already stained the weapon. And now it would sever my head from my body.

As he took a breath and raised his sword higher, I closed my eyes and prayed for death to take me rapidly.

A screech rent the air above us. Before I knew what was happening, a burst of fire hit the squire holding the sword. Flames immediately engulfed him, the heat so intense I could feel it roasting my skin.

His screams rose into the air, and he flailed in an effort to escape the fire. But it was too consuming.

Another shriek was followed by a second burst of fire, this aimed at the other squire on the rock beside me. He dove out of the way, scrambling on his hands and knees to avoid the same fate as his companion.

"Shoot it!" Sigfrid was shouting, even as he fumbled with an arrow of his own.

But already Casper and the remaining squires were racing away, trying to find cover.

Sigfrid released an arrow into the sky. I visually followed its path. He was aiming for a draco. As if things couldn't get any worse, now a red draco was attacking. The creature was reminiscent of the dragons of old, but smaller, more the size of an enormous eagle. Like all dracos, it had thin wings, a scaly back, and an underbelly with a square pattern of black, red, and white.

The draco swirled away from the arrow before swooping down and breathing its fiery breath at Sigfrid. The young knight, like his companions, had no choice but to retreat. As he did so, I attempted to stand. I had to make my escape while they were distracted.

But the moment I pushed myself to my feet, the draco dove directly toward me. I reached my arms up to cover my head and protect myself from the creature's fiery breath. But instead of shooting fire at me, it wrapped its talons around my arms and lifted me off the rock into the air.

My legs and body dangled, suspended in the air while the talons locked me firmly in place. I knew I needed to squirm and fight my way free, but I'd already lost a great deal of blood and was too weak to do anything. As the draco carried me higher above the treetops and out of range of arrows, I glanced at the frightened faces below.

I was being carried off like a sheep to the slaughter, no

doubt the draco's next meal. The only thing I could do was fight my way free once it put me down—if it didn't drop and kill me first.

Chapter 8

Lis

Something wasn't right. I could sense it in my bones. Nevertheless, I swung the scythe alongside my father, both of us laboring in the silent rhythm we'd always shared as the dry barley toppled to the ground, ready to be gathered and threshed before winter.

While the barley was the last of the grain crops to be harvested, I still had much to do. I needed to dig up the root vegetables and store them. I also wanted to gather more berries from the outfields, cut more firewood, and strengthen the barn roof in several places. All before the first snowfall.

It was like this every autumn. We engaged in a frantic race to prepare for winter to ensure survival through the months when both fresh produce and game were scarce. With Mother gone, her work of preserving food fell on my shoulders. And with Father's leg paining him more every year, I'd taken on some of his responsibilities too.

All throughout the morning, I hadn't been able to

shake the strange disquiet having to do with Red. I sensed a shift in my relationship with the draco, and I had the feeling it had to do with Ansgar. I could admit, I hadn't been myself since returning from my meeting with Ansgar two days ago. He filled my thoughts in a way that was entirely too overwhelming.

I'd relived our encounter in the cavern more times than I could count. And I'd done the same with his kisses. Perhaps they'd meant nothing to Ansgar, only a part of the pretense of our meeting. But they had shaken me to my core.

He'd shaken me to my core.

Everything about him was engaging—his determination to protect the king, his effortless way of conversing, his intelligence and wit, his strong and compelling presence.

And the way he'd kissed me, as if I mattered, as if he was as attracted to me as I was to him.

My heart fluttered with the same sensations he'd awakened in me during the kisses. The simple fact was that I adored him. Yes, I truly did. And my quick infatuation frustrated me.

A trilling sensation reverberated in my ears. I paused and looked to the sky, letting the familiar sound comfort me.

"Where have you been?" I whispered, unable to keep the chastisement and worry from my tone.

The murmuring response was low and repentant.

Father stopped and glanced overhead too. His sun-darkened face wrinkled in concern. "Red?"

I nodded.

He tugged his heavy wool cap down over his gray hair and red ears in an attempt to keep himself warm.

But the knitted material was old and loose and didn't fit well anymore. "Then he's finally back?"

"'Twould appear so." I shielded my eyes with my hand, the morning sun blinding but warm. I searched the sky for a sign of him, but only a few clouds floated overhead.

Since the day ten years ago that I'd stumbled upon Red as a hatchling, abandoned and dying, I'd never gone more than a few hours without communicating with the draco. Even when he was off hunting, he always stayed connected with me.

But I hadn't felt his presence nearby or heard him since last night.

I'd tried not to worry, but as the morn had progressed, the pressure in my chest kept mounting. After involving Red in the battle with Swaine last month, I speculated it was only a matter of time before draco hunters came after him. The Ice Men, who made a fortune from capturing the flying lizards in the Snowden Mountains, would have their sights set upon Red. If they could not have him for their own, they would at least attempt to eliminate him.

The moment I'd stood on a cliff in the Valley of Red Dragons overlooking the battlefield and realized King Ulrik and the Norvegian soldiers were being slaughtered by a Swainian draco, I'd summoned Red without a second thought.

Now, weeks afterward, I wondered if I'd done the right thing by involving him in the battle. I couldn't change what I'd done by exposing him. All I could do was chastise him to be careful of being seen. I wanted him to stay out of sight until the Ice Men tired of searching for him this autumn.

Red trilled again, this time more urgently.

Something *was* amiss.

I lowered my scythe and attempted to gauge the pattern of Red's communication. Though we spoke different languages, I'd learned to interpret his as best I could. Thankfully, he was much better at understanding mine.

Father watched my face expectantly. "What is it, Lissy?"

I listened again more intently but then shook my head. "I cannot decipher what he's communicating. It's not familiar." Clearly, he'd done something new, and I didn't have the ability to understand what it was.

"Where are you?" I whispered, knowing he was within range again of hearing me. Our bond was so strong, I needed only to breathe and he would find me.

His soft response indicated he was arriving at the tunet. Though he didn't say so, I got the impression he wanted me to meet him there. As fast as I possibly could.

Was he injured?

My body tensed. "I think he's hurt. I must go to him."

Father nodded, having long past accepted the unique bond I shared with the draco. "Where is he?"

"He's aiming for the tunet." I started across the field, picking up my skirt and running. I didn't wait to see if Father followed. I already knew he would. Red had become part of our family, and Father would want to help me doctor the draco in any way he could.

Thankfully, the barley grew in the infields, and the distance to the tunet—the farmyard—was only a quarter of a league. Though the infields were cleared of trees, most farmers left the thick shrubs and trees surrounding their tunets as a way to not only fence in their livestock but also provide a buffer against the blowing snow during the severest parts of winter.

By the time I burst through the woodland that surrounded the barns and lofthouse, I was frantic with worry. I searched the sky again before scanning the woodland.

Red was still nowhere that I could see. "Red?" I shouted his name.

He replied with a shriek, his version of a shout.

I spun in time to see him flying from the west, just barely above the treetops. He was carrying something. A gift for us? Prey that we could smoke and eat over the winter?

As he drew nearer, my pulse stopped. This was no prey. Red had a human. A man.

Why was Red bringing me a man? He'd never done anything like this before.

"Who is he?" I whispered.

Mate.

Red's low response made no sense. "Who?"

Belongs to you.

I still couldn't understand what Red meant. But I refrained from any other questions as he dipped nearer. Arrows riddled the man's body, and blood stained his garments. Something about the man seemed familiar. With the drooping angle of his head, I couldn't see his face, but I could tell he was unconscious.

As Red flapped his large wings and slowed, I raced forward, knowing I needed to grab this injured man before he hit the ground to prevent further trauma to his already battered body. He was wearing mail, but the arrows had penetrated, the one in his leg having gone the deepest.

I took hold of his torso, hoping I could hold his weight. When Red released his grip, the man's weight sank against me, nearly sending me to my knees. As I held on tightly and propped him up, his head lolled, revealing his face.

I couldn't contain a gasp. "Ansgar?"

His head fell forward again, his chin resting on his chest, revealing a wound on his neck.

A swell of horror rolled through me. Ansgar had clearly been attacked with the intent of murder. But why? And by whom?

Red began to flap in an upward movement. *Mate.*

The draco's soft trill penetrated my roiling thoughts, and I finally understood what Red was saying. He thought Ansgar was my life partner.

I wanted to tell Red no, that he was wrong, that I hardly knew Ansgar. But Red had sensed my new feelings toward Ansgar, and he'd known Ansgar was in trouble, the same way he always knew when I was in trouble.

As much as I wanted to question Red further about where he'd found Ansgar and who had been attacking him, I could sense Ansgar was quickly fading.

"Who is it?" Father called as he jogged into the yard as fast as his limping gait would allow.

I'd spoken to Father about Ansgar before leaving to deliver my message. And after getting home, I'd also relayed what had transpired during the recent secret meeting, leaving out the kisses, of course. I'd also refrained from disclosing my feelings about Ansgar. I'd been too embarrassed and confused to make sense of them for myself, much less attempt to explain them to my father.

And now . . . Red had brought me Ansgar because he assumed my fledgling attraction to the man meant we were a couple, that Ansgar belonged to me.

Now wasn't the time to explain Red's mistake. "'Tis Sir Ansgar." I strained to keep him from slumping out of my arms. "Help me. We need to get him into the house."

When Father reached me, his breathing came in heavy gasps. Regardless of the strain to himself, he eased Ansgar back until he was supporting the body and I held the legs, then we transported him into the lower level of the lofthouse, which was already crowded with what we'd harvested thus far.

Our living quarters were above the storage room, accessed by a ladder by the door. But we couldn't attempt to carry Ansgar up the ladder, not in his current condition. Instead, we cleared a spot on the floor near the hearth. The embers still glowed from earlier when we'd banked them, and now Father stirred them and added fuel before swinging the cauldron of mead away from the heat and moving the iron pot full of water into position above the growing flames.

Meanwhile, I staunched the flow of blood in Ansgar's neck, then carefully worked the arrows from his flesh—except the one in his leg that would require much more finesse.

Father helped me remove the chain mail and insisted I leave while he finished undressing Ansgar down to his linen breeches. When we could finally access the leg wound, we labored together to extract the last arrow. Ansgar thrashed, no doubt feeling the excruciating pain even in his unconscious state.

By the time we completed cleaning and stitching each wound and then lining them with a healing poultice that Mother had developed, the afternoon was mostly spent. Ansgar remained restless, but as long as none of his flesh putrefied, he would likely live. Father wasn't sure if the wound to Ansgar's leg had damaged muscles and nerves, which would make for a more difficult healing and possibly give Ansgar a limp. But overall, we'd spared his life, even if we hadn't spared him pain.

Though I was strangely loathe to leave his side, I didn't want to cause more work for Father. I returned to the barley field to retrieve our tools, then corralled and fed the livestock. As I threw fresh hay into the sheep pen, I could feel Red nearby, likely in the hills to the north where he oft stayed.

I paused, pitchfork in hand. "Thank you."

The vibrations of his response reached me a moment later, the warmth of his affection letting me know he'd do anything for me and my family.

I still didn't have the heart to tell Red that Ansgar wasn't kin, wouldn't be my life partner, and wouldn't stay after he had healed. Once Ansgar left, Red would learn that lesson for himself.

Chapter
9

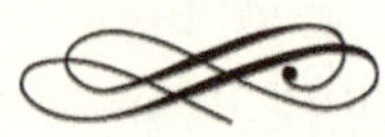

ANSGAR

PAIN WAS MY CONSTANT COMPANION. I SEEMED TO LIVE IN A LAKE of fire. Every time I awoke, I cried out with the agony of the flames lapping at my flesh. Someone was always there to give me a sip of a bitter drink, press a cool cloth to my face, and attempt to ease the burning in my back and limbs.

I didn't know where I was, who was around, or what had happened. The torment made coherent thoughts too difficult. The only thing I longed for was to fall back into the oblivion where I didn't have to feel anything.

I wasn't sure how long I hovered in and out of consciousness, but at some point, I awoke. And the heat was gone.

With my eyes closed, I remained unmoving, using my other senses to take stock of where I was. A feather-stuffed pallet cushioned my body, and my chest and cheek rested against it. The chill in the air bathed my exposed skin. But heat emanated from a crackling fire. I breathed in the scents of comfrey, chamomile, ginger, and other herbs I couldn't name.

The rattle of the door and the whistle within the chimney told me the day was windy. And the soft limping scuff of footsteps indicated I wasn't alone.

I pried my eyes open to find that I was lying near the hearth. The steam rising from a bubbling pot was likely some kind of medicinal tonic containing some of the herbs I was smelling.

Gritting my teeth, I pressed up on my elbows until I'd arisen enough to see my surroundings better. I was inside the low-ceilinged room of what appeared to be a lofthouse, the typical home for many farmers in Norvegia.

The movement seemed to set me on fire again, and I dropped with a grunt back to the feather pallet.

The shuffling steps ventured my way, and in the next instant someone was kneeling beside me. "Praise be," came a grandfatherly voice. "You're awake."

I glanced up to find kind eyes peering down at me from a leathery face framed by tousled gray hair and brows. "I'm Nils."

My mind flashed with images of my pursuers surrounding me, of Sigfrid turning against me, of fighting upon the rock, and the draco lifting me away. This older man had somehow come to my rescue. Had he found me after the draco dropped me?

With frail features and a gentle smile, he seemed harmless enough, but did I dare tell him my true name? If I did, he'd likely inform others of my location. Then Sigfrid and Rasmus would learn I remained alive. Erelong, they'd find a way to finish eliminating me.

"I'm honored to have you here, Sir Ansgar," Nils said with a bow of his head.

I should have known he'd figure out who I was. "Thank

you," I managed, though my voice was hoarse. "But please don't tell anyone I'm here. I fear doing so will only put both of us in peril."

"No need to worry, sire." Nils pressed a hand to my cheek. His fingers were rough but cool and soothing. "We won't speak of it to a soul. You're safe with us."

Relief flooded me along with a sense of peace. For a reason I couldn't explain, I trusted this stranger.

My eyes felt suddenly heavy, and I struggled to keep them open, wanting to learn more about all that had transpired to bring me to this farm. But I gave in to the need to shut them, letting myself fall into a deep, restful slumber.

The next time I awoke, Nils was by my side, this time with a bowl of broth. He fed it to me by spoonfuls and offered me an herbal drink. I eagerly accepted his ministrations, too hungry and thirsty to make conversation. When I finished, weariness overcame me and I slept again.

Sometime later, a gust of cold air and the shutting of a door jerked me from my oblivion. I blinked, gathering my bearings. The room was decidedly darker than earlier, which meant eve was falling.

"How does he fare?" came a woman's voice from behind me, one that sounded familiar.

"The fever broke at noon," Nils responded. "And he awoke then, as well as midafternoon."

"Thanks be to God."

My pulse sputtered. Was Lis here?

"Aye. Many thanks to God."

"Then you think he is through the worst?" Though tinged with worry, the voice belonged to none other than Lis. Was this her farm? Her father? Had her draco rescued me?

"His wound is no longer so red." Nils spoke in his gentle tone. "And the discharge is gone. I believe he will heal now."

One of my wounds had apparently putrefied and caused me to have a fever.

"Truly?" Lis asked. "Please do not say so to ease my mind."

"Truly. He's on the mend."

She released a long, shaky breath. Her tangible relief did something to my insides I couldn't explain. All I knew was that the warm energy coursing through me had nothing to do with a fever or hot herbal drinks.

"I'll go out and tend to the livestock tonight," Nils said.

"I don't mind."

"You've done the labor of two people the past few days, and now you must rest."

"But you've hardly slept—"

"Let me do this, Lissy."

I could sense her hesitation even though I couldn't see it. A moment later, the door opened and then closed, bringing another gust of cold air.

Nils had gone out. And I was alone with Lis, the feisty maiden I'd tried not to think about but who had invaded my thoughts nonetheless.

My blood pumped harder. I didn't want to feel this way, but my attraction to her had come swiftly and powerfully that day we'd met at Lover's Lane. As much as I wanted to deny a potent pull existed, as much as I'd hoped it had been only a one-time feeling, it was there again, coursing through me even stronger. In fact, I'd never experienced such an immediate and intense connection with a woman.

I needed to let her know I was awake, but as her

footsteps approached, I couldn't find the words to thank her for bringing me here and saving my life. How long had I been unconscious?

She stopped behind me, out of my line of vision. I could feel the chill radiating off her garments and body. If her father had been inside doctoring me, then the burden of the harvesting had fallen on her shoulders. As a result, it was likely she and her father wouldn't have time to complete all the work before winter set in.

I opened my mouth to apologize for imposing on their goodwill, but I heard her bend, and in the next instant she touched my bare back. I was suddenly conscious of the fact that I was wearing only breeches and covered in a thin linen sheet that had fallen partially away. With the lure I felt toward her, the situation was entirely indecent, and I was surprised her father was allowing us to be alone this way.

Of course, he believed I was asleep. And incapacitated.

But as she caressed the flesh near my shoulder wound, I felt anything but incapacitated. I wanted to roll over, take her hand in mine, and kiss her fingers.

I pinched my eyes closed. I needed to slumber again and rapidly. Then I'd be able to refrain from putting Lis into a compromising situation. But as her fingers made a trail down my spine to the wound by my side, I awakened more than I ever had been. I would get no sleep, not now, maybe not ever again.

Her touch is innocent. She's only concerned about my wounds. I silently repeated the words several times. But my internal warning didn't matter. The merest graze of her fingers was stoking a fire inside me, a fire that scalded me, a dangerous fire that could only lead to no good.

I had to put an end to her touch.

With a resolve that came from deep within, I released a long breath, hoping it would alert her to my wakefulness.

Immediately, she jerked her hand away.

I opened my eyes again and tried to roll to my side. I only made it halfway before sucking in a breath at the sharp pain that shot through my leg.

She gently prodded me to my original stomach-down position. "You shouldn't move yet."

"I'm fine." I wasn't fine, and we both knew it. But I didn't want to admit I was helpless.

"It's about time you woke up." If I hadn't heard the worry in her tone moments ago, I wouldn't have guessed how relieved she was. Her skirt rustled as she rose. "You must be hungry again."

I was, but not for food. I was hungry for the sight of her, but I bit back my response. I'd already given myself too much leeway concerning this maiden.

"We could try some solid food." She crossed past me toward the fire. With a rag in hand, she lifted the lid off the pot, dipped a ladle inside, and stirred.

The scent of venison stew greeted me, and my stomach answered her statement for me. It growled its need for sustenance.

I waited for her to turn, suddenly breathless to see her face, to look into her eyes, and to take her in fully. But she stirred for another minute before reaching for a bowl and scooping in two helpings of stew.

Hot steam wafted from the bowl. She blew noisily and stirred it, clearly attempting to cool it down. Or was she stalling, doing her best to prolong facing me? Was she uncomfortable with me? Embarrassed to have been caught touching me?

"How long have I been here?"

"This is the third day." She continued to blow and stir.

"Have you seen signs of anyone searching for me?"

She shook her head, her long braid swishing. "No doubt your attackers will assume you are dead."

"I pray they'll believe your draco took me away as his next meal."

She didn't immediately reject my statement about the draco being hers as she'd previously done.

"Thank you for instructing your draco to watch over me—"

"I didn't instruct him regarding any such thing. He did it of his own volition." She finally turned her head enough that I caught a glimpse of her beautiful face, her cheeks rosy from being out in the cold, her green eyes bright, and her lips pretty enough to kiss.

No. I couldn't kiss her again. Not if I wanted to retain a shred of my dignity and maintain boundaries that wouldn't lead her to believe anything more could exist between us besides friendship.

As if recognizing she'd given away her connection to the draco, she twisted away, her shoulders stiffening. "Perhaps he remembers you from the battle last month. Or perhaps he has seen you at other times and likes you."

"Maybe he likes me as much as you do." I tried for light and teasing.

Instead of sparring words with me, she ducked her head and blew on the stew once more.

My pulse gave an extra beat. Did her lack of protest mean she liked me more than she let on? "The draco was kind to bring me here to you and your father, although I regret the delay in harvesting I'm costing you."

"We are mostly done. Another week or two and we'll

be well prepared."

"I aim to be on my feet again soon and will help you—"

"You'll do no such thing." She spun and glared at me. "You'll rest until you're well healed."

I let myself stare, getting my first full view of her, taking her in from her wind-blown hair down to her muddy boots. She was my feast. I needed nothing for my famished soul but her. "You're as beautiful as I remembered." The words slipped out before I could stop them.

She sucked in a breath and dropped her gaze to the bowl, her long lashes shielding her eyes, but she couldn't hide the pleasure in her expression. She was silent several seconds before she glanced at the door, as though her father might burst through and chastise us for our exchange. "You mustn't say things like that. My father doesn't know about the . . . that we . . ."

I let her unspoken word hang for only a moment before filling it in for her. "That we kissed?"

Her lashes rose, and her eyes rounded. "*You* kissed me."

"And you kissed me back."

"You took me by surprise."

"Very well. Next time, I'll warn you well in advance." With each word of our conversation, I could feel the strength infusing my blood. The mere sight of her, the mere exchange of banter, the mere power of her presence was healing to my body.

She nibbled at her lip.

"Next time, I'll allow you to kiss me first."

"There cannot be a next time." Her voice lacked conviction. "And if there was a next time, I would never kiss you first."

I shrugged, although the motion pained my wound. "Is that a challenge, my lady?"

"I'm no lady." She moved toward me, avoiding my gaze. "And I am not challenging you to anything."

"Because you know I would win."

"And how, exactly, would you win?"

"The next time we kiss, you'll be the one who initiates it. I guarantee it." Why was I letting myself get carried away with this ungodly exchange? I needed to put an end to it. So why couldn't I?

"I guarantee I shall not initiate anything." As she knelt beside me, her hands trembled as she lifted the spoon. Though she might deny our attraction, it was obvious she felt something too. "Now, let's get you fed before you become too full of yourself."

I couldn't keep from chuckling, but the movement wracked me with pain and quickly cut off my laughter. Slowly, I pushed myself up to one elbow, then reached for the spoon.

She lifted it out of reach.

I went for it again.

"I shall feed you."

"I can feed myself."

She released an exaggerated sigh even as her lips twitched with a smile. "I have never met a man as obstinate as you."

"Obstinate." I released a scoffing huff. "I'm behaving as docilely as a kitten."

"Then I should like to see you behaving as a lion."

"Maybe one day you will." There was no *one day* with this maiden. Was there? What if I'd been too rash in making my vow to remain single and devoted only to the king? What if I was destined for more?

She tipped the spoon toward me. "I intend to feed you today, so please resign yourself to the task of opening your mouth."

Ought I protest again? I was fully capable of feeding myself, although from my odd angle, I'd have a difficult time reaching for the food. I settled my head on my bent arm. Letting her feed me might actually be enjoyable and prolong this irresistible tension between us.

She moved the spoon closer.

I opened up and at the same time locked my gaze with hers.

Her eyes were a lush and thick green, like the richest summer foliage. As she placed the spoon between my lips, her attention shifted to my mouth.

I closed my lips around the bite, conscious that she was watching me. Was she thinking about how my mouth had touched hers only a few days ago? Was she remembering the warmth and pleasure of our kiss?

She nibbled at her bottom lip again. Even if she wasn't thinking about the kisses we'd shared, they were uppermost in my mind again. And I wanted to reach for her and pull her down into another one.

How many days of recovery did I have left? Whatever the amount, I'd only torture myself if I didn't gain control of my runaway thoughts. I had to change the subject, turn the attention away from the physical attraction that was a very real and compelling force between us.

I quickly chewed and swallowed the first bite, not tasting it at all. "Tell me about your draco."

She focused on digging the spoon into the stew.

"'Tis clear you have a special bond with him." I infused seriousness into my tone, wanting her to understand I was no longer teasing her and that I genuinely cared about her relationship with her draco.

She lifted another spoonful of stew to my lips.

I took it, and this time I didn't linger over it. Instead, I pulled back and chewed, waiting for her to say something more.

"I'm not allowed to speak about Red." She twisted the spoon. "I don't want to put his life or mine in danger."

She had already done so, but I refrained from reminding her. "You can rest assured that the last thing I wish is for you to face danger on my account." The confession came out low and earnest.

When her eyes met mine again, the power of her gaze wrapped around me, binding me to her. I wasn't sure I'd ever be able to liberate myself. Or if I'd even want to. I quavered, afraid of what might happen if she knew just how much she'd captivated me.

Chapter 10

Lis

Ansgar was much too easy to confide in. Before I knew it, I'd told him all about how I found Red when I was but a girl, how I'd raised him, how he saw me as a parent figure, and how we communicated.

By the time Ansgar finished most of the bowl of stew, his eyes were heavy, and he struggled to keep them open. I was flattered he was trying so hard to stay alert to talk to me and share my company. But he soon succumbed to slumber, allowing me to stare at him to my heart's content as I'd done the previous few times I'd stayed with him so Father could sleep.

With the firelight reflecting off the strong lines of his face, Ansgar was more handsome than I remembered. Even with the bruises and cuts, he radiated purpose and possibility. And somehow I wanted to be a part of whatever those purposes and possibilities were.

He didn't stay on his pallet for too many more days. Though the wound in his leg pained him, he hobbled around with the simple crutch Father carved for him. Ansgar couldn't go far and tired easily, but he was clearly determined to make use of his leg again soon.

Father spent most of his time with Ansgar, changing bandages, aiding with personal needs, and allowing Ansgar to help him with easy tasks around the farm. All the while, Father relayed escapades from the days when he'd been a soldier in service to King Ulrik's father, Erik Bloodaxe, when Norvegia had been at war with the invading barbarians from the Wend. I'd heard the tales many times over and smiled as Father enjoyed telling them to someone new.

As one week of Ansgar's stay passed into two, I was busy most days finishing tasks in preparation for winter. Though I was exhausted by the time darkness drove me home, I relished the time in front of the hearth every eve with Ansgar and Father while they played dice and rocks, a board game Father had tried to teach me but that I'd never had the patience to learn.

"Rasmus won't stop with eliminating me," Ansgar said while he waited for Father to take his turn.

I sat nearby patching a pair of Father's stockings. I wasn't nearly as proficient with sewing as Mother had been, but the task fell to me, and I'd learned to do it because I had no wish to watch Father suffer from holes in his garments.

"He won't be satisfied until he destroys anyone who poses a threat to his authority," Ansgar continued. "He'll become the strongest man in the land and rule through whomever he puts on the throne. I can't sit by and let that happen."

"I thought you said Rasmus will allow the sword to

choose the next king." I paused in my stitching to watch Ansgar as he leaned on his elbows and studied the board. "Do you think he has some sort of magic that will cause the sword to come loose at his bidding?"

"Though some believe the Sages wield magic, I have never seen it in my years at court. No, more likely Rasmus will use his influence to put a man of his choosing on the throne, though I know not how."

I poked my needle again into the thick wool. I should keep my thoughts to myself, but I couldn't. "Rasmus and the sword's choosing are no longer your concern. Everyone believes you're dead. You can live out your life in peace." On the farm. With me.

He was becoming a part of our family. His presence brought life and energy in a way we hadn't experienced before, even when Mother was alive.

Yes, I'd entertained the possibility of him staying and helping take care of the farm and Father. And maybe one day, he'd ask me to marry him. I was ashamed to admit I'd considered such a thing, even more ashamed to admit how much I wanted it.

Carefully, Father moved one of his pieces, letting his finger linger on it as he scanned the rest of the board.

The moment Father removed his finger, Ansgar made his next move, quickly and decisively, then settled his elbows back on his knees. "I wouldn't be able to live out my life in peace knowing I'd turned my back on the king during his time of need."

"The king turned his back on you."

"Only because he's not in his right mind."

I knew Ansgar was correct. He'd spoken previously of his frustration at having failed to protect the king.

Even so, longing welled up within me—longing for a future that would never be mine.

I jabbed the needle and pricked my finger. As I lifted it to my mouth to nurse the wound and keep the blood from spreading, my gaze snagged with Ansgar's.

He hadn't moved but was watching me through half-lidded eyes, the fire within them barely banked.

I'd caught him looking at me that way occasionally, and each time it elicited the same response inside me, the response I felt right now—warmth spilling through my middle, breathless anticipation seizing my chest, and a longing in the air between us I couldn't deny or explain away.

His words about kissing me again were also never far from my mind. He'd said the next time that he'd wait for me to kiss him first. And true to his word, he hadn't approached me or even hinted at the intimacy.

Of course, with Father's constant supervision and watchfulness, Ansgar wouldn't dare. Nor would I. But it didn't diminish a growing need within me.

Could Ansgar sense it?

Father stood, bumped the game board, and had to catch several pieces as they fell over and rolled toward the edge. "Time for a breath of cool air. Don't you agree, Ansgar?"

Ansgar straightened and avoided looking my way. "I agree."

Father attempted to set the pieces upright on the board but fumbled with them, avoiding looking at me too.

As the two grabbed their cloaks and shuffled toward the door, embarrassment stitched through me as surely as my thread through the stockings. Father could feel the growing connection between Ansgar and me. And somehow, he knew it was getting hotter each day. How long could we all last before someone was burned?

A few days later, as I worked in the field, snow began to float down around me. I paused in my digging and lifted my face to the feathery-light flakes. Was it wrong to pray the snow would trap Ansgar at the farm for many more days, if not through the winter?

Even as I wished for him to be stuck, I suspected he would only grow miserable if he couldn't do his part in saving the king. He would never be the type of man who would sit back and do nothing when duty was calling. While I respected that about him, each day we were together, I couldn't keep from wishing both of us were free to pursue a future together.

I sighed and thrust the shovel back into the hard earth, pressed my boot against it, and wiggled it. The turnips came loose. I grabbed the handful, banged the dirt free, and tossed them into the basket. As I rose, I caught sight of Ansgar limping without his crutch across the field toward me.

He'd been smoking game Father brought back from his hunting. It was an easy task, one that allowed Ansgar to feel useful but didn't put too much strain on his leg.

I straightened and, for a moment, let myself enjoy the fine figure he made with his strong shoulders, rigid back, long legs, and determined steps. I could go on watching him forever to the neglect of all my work.

At the wanton thought, I ducked my head and dug the shovel into the next mound. Why was he coming out to the field? To help me? Or to practice traveling a longer distance? Regardless, I didn't want him to see just how eager I was for his presence, especially since I'd seen him but an hour ago when I'd delivered another bag of root vegetables to the cellar. Father had been out hunting, so I hadn't stopped to speak with Ansgar though I'd been tempted to.

From the corner of my eye, I gauged his approach, my body tingling with awareness, especially because he was staring at me boldly and not bothering to hide his interest the way he did when Father was present.

As he halted several paces away, I cast him a glance.

"I've come to say good-bye."

I stopped in the middle of a jab. I didn't have to question him to know he was serious. The gravity in his expression told me he was going, and nothing I could say would deter him. Even so, my question tumbled out. "Why now?"

"Nils ran into friends while hunting and learned the king has officially disinherited Princess Elinor."

Another snowflake floated down, this one landing on my nose. "Has he chosen his replacement?"

"The Royal Sages and Noble Council are searching the Oldenberg family history for anyone else who might share the royal family bloodline. If they cannot find such a person, they have agreed that the man who frees the Sword of the Magi—commoner or nobility alike—will become the heir to the throne so long as the king gives his approval of the man."

My pulse gave a slow and awkward stumble. My

thoughts returned to Maxim's insistence that I was the firstborn child of Princess Blanche, who had been King Ulrik's sister. If that was true, I was Elinor's older sister and shared the bloodline. In fact, I was next in line to the throne, even above Elinor.

I didn't want to think on the prospect now any more than I had over the past weeks. "And can you stop what has been set in motion?"

"I must at least try." Ansgar favored his uninjured leg, the walk to the infields clearly having taxed him.

A sudden desperation clawed up inside me. "You cannot go back and stop Rasmus. He'll kill you." Ansgar had told us about the bounty Rasmus had placed upon him if he ever returned to the capital. If Ansgar went back, he'd be captured and beheaded. There would be no way for Red to rescue him the next time.

"I must continue my journey to find Maxim and the princess. Maxim is the only one who can rival Rasmus in his wisdom and wile. He can help me change the course of events and restore the king to his former state of mind. Once the king is in his right mind, he'll give the throne to Princess Elinor. I am sure of it."

"You won't be able to do anything if you are dead."

"I won't die. Not until I accomplish this."

My helplessness swelled. "I suppose that's what you said when you fought the men sent to murder you."

"You sound as though you care whether I live or die." His voice took on a note of teasing, one I loved but didn't want to hear at this moment.

"If you insist on leaving for certain death, then go." I jerked the shovel, then jabbed it into the ground. He was right. I did care about his life. Too much. Clearly more than he did.

Blindly, I uncovered another cluster of turnips. I grabbed them and threw them in the basket. As I straightened and stuck the shovel in again, I could feel him watching me.

"Lis. I'm sorry."

I shoved hard at the dirt, letting it receive the brunt of my frustration. "Sorry for what?"

"Sorry I'm not a different man in a different position."

I understood what he meant—that he wasn't the man for me, not when he took his task of guarding the king so seriously. But now that he was in my life, I loathed the thought of losing him, especially forever.

Ansgar took a step closer, then another. He was but an arm's length away, the closest we'd been to each other since that night when I'd knelt next to his pallet and fed him.

I didn't stop. I bent and tugged loose another turnip.

When I straightened, he moved in again, only a hand's span from me. "If I were a free man"—he spoke in a whisper laced with desperation—"I would have you."

The words silenced the raging inside me and replaced it with a quiet desperation of my own. "You are free. Everyone believes you're dead."

"I am beholden to the truth regardless of anyone else."

I wanted to protest but restrained myself. He was a man of great honor and integrity, and I wouldn't want him to be any other way, no matter how difficult the travail for me.

A snowflake drifted on the air between us. Finally, I nodded, my throat cinching with a strange emotion I couldn't name.

His gaze traced my cheek, leaving warmth in its wake. He lifted his hand as though to follow that path but then fisted his fingers and dropped them to his side.

If there was nothing I could do to change his mind about leaving, then perhaps I could give him a reason to fight harder to live, a reason to come back when he completed his work of saving the king.

I'd told him if we kissed again I wouldn't initiate it. He'd boasted that I would. Though I didn't want him to be right, urgency prodded me. I finished closing the span between us, reached around his neck, and rose until my lips met his. I pressed in with the intensity of a woman trying to rescue someone she was losing.

His arms wrapped around me, drawing me close while he responded to the kiss almost fiercely with a need that matched my own.

Thus far during his stay, we might have been able to skirt around whatever was happening between us. But at the moment, our attraction was too powerful to deny.

This wasn't a farewell kiss for me. Instead, I wanted it to awaken him to all the possibilities between us, especially the possibility that we could still have a future. But as his kiss deepened with a consuming fervor, I sensed this was his farewell.

"No!" I broke away, tears stinging my eyes.

He clung to me, his labored breathing echoing in the barrenness of the field. He paused but a heartbeat before angling in and chasing my lips.

I shifted my head, denying him access.

Instead, his lips grazed my cheek.

I closed my eyes and fought the urge to kiss him again, knowing the next time I wouldn't be able to make myself stop.

"Lis." My name on his lips was a soft plea that brushed my skin. He wanted me to understand, to let this be our farewell. A forever farewell.

"No!" I said louder, this time releasing my hold and pushing his chest. I didn't want to say good-bye. Not today. And certainly not forever.

I struggled to break free. His grip tightened but a moment, then he released me. I stumbled backward, away from the shovel and basket of turnips, away from him, and away from his leaving.

Maybe if I didn't utter a farewell, it wouldn't be so final. I spun and ran away from him, my feet slipping in the dirt clods. As I reached the edge of the field, I saw Father standing in the clearing, his hands in his pockets, his shoulders stooped, his expression sad.

He'd witnessed the kiss. Was he disappointed in me?

I rushed past him onto the trail that led to the tunet. I expected him to call out and gently chastise me. But he said nothing.

Tears filled my eyes, but I wouldn't let them spill over. My lungs ached with the need to cry out, but I kept the cries buried. As I reached the tunet, I raced across the yard and into the house. Once there, I closed the door and paced the length of the storage room, which had grown fuller every day with the various herbs and plants I'd bundled or strung to dry.

I could hear Red's trilling concern. He sensed my

dismay and wanted to help. But in this case, he couldn't do anything to take away my pain. No one could. I whispered my assurances to the draco but didn't know how I'd ever feel assured again.

Why had I allowed myself to care about Ansgar so swiftly and so deeply? Why hadn't I been more careful?

As the door opened and Father shuffled through, I lowered myself onto the nearest stool and buried my face in my hands, too embarrassed to look at him. He closed the door quietly and paused, likely not knowing what to say or do to a daughter who'd just thrown herself at a man.

This situation was forcing us to have an awkward conversation about love, relationships, and marriage, one he probably wanted to avoid as much as I did.

I waited for his rebuke. But when the silence dragged on, I lifted my head and faced him as I knew I should. "I'm sorry. I was forward with Ansgar, and I should have refrained—"

"'Tis clear you love him."

Love him? Was that this heart-pounding bond I felt with Ansgar? One that felt impossible to sever without causing something to wither and die within me?

"You must go with him." Father leaned against the door as if he'd lost the strength to stand.

I shook my head. "He doesn't want me."

"He loves you too—"

"No . . ."

"I may be a weak, old man. But I'm not blind. Even if I were, the strength of the attraction between you is unmistakable."

I knew he'd been aware of our attraction but hadn't

realized he'd guessed how much it crackled in the air every time we were near to each other. "It doesn't matter. He's leaving to do his part to save the king."

Father nodded and stroked his beard, something he did only when he was nervous.

"Besides, I won't ever leave you—"

"You were born Princess Elisbet."

Chapter 11

ANSGAR

PRINCESS ELISBET? I FROZE, MY HAND POISED ABOVE THE DOOR handle. I hadn't meant to eavesdrop, but when I approached the door, I'd heard Nils tell Lis I loved her. I wanted to deny his statement, but somehow the certainty of his words reverberated deep inside.

I'd liked Lis from the moment I first met her, admired her inner strength, her command of the draco, and her willingness to put herself at risk to help the army. When I'd visited with her at Lover's Lane, the attraction had been just as instantaneous as the first time, only stronger. And during this stay at her home, I'd only fallen for her more deeply. Now I was so far in, I doubted I'd ever get out.

What did Nils mean by calling Lis the Princess Elisbet? Wasn't Princess Elisbet King Ulrik's niece who had vanished many years ago with her mother, Princess Blanche? The child had only been a year old at the time. No one knew what had become of the mother and infant. And no amount of searching had brought about any clues.

Surely Nils was going slightly mad, and Lis would cry out against such a bold and treasonous statement.

But the silence inside stretched, and with each passing moment, my muscles stretched tighter too, reminding me of the throbbing in my leg.

"Maxim discovered my identity during his time here." She finally spoke, her voice containing a resignation that stunned me and forced me back a step. She wasn't denying being a princess. She was, in fact, agreeing to it.

"How?" Nils's one-word question was strangled.

Because Maxim was the most intelligent man in Norvegia. But I didn't speak, only quieted my racing heartbeat so I could listen.

"Does it matter how?" Lis asked. "The real question is why you and Mother never informed me."

Again, silence fell. I could almost sense Nils's inner debate, whether to tell Lis the truth or to give her some other more palatable explanation.

"I can understand not saying anything when I was younger. But in recent years?" Her tone softened with hurt. "Why did you withhold the truth?"

"Lissy. Please." Her hurt must have tugged at Nils's sensitive heart. "Your mother, the Princess Blanche, made us swear an oath that we'd never tell you."

"I don't understand."

I let my hand fall to my side, disbelief and confusion making me almost dizzy. Lis was the Princess Elisbet. Lis was royalty. Lis was a princess.

"Please try and explain," Lis pleaded.

Nils sighed. "When your mother brought you here, she was dying of a disease she claimed was a curse that afflicted only firstborn daughters in the royal house."

"And she was the firstborn princess."

"As are you. She hoped by giving you to a poor, childless farmer and his wife, we could keep you away from the royal city and royal life and in doing so break the curse."

"If I am cursed, does it matter where I live or who my parents are?"

"Your mother believed escaping the royal life would break the power of the affliction."

"And did it help her? Did she run away to some place where she found safety?"

"She didn't tell us where she was going, but I suspect she was seeking a healer woman in the Snowden Mountains, one who could help her break the curse. But she never returned."

"Then she wasn't healed?"

I shook my head, trying to clear it, trying to make sense of everything I was hearing. Some sort of affliction was passed from mother to daughter, a curse Lis could avoid by cutting ties with her family and living in obscurity.

If being on this rural farm would keep Lis from catching the disease, then why was Nils telling her now? After all these years? He'd made a vow, and he'd broken it. What if Lis suffered as a result?

Something twisted in my gut, something akin to anger. Nils should have left things the way they were. He hadn't been under any obligation to speak up. But even as the frustration tightened within me, I knew I couldn't entirely blame Nils. For some reason, Maxim had already told Lis the truth.

Lis had known for weeks—or at least suspected—she was the Princess Elisbet, and she'd kept the news to herself. Had she wanted to deny the truth? Even now, though she seemed to be accepting her identity, her voice held no enthusiasm for it.

The knot inside loosened slightly. I wouldn't have to try hard to convince her to remain here at the farm and stay safe, the way Princess Blanche would have wanted.

"If you vowed to Princess Blanche you would say nothing to me, why are you telling me now? After all this time?" Lis's questions echoed my own, and I held my breath, waiting for the answer.

Nils was silent for a few moments before expelling a long sigh. "The same reason Ansgar is leaving. 'Tis my duty to the king and country."

If I'd thought the knot was loosening, now it cinched tight. Nils couldn't compare Lis to me.

"With the royal lineage in jeopardy," he continued, "who knows but that perhaps Providence brought you to us to keep you safe for such a time as this, so you can present yourself before the king as his heir."

I shook my head, frustration rising swiftly. I wouldn't let Lis leave this secluded farm. Not with a curse hanging over her head. I pounded several obnoxious thuds on the door before Nils swung it open.

"No." I ducked inside and straightened under the low ceiling as best I could. "Lis—Princess Elisbet—cannot go to the king."

Lis stood so quickly the stool tipped over behind her. Her eyes rounded with her surprise at my words.

Nils only watched me with his gentle and probing gaze. Had he known I was standing outside listening to their conversation? If he hadn't before, he knew now. "After all these years of sheltering her from the curse, would you put her at risk now?"

"The king and this country need her," Nils said. "If

you're willing to sacrifice yourself for your king and country, then you should allow Lis to do the same."

"She doesn't want to do the same—"

"Don't speak for me." She drew her shoulders up, and as she glared at me, I could see the resemblance to the king in her stance and features. How had I not noticed before?

I bowed my head. "Your Highness—"

"And don't call me that."

"I beg your forgiveness—"

"Oh saints above." She rolled her eyes. "Don't put on airs around me now, Ansgar. I'm still the same person. Nothing about me has changed."

Everything had changed. She was royalty. While I'd never seriously contemplated the possibility that we might one day be able to have a life together, I couldn't deny a part of me had wished for it. Especially after sharing another kiss. My body had ached as I'd watched her run away, not only because she was hurting but because a battle raged inside me, one pushing me to go after her, wrap her back in my arms and never let her go.

Now I had to put those desires far from my mind.

"You cannot put yourself in jeopardy," I insisted. "You must do as Princess Blanche wanted and keep away from the royal house. Otherwise, you'll suffer the same fate she did."

Lis's cheeks were still a healthy rosy glow from her morning outside. She radiated such beauty and vitality that it was difficult to believe a curse lingered under the surface, just waiting to bring her harm.

She lifted her chin and glared at me. "We don't know her fate."

"She obviously died," I answered. "If she had overcome

her disease or broken the curse, she would have come back for you."

Nils nodded. "I suspect as much."

"You cannot take the same chance." I folded my arms over my chest and spread out my feet, intending to block the door to keep her from leaving.

"If you can take risks, why can't I?" Narrowing her eyes, she started toward me, as though sensing my challenge. "You're willing to forfeit your life for the greater good of the kingdom, but you would deny me the same opportunity?"

I steeled myself. "I'm not living under a curse."

"You're living under hypocrisy."

She had a point. But it still didn't matter. "I don't care if I'm giving myself permission to die for the cause but am unwilling to allow you to do the same. If you call me a hypocrite and hate me for my stance, so be it."

She stopped a foot away, as regal and proud as a future queen ought to be. "If I have the power to save the king and the kingdom from the control of one as evil as Rasmus, then Father is right—perhaps God has guarded and saved me for such a time as this."

I clenched my jaw. A part of me knew her words were true. But the other part couldn't release her into the dangers of facing her curse or facing Rasmus. "Rasmus has already gone to great lengths to put his own plan into place. He will not accept you coming in and disrupting his schemes. He'll find a way to eliminate you."

"You'll find a way to keep Lissy safe." Nils had crossed to a stool and now lowered himself.

She shook her head. "I have no need of Ansgar. I'll have Red."

I met her defiant gaze with one of my own. "Red

won't be able to save you once you're in the castle and in Rasmus's clutches. Not only will you risk people learning of your connection to the draco and branding you a witch, but you'll also put Red in peril as he attempts to free you."

Her stance wavered. Uncertainty flashed in her eyes.

Lis was a smart woman. She'd understand my reasoning. If not, I would take her in my arms and kiss her again until she understood the depth of my feelings and my need to protect her, a need that seemed to run even deeper than my need to protect the king.

I hadn't realized I was staring at her mouth until she nibbled her bottom lip.

She was close enough that I could bend in to kiss her. I fought against the overwhelming urge to reach for her and drag her against me.

Nils cleared his throat.

Lis dropped her gaze and took a step away, her chest rising and falling more rapidly.

My chest was doing the same, moving in tempo with my runaway heartbeat.

Nils's voice rang with quiet conviction. "I've been praying these many years for Providence to reveal when I ought to tell Lissy about her heritage. I didn't realize I was waiting for one such as you, Sir Ansgar, to come along. One who loves Lissy enough to take her to her rightful place and protect her there."

At his pronouncement, heat burned through my chest. Once again, as when I'd been eavesdropping, a part of me wanted to deny my love for her. But I was a man of truth and honor. And I couldn't lie, even about this—not to myself or to him.

I did love Lis. And I would do just as Nils said. I would

defend her life above my own.

Was that, then, my purpose? I'd believed my destiny was in protecting the king. But maybe God had ordained the entwining of my life with Lis's instead. How else could I explain this bond that had so rapidly formed between us along with my need to keep her safe?

Nils had mentioned that Lis loved me too. Though her kiss from the infields had contained the depth of her feelings and desire for me, it wasn't possible for her to love me the way I loved her. In fact, it was better for her if she didn't dwell on her feelings.

As much as I wanted to continue to protest her joining in this fight to save the king and the kingdom, I sensed she'd made up her mind to persist whether I wanted her to or not. I would need to develop a plan for taking her before the king and proving she was Princess Elisbet, the uncontested heir to the throne.

"I'll take her to her rightful place." I spoke solemnly, repeating Nils's admonition. "And I'll spend my life protecting her there. But before we go, we must have proof Lis is the Princess Elisbet. And it must be strong enough that Rasmus cannot refute it, for he will surely try."

Nils rubbed at his gray beard and stared into the fire. "Princess Blanche gave us nothing to verify Lissy's birthright. I suspect she did so in order to erase every trace that Lissy was her daughter."

"Lis shares many family traits." I studied her again. She was as beautiful as Princess Elinor, perhaps even more so, but I couldn't make myself say it—not in front of Nils. "But family likeness will not persuade Rasmus. He'll demand much more than we'll be able to produce and will do his best to cast doubt upon Lis's authenticity."

Nils continued to peer into the hearth, his brow wrinkling as if he was deep in thought.

Lis released a frustrated sigh, then spun toward the ladder leading up to the loft. "Regardless of proof, I shall go to court and to the king to plead my case. If Maxim and Ansgar both recognize the truth of my identity, then others will too."

Both Maxim and I were considered outlaws and enemies of the king. Few would dare accept our testimony regarding Lis, even if they wanted to. "We won't go until we have evidence." I didn't care that my tone was hard. I intended to keep her alive, and to do so, I would be in charge of this venture, not her. It didn't matter if she was the princess and I but her servant. She didn't have experience with the royal court like I did.

Lis stiffened and paused her ascent. "You heard Father. I have nothing. All I can do is offer myself."

My mind scrambled to find an answer, anything that might help our cause. There had to be something, somewhere, that would prove Lis was the princess.

"The healer woman." Nils sat forward and snapped his fingers. "She requires a trade before offering her skills. Princess Blanche must have come prepared to give her something of value."

I'd heard of the healer woman. Her name was Ulla, and many believed her to be a witch. She'd lived in the southern hills of the Snowden Mountains for as long as anyone could remember. Some said she was as ancient as the hills themselves, but I'd heard others say she wasn't more than a hundred years in age.

Seeking her out could waste precious time. We had no guarantee Princess Blanche had reached Ulla those many years ago. Even if the princess had, we couldn't know for sure if she traded anything that would give Lis proof of royalty.

In addition, the skies bore the telltale signs of snow. 'Twould not be long ere the snowfall began in earnest, making travel into the Snowden Mountains treacherous.

Lis continued up the ladder. "I'll pack and seek the healer woman."

"You cannot go anywhere without me."

"I have been traveling alone my entire life. I don't need you serving as a nursemaid."

I could only imagine all the dangerous places this headstrong maiden had gone by herself—the battle with Swaine and Lover's Lane were just two recently. Of course, she could summon Red, but every time she ventured out on her own, she was taking a chance.

"As your devoted servant and protector," I said more emphatically, "from this day forward, I'll accompany you anywhere you go and serve as your guard when you are resting."

She reached the top rung, her head already out of sight. "You need more time to recuperate."

Though my leg wound still pained me, it was healing well, thanks to Nils's diligent ministrations. "I shall be fine. I have ridden farther with worse wounds."

"That may be." She climbed into the living quarters above, and her voice became muffled as it filtered down through the floor. "But I would have you rest and regain your strength."

A growl pushed for release, but I held it at bay. "Don't think I'm a fool. If I let you go without me, you will not only travel to the healer woman but go directly from there to Vordinberg."

She hesitated long enough for me to know I was right. "'Tis inappropriate for us to travel together alone without a chaperone. Father won't allow it."

My ready response fell away. She was correct. As both of us were unmarried, I didn't want to do anything to stain her reputation or cause people to think ill of her on account of me.

If Nils had easily deduced the feelings between us, then others would as well. I would have to do a better job of containing my attraction. Nevertheless, even if I vowed to remain completely chaste, people would still assume the worst.

Nils had begun gathering food into a pack.

"What do you suggest we do, Nils?" I lowered my voice.

"I trust you." Nils wrapped several hunks of recently smoked venison into a cloth. "You're a man of great integrity and honor and won't do anything to harm Lis or bring her shame."

I appreciated his trust and his words of praise. But I was only a man. "You saw me kiss her." If he hadn't known how attracted to her I was, the kiss had most certainly shown it.

He paused with the wrapped meat halfway in the sack, then he lifted his serious gaze to mine. "The greatest honor a man can experience is dying to himself and living for a greater cause."

Was Nils speaking from experience? Had he and his wife chosen this isolated and lonely existence to protect Lis? Perhaps the keeping of so difficult a secret from Lis had required sacrifices. Perhaps he'd sacrificed friendships and relationships with family to live here. Whatever the case, I knew what he was telling me. I needed to die to my desire for Lis for the greater cause of the kingdom and the future of Norvegia.

For her, for me, for the good of everyone, I had to let my longings go unattended, and I would need to start burying them deep where they couldn't find release, deep where, eventually, I might be able to forget about them.

Behind us, Lis climbed down the ladder, a sack slung across her shoulder. "Should I take the snowshoes?" She hopped to the ground.

"Yes, *we* will take the snowshoes." I met Nils's gaze a final time, letting him see my resolve.

He reached out and squeezed my hand.

At the sight of Nils's gesture, Lis glanced between us. "You're allowing us to travel together without a chaperone?"

Nils resumed packing. "Ansgar is your guard and chaperone."

That's all I'd ever be—her guard and chaperone. And I needed to begin acting like it.

Chapter 12

Lis

Ansgar's demeanor toward me had changed.

I slid a sideways glance at him on his horse. A dusting of snow covered his hood and cloak. His expression was stoic, his attitude brusque, and any conversation brief.

For the past hour of riding since we left the farm behind, I'd waited, hoping he'd unburden himself of whatever was bothering him and return to his normal self. But he hadn't done so yet, and I was beginning to suspect he wouldn't unless we talked about the problem.

"Ansgar?"

"Yes, Your Highness?"

I blew out an exasperated breath. I'd told him numerous times I didn't want him using such a title, but he'd taken to calling me by the proper address anyway. If I brought up my distaste for it again, he'd probably keep saying it regardless.

The title only served to remind me of my

inadequacies. Even though I wanted to go to Vordinberg and present myself as royalty, why would anyone want me, a poor country girl without any experience, to become Norvegia's next ruler? Likely, they'd weigh their options and decide Elinor was better, no matter how great her trespasses.

The foothills stretched out ahead of us, rocky and rugged. The white peaks of the southern Snowden Range rose in the distance, at least a day's ride. Once we reached them, according to Father's instructions, we were to take the mountain trail to the west of the tallest peak. Although he'd never been to visit Ulla for himself, he had a general idea of where she lived.

If the snow continued only lightly and didn't impede us, we'd be able to travel halfway there by nightfall and would need to make camp somewhere secluded. Father suggested finding a grouping of caves past the Twin Lakes. There, we'd have shelter and be able to start a campfire to warm up.

Though our journey was dangerous, I couldn't deny the thrill whispering through my blood to be on so great an adventure, as if I'd been a caged bird now set free.

"You're upset with me, aren't you?" I released the question nagging me.

"No." His answer was too quick.

"Then why don't you want to talk with me?" I drew my heavy fur cloak about me tighter to ward off a chill that was less from the cold of the day and more from the chill in his attitude.

"I'm busy guarding you." He scanned the terrain ahead, taking in a cluster of evergreens, his eyes not seeming to miss a single detail.

"Yes, I can see the need with all the wild creatures and dangerous enemies just ready to accost us at any moment." With the fresh layer of snow, the landscape was still and peaceful. In fact, it felt as if we were the only two who existed. If I hadn't been so consumed with wondering what was amiss with Ansgar, I might have enjoyed the beauty of the day.

I waited for him to banter back, to repay my sarcasm with his own. But he remained silent, his lips pressed in a straight line.

I was tempted to exhale another frustrated breath. Instead, I decided to use guilt in prodding him to share. "For a man who prides himself on the truth, you are being less than truthful to me now."

His jaw flexed. With guilt. But still he didn't reply.

When we first started out, I'd anticipated this trip together. I'd even reveled in the fact that Ansgar wasn't leaving me after all, that he was willing to stay and help me. I thought he was doing so because he cared about me. After all, he hadn't denied Father's statement about loving me.

But now my heart sank in my chest with the growing reality of our new situation, the reality that things were changing between us in a direction I didn't like. He didn't behave like a man in love. Instead, he seemed to be purposefully putting a gulf between us, acting as though I was royalty and he was a servant.

Was that what he and Father had been talking about while I packed my bag? Had Ansgar reassured Father he had no aspirations toward me, that he had never intended to pursue a future with me, and that with the knowledge of my identity, he was less inclined to do so?

"So is this the way you plan to interact from now on?" I couldn't release the issue, not when I yearned for Ansgar more than I yearned for anything else.

"What way?"

"Formal and aloof."

"Respectful and conscientious, as befitting our differences." His rebuttal was more typical of our usual interactions.

I took heart from it. Perhaps he simply needed time to adjust to the revelation about who I was. "The only difference is that I'm not willing to allow a title to change who I am."

"'Tis much more than a title. 'Tis who you were born to be, with a destiny that cannot be denied."

"Denied, no. But decided, yes. I shall fulfill my destiny, whatever that may be, but I still retain the right to decide whom I want to love." As soon as I spoke the word *love*, I focused on the tiny braids in my horse's mane, unwilling to meet Ansgar's gaze lest he see the truth—that I was falling in love with him just as he was with me.

The patter of our horses' hooves was muted by the powder. Even so, in the distance, a herd of reindeer lifted their heads from where they were grazing on long grass not yet flattened by the falling snow. Their dark eyes watched us, their bodies tense with the need to flee.

"Do you really want to hear the truth?" he asked, his voice low and raw.

"Always."

He hesitated, then seemed to push forward. "If I am to guard you the way you need, I cannot let my emotions get in the way. I must remain objective and unattached."

"And what if I don't want you to be my guard but would prefer you to take another role instead?" I was being bold, but under the circumstances, I had no other choice.

The reindeer flicked their ears, then started to race away. Did they think Ansgar and I were a threat? Or had they caught the scent of Red, who was following us out of sight but always close at hand?

Ansgar didn't answer, and silence settled between us.

My chest tightened with each passing moment until it hurt to breathe. I desperately wanted him to choose us, the way I was.

Finally, he expelled a taut breath. "You're royalty, and I'm a man from common stock. One day you'll rule this country. God willing, I shall remain by your side, but only as your most loyal and devoted knight."

The tension and hurt radiated into my limbs. He was letting go. He didn't want me enough to fight for me or my love.

With a nudge of my heels, I urged my horse ahead until I was galloping away from Ansgar. The pressure of tears pushed for release, but I wouldn't allow myself to cry.

He was the first man I'd truly known. The first I'd truly loved. And at the moment, I doubted I'd ever find another I cared about half as much.

One thing was certain: I wouldn't allow myself to plead with him again. If he could cut me out of his heartstrings, then I would do the same to him.

ANSGAR

I'd hurt Lis. And as much as I hated myself for it, I needed to establish boundaries now before too much time elapsed.

She rode ahead of me, her back rigid. Though I wanted to pull alongside her, throw caution away, and assure her that I cared, I held back. I was building a necessary wall between us, but it was fragile. It was a good thing she didn't know just how fragile. With but one touch, she could easily break it down. With but one kiss, I would be hers to do her bidding. With but one of her becoming smiles, I would turn to clay in her hands.

The snow grew thicker and our way more difficult. We slowed our pace to keep from taxing our horses, and we stopped several times to scrape ice from their hooves. But by the time the darkness of the coming eve began to fall, we'd reached the far side of Twin Lakes.

I located a cavern large enough to provide shelter not only for us but also for our mounts. Silently, Lis and I worked together to start a fire. Once we had light and warmth, we hurried to tend to our horses.

After the horses were groomed and fed, we unpacked a portion of the food from Nils and ate with the crackling flames and the distant howl of foxes the only sound. When finished with her meal, Lis curled up beside the fire and wasted no time in falling asleep.

From across the fire, I reclined against the cavern wall, half my gaze trained upon the opening and the other half upon her. Now, with her slumbering, I could study her without her knowing I was doing so.

I knew I shouldn't allow myself even this small pleasure, but surely this looking from a distance from time to time wouldn't hurt my resolve to keep our relationship from growing into something it could never be.

I'd been honest with her when I explained that I couldn't let my emotions distract me. I could be more alert if I wasn't constantly thinking about how much I wanted her.

But the other truth was that even though Rasmus had already set in motion changing the law regarding royalty being able to wed a commoner with the king's approval, I wouldn't entertain the notion that I might ever have a life with Lis. Already, Elinor had lost her inheritance of the throne over her choice of spouse.

In comparison, Lis would have more obstacles to overcome by nature of her upbringing. She'd have to tread carefully as she entered the royal and political life of Norvegia. That meant she would need to choose a husband the traditional way to prevent anyone from finding excuses for why she shouldn't become the next queen.

The firelight flickered over her face, highlighting her high cheekbones, her elegant nose, and the perfectly rounded curves of her lips. The memory of those lips pressing into mine earlier in the day came rushing back, sending a cascade of warmth through my veins.

While recuperating, there had been moments when I'd considered following her into the barn or one of the other outbuildings to get away from Nils's watchful eyes and stealing a kiss from her—regardless of my resolve to wait for her to initiate.

Now I was glad I'd refrained. I was having a difficult enough time cutting off my feelings. How much more challenging would it be if I'd pursued her more ardently?

The battle of watching her but not being able to have her would only get harder when I had to stand by at her wedding, when I had to witness her new husband lead her away to their chambers, when I had to sit at the head table and listen to her interact with her new spouse. How would I be able to endure the torture when I wanted her for myself?

Had I been rash in promising to protect her the rest of my days? Maybe I would need to pick one of the other Knights of Brethren to guard her in my stead. On the other hand, how could I go anywhere away from her? I'd only worry about her and wish I were near to keep her safe.

I released a sigh and lifted my gaze. Her eyes were open, and she'd caught me staring.

Her eyes beckoned to me, an invitation I sensed would be her final one, an invitation to accept her for who she was, regardless of her royalty. For several heartbeats, I had the overwhelming urge to toss aside the caution I'd donned over the past hours. My love for her surged with a force that nearly drove me to my feet.

No. My inner command was harsh. I quickly brought up the image of Nils's face, the trust in his eyes as he'd watched us leave the farm. He believed I was a man of honor. I was the one he'd been waiting for these many years to take care of Lis and see that she was restored to her rightful place.

I jerked my gaze away and focused on the flames, even though the longing within hammered hard, chipping at my heart.

A few seconds later, Lis rolled over, turning her back to me.

I let my attention flicker to her, knowing I'd severed our bond completely. I'd done the right thing. If only my heart didn't feel like it had crumbled into a hundred pieces.

Chapter 13

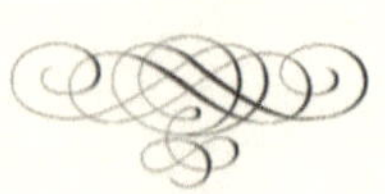

Lis

The climb up into the mountains grew treacherous. The snow was already hardpacked from earlier snowfalls, and the fresh layer made the trails slick. For a time, we strapped rags to our horses' feet to keep them from slipping.

We located a safe alcove for the horses to rest while we continued by snowshoe. A thin curl of smoke rose in the distance and guided our way to Ulla's mountain home. I could sense Red nearby, but I hadn't seen him over the past day since I'd warned him to stay out of sight. Though we hadn't seen any Ice Men who populated the mountains, I was using caution anyway.

As I took a few final steps up a snow-covered hill and crested the top, a log cabin came into view at the base of a steep cliff. The wisp of smoke we'd seen from a distance now puffed from a stone chimney.

I paused to catch my breath, glancing behind at the way we'd come—the trail winding up the side of the mountain in a zigzag. Had Princess Blanche climbed this same path all those years ago? Or were we on a doomed mission?

I'd had plenty of time to think about Princess Blanche during the journey. She'd obviously been feeling the effects of her disease or curse or whatever ailed her when she brought me to Mother and Father. How close to death had she been at that point? And why hadn't she told anyone else what she was doing or where she was going?

From the little bit I'd gleaned about the royal family in recent years, I knew that Princess Blanche's husband had died while searching for his missing wife and daughter, which left Elinor an orphan. Queen Inge and King Ulrik had raised Elinor as their own daughter, lavishing their love upon her since they'd never had any children of their own.

What would Elinor say once she learned of my intent to present myself as an heir to the throne? Would she feel threatened and hate me?

Ansgar stopped beside me, scanning the dark forestland that spread out to the east and covered the mountainside until reaching the barren, rocky peaks frozen with snow and ice. He'd spoken little all day, and I'd felt too hurt and rejected to initiate any conversation beyond what was necessary.

I hadn't imagined the stark longing in his eyes last night when he stared at me from across the fire. Though I'd willed him to say something, to acknowledge that what we had was real and could lead somewhere, he'd done nothing. Nothing but make clear his determination to put an end to his feelings for me, no matter how hard and no matter what it cost him.

I'd decided to make his decision easier. If he aimed to forget about his feelings for me, then I could do the same about him. I'd worked all day to squelch my attraction, frustrated that it crept out regardless of my efforts, frustrated that he was so stubborn, frustrated that our lives weren't simpler.

"I don't feel good about this." Ansgar narrowed his eyes on the forest. "There are too many moving shadows."

I tried to view the scene from his perspective, but I couldn't see anything but thick evergreen limbs. I moved forward, my snowshoes keeping me on top of at least two feet of snow. "If we hurry, we can be off the mountain passes before nightfall."

He studied the landscape a moment longer before plodding after me.

We crossed the open hillside toward the cabin. As we drew closer, I realized the cabin front was a façade built against the cliff and that the home had been carved out of the mountainside.

One lone window next to the door was shuttered tightly. There weren't any fresh prints in the snow in front of the home. And the air was eerily silent, the way it sometimes was before a storm.

As I approached the door and lifted a hand to knock, it creaked open.

"Come in," spoke a wobbly, old voice from within.

I discarded my snowshoes, then pushed the door wider, squinting through the darkness of the cavern-like interior. A small fire was lit on the hearth, giving forth a scant amount of light, only enough to see the outline of someone sitting in a chair near the fire.

"Princess Elisbet?" This time I could tell the voice

belonged to a woman.

"Ulla?" I replied, breathing in a musty, smoky scent along with the spicy aroma of brewing ale.

"Yes, I'm Ulla."

I stepped farther in with Ansgar on my trail. He'd pushed aside his fur cloak to rest his hand on his sword.

The log cabin part of the structure jutted from the stone walls, the two forming an interior with only enough space for a bed, table, and chair. Artifacts and trinkets crowded the room, sitting on wall shelves, hanging from the ceiling, gathering dust in piles, and dangling from the walls. Embroidered tapestries, colorful glass globes, intricately beaded necklaces, bright linen scarves, and other items I couldn't begin to name.

The far wall was also stone but contained an arched opening that led to an unlit passageway. It was possible such a tunnel wound to other caverns or rooms or perhaps led deeper into the heart of the mountain.

"Close the door," Ulla said without moving from her chair. "I can ill afford to use all my fuel in one day."

Ansgar obeyed, shutting out the daylight.

A low, menacing growl came from beside Ulla, and the dim firelight revealed a creature pushing slowly to its feet.

At the rasp of Ansgar's sword leaving its sheath, the creature snarled again, rising to its full height, its hackles spiking. From what I could tell, it was a mangy white wolf, too frail and bony to put up a fight, likely as ancient as Ulla herself.

"Sit, Angel. Sit." Ulla reached out a gnarled hand and stroked the wolf's head. "I told you there's no reason to worry." Her murmur was gentle, as if the wolf were a child instead of an animal.

"How do you know who I am?" I tried to glimpse Ulla's face, but the hood of her cloak was pulled so far forward, I could only see the wayward strands of curly gray hair. Was she as old as everyone said?

"Angel alerted me to your presence late last night."

"But you know my real name." I prayed that meant she knew of Princess Blanche and that she'd be able to help us. "I haven't revealed it to anyone else yet."

"Who else would seek me at a time like this?" Ulla's stroking seemed to calm Angel. Though the wolf didn't lie back down, it sat on its haunches.

"A time like what?" Ansgar asked, his tone low but measured. He still held his sword, clearly sensing peril that I didn't.

"This is a time of great upheaval in our country—a time when the kingdom is in trouble, a time when evil seeks to overcome good." Ulla's raspy voice seemed almost prophetic.

Ansgar must have been satisfied with Ulla's answer, because he refrained from plunging his sword into her and the wolf.

"Since you are aware who I am," I said, "then perhaps you can tell me what became of Princess Blanche?"

Ulla waved to the items all around her. "I can only provide information when payment is given."

I fingered a string of colorful beads hanging from the wall. Were all the things around her home payments from people who'd sought her out? Perhaps Blanche had left one of these trinkets as payment.

Everyone knew Ulla never gave anything for

nothing, which was why Father had provided me with a small pouch of coins. I wasn't sure how he'd amassed the sum, but I opened the drawstring, withdrew a coin, and placed it on the table.

Ulla remained silent.

I took out another coin and placed it next to the first.

Ulla nodded, the amount apparently satisfying her. "When Princess Blanche came to me, the disease had already spread through her body, and nothing I did could heal her. She resided with me a fortnight before passing on."

"What was her disease? And was it truly a curse?" While I didn't want to think about Blanche's curse, I couldn't dismiss it as a fairy tale. From a young age, my mother had taught me that Holy Scripture spoke of curses as well as blessings being passed from one generation to the next.

Ulla nodded at the table.

I took out two more coins. I had to be careful with my questions, or I would soon have nothing left.

Ulla waited for the clink of the coins against the table before continuing. "Princess Blanche was afflicted with a bleeding disease, one inflamed by her monthly courses. In the end, we couldn't stop the flow, and she bled to death."

I waited for the healer woman to answer the second part of my question. But when she lapsed into silence, I sighed and pulled out two more coins. "Is her curse passed on to me?"

"Only time will tell," Ulla said in her raspy voice. "But 'tis a condition that afflicted her mother and grandmother, both firstborn daughters. So, yes, it appears to be a curse, something you could suffer from one day."

"Why did she think cutting me off from my true identity would prevent me from getting the disease?" The question was out before I could stop it.

Ulla didn't respond. Though I was tempted to give her additional coins, I couldn't afford it. I needed to save the rest for making a trade.

"You've probably guessed I come seeking a possession that once belonged to Princess Blanche. 'Tis possible she may have given you an item I could use to prove she was my mother."

"Yes. It's possible."

"Do you have something or not?" Ansgar spoke calmly, but the authority in his tone said he wouldn't accept anything less than the truth.

Ulla hesitated.

Did she expect more payment before she would tell us?

I started to reach for my pouch, but Ansgar stopped me with a touch to my arm.

For a long moment no one moved, not even the white wolf by Ulla's side. Finally, Ulla began to rise from her chair. Each small movement upward seemed to cost her dearly, and I was tempted to rush over and assist her. But again, Ansgar pressed his fingers against me, halting me.

As Ulla stood, Angel did too. The old woman, hunched with age, leaned against the wolf. "I have the thing that will prove she is your mother."

I breathed out the tension I hadn't known I'd been holding, then I dug in the pouch for the remainder of what Father had given me.

Ulla shook her head. "No, you cannot pay me in coins for this. It is much too precious for that."

I placed the money on the table anyway. "I have nothing else. Surely, this will be enough."

"No."

I could feel Ansgar stiffen, and this time, I placed a steadying hand on his arm. What harm could this old woman and ancient wolf do to us?

"One can never gain something truly valuable without sacrifice." Ulla's tone took on a reverent quality.

"What would you have me sacrifice?"

"You need not sacrifice anything," Ansgar whispered. "She has no right to demand anything of you."

"Of you both," Ulla interjected. "I require it of you both."

"He has nothing to do with this."

"As your husband, Sir Ansgar will have much to say."

I withdrew my hand from his arm, clearly having given Ulla the wrong idea. And how had she known his identity? "We're not married—"

"Not yet." Though the room was dark, I somehow sensed Ulla could view Ansgar and me as clearly as if we'd been standing in bright sunshine. "But when you are, you will pay me then."

"You don't know what you're saying," I said at the same time Ansgar released a murmur of protest.

"I know very well what I'm saying," Ulla responded. "I can sense the bond between you and know it will not be satisfied by anything less than a lifetime together."

How could I respond to her bold statement? What could I say to explain the challenges already keeping us asunder and the myriad more we were sure to face? It wouldn't do any good to argue with her.

As though coming to the same conclusion, Ansgar spoke again. "Tell us what you require in payment for the article that belonged to Princess Blanche."

I stiffened in preparation for whatever the old woman would demand of me. I could relinquish it. Surely I could.

Ulla stroked the wolf's head again. "I require the payment of your firstborn daughter, to be given to me when she enters the age of adulthood."

I sucked in a sharp breath.

"No." Ansgar's answer was firm. "Princess Elisbet will never give you her firstborn daughter."

"She will be your daughter too."

He shook his head. "Never."

I knew what he was saying, that we would never be married and never have a daughter. But Ulla believed otherwise. "What if we don't have a daughter?"

"Then you are not beholden to me."

"And if we don't marry?" I asked the question before Ansgar could.

"Then you are also not beholden to me."

Through the darkness, I glanced at Ansgar at the same moment he looked at me. I couldn't read his expression well, but I sensed he was thinking the same, that we had nothing to worry about. We'd already decided to deny ourselves any future together. Thus, we would never owe Ulla anything.

"Very well." I wanted to accept her bargain before she changed her mind and decided to require something more difficult.

"You and Sir Ansgar will give me your firstborn daughter?"

"You'll find yourself disappointed with such a request. But if you insist on the payment, then yes, I vow to offer you my firstborn daughter."

"You will have her delivered here upon her sixteenth birthday and not a day later?"

"Yes." It would never happen because we would never get married.

"And you vow it too, Sir Ansgar?" Ulla asked.

He hesitated. "And if I don't agree?"

"Then I cannot give you the item you seek."

Beside me, his presence was as magnetic and overwhelming as always. *Ignore it*, I silently chastised myself. Perhaps with more practice, I would forget about this attraction to him.

"I will vow it," Ansgar answered. "But I don't feel comfortable with the bargain."

"Good." For the first time, Ulla's tone hinted at a smile. "Then you have reassured me that I have chosen wisely."

"Is there naught else we can give you?" he asked.

"We need give nothing else," I said. Why was he stalling? He'd already clarified that he had no plans for a future with me.

"This item," Ansgar persisted. "Will it convince everyone Lis is Princess Elisbet?"

Ulla shuffled several steps forward to a shelf on the wall, using her wolf to aid each step. She opened the lid of an engraved box and lifted something out. Then she made her way toward us, leaning upon her wolf again.

"The Princess Blanche didn't want to give this to me. She offered gold instead." Ulla opened her hand to reveal a beautiful bangle made of intricate leaf engravings and decorated with emeralds of various sizes and shapes. "But I would only accept this in payment. The bangle she was given by her mother."

I pictured Blanche in this very spot, bargaining with Ulla the same way I was. "If you couldn't break the curse, then why did you demand this of her?"

"She agreed to give it whether she lived or died. As I said, one can never gain something truly valuable without sacrifice."

"And if she died, what did she gain?"

"Her sacrifices will save Norvegia." Ulla spoke with a certainty that somehow quieted my doubts. "Her sacrifice in giving you away to new parents saved you from being ensnared in the evils at court. And her sacrifice of this bangle will allow you to free the land from the grip of evil that now threatens it."

"She couldn't have known all that when she came here."

"No. We never know the way everything will work out, only that Providence is weaving together all things for his purposes."

Was it possible everything that had happened was somehow entwined? That Blanche's curse and her sacrifices would now lead to my saving the kingdom? Was it also possible that someday I would see what I'd sacrificed and that it would end up being more than I anticipated?

No matter the reasoning, I was willing to do it.

Ansgar shook his head. Before he could stop me, I pushed aside my fur cloak and slid up my sleeve.

Without further hesitation, I took the bangle from Ulla's outstretched hand and wrapped it around my upper arm.

When it was firmly in place, I nodded at her. "We have a bargain."

Chapter 14

ANSGAR

I DIDN'T LIKE THE DEAL LIS HAD MADE WITH ULLA. BUT HOW could I protest any further without turning myself into a fool?

As we strapped on our snowshoes and headed back down the mountain, my emotions warred within me, just as they had on the ascent. Lis was a princess, and I was her guardian. That was all I could ever be to her. Nothing more and nothing less. In light of that, the arrangement with Ulla appeared harmless enough. We would never have to give up our firstborn daughter, because we would never have one together.

Even so, Ulla's warning repeated itself: *"One can never gain something truly valuable without sacrifice."*

She never made bargains that weren't costly. Yes, she required something for each question asked and each question answered. The coins and beads and other items around her home attested to the trading she'd done in her lifetime. But I suspected her trading had less to do with greed than with teaching people they couldn't get something for nothing.

What, then, was the purpose of this agreement Ulla had made with us? It hadn't cost Lis or me anything now or in the future. In fact, it made me all the more determined not to give our relationship a place in my life.

"Can we make it to the cave near Twin Lakes by nightfall?" Lis asked over her shoulder as she maintained a steady pace through the heavy snowfall on our way back to where we'd left our horses.

Now that we'd descended the more treacherous mountain trails and were in the valley between the peaks, our trek would be easier. Even so, we'd be sorely pressed to be at the cave by the time darkness settled.

Before I could answer, she stopped abruptly, her face pointed upward. She whispered something, and I knew she was communicating with Red. She'd done so several times already on our journey. But this time, her expression turned more severe and her whisper more urgent.

I stopped alongside her and scanned the cliffs on either side of the canyon-like valley. The high rock walls acted as a fortress against the wind, protecting us from the battering cold we'd experienced in the higher elevation. The descent here was more gradual and the snow accumulation not as heavy.

Her scowl deepened.

"Is something amiss?" I asked.

"Red senses a threat and wants to fly closer to us."

My muscles tensed, and again I surveyed the surrounding area, this time looking for anything amiss. "What kind of threat?"

"People."

"What kind of people?"

"Red can't communicate that." Her voice contained a note of exasperation, as if I should know better.

"Can he at least tell us where the people are?"

"Close enough that he wants to hover lower—" Her words were cut off by warlike cries that echoed off the canyon walls and turned my blood cold. That kind of shouting belonged to one group of people I'd hoped to avoid—the Ice Men.

They were running up the slope from the front of the canyon. Thickly boned and with heavy girths, they always appeared giantlike. Their bulky fur garments and tall fur caps only added to their imposing stature, and their heavily bearded faces were always covered with bear grease to protect them from the elements. So fierce an appearance served to intimidate most people.

But I'd waged war against the Ice Men not many years past, when they'd invaded the moors and the plateau. If I'd once been afraid of these warriors, I no longer was. I'd fought them oft enough to learn their weaknesses and drive them out of the land.

Regardless, I was one against half a dozen, and I had Lis to protect.

I unsheathed my sword and shoved Lis behind me, positioning her within the shield of my broad back.

As the men at the forefront raced nearer, more screeching trills behind us told me all the shadows I'd seen in the woodland near Ulla's home hadn't been my imagination. The Ice Men had guessed we were traveling to visit the healing woman and had waited to trap us in this valley from behind and in front.

The question was, why? They didn't know Lis was Princess Elisbet. We'd told no one—although somehow Ulla had guessed the truth.

Were these Ice Men after me? Perhaps Rasmus had learned I hadn't died in the murder attempt. After hearing of my escape, had he proclaimed a bounty on my head throughout Norvegia? Was I now in danger anywhere I went?

I shifted so Lis was positioned between my body and the valley wall. She'd be safe as long as she stayed behind me. "Don't come out!" I handed her my knife, wanting her to have something for protection.

She unsheathed her hunting knife and held it up, her expression holding no fear, only determination. "I have my own weapon and can fend for myself."

"I don't want you to do anything but stay behind me." In fact, I'd concentrate better on my fighting if I knew she wasn't engaging in the battle. Otherwise, I'd end up worrying about her and not focusing the way I should.

The Ice Men trudged nearer, the snow slowing their steps. Even so, their battle cries echoed with increasing volume.

"You can't fight all these men by yourself." She thrust her knife toward them. "I'm able to do more than you think."

As the first group of men closed in, I eyed each one, planning a course of action, who I would eliminate first, then second, and so on. Before I could engage any of the men in battle, a shriek echoed overhead—the shriek of a red draco.

"No!" Lis commanded Red quietly from behind me, her tone filled with worry. "Wait."

Red either didn't hear her or was choosing not to listen. He clearly intended to blow his fiery breath upon our attackers before they came too close to Lis, preventing them from harming her even as he scorched them.

As he dove between the rocky cliffs and angled toward the oncoming Ice Men, a chain-mail net flew off the ledge overhead. For a moment, I could only watch it fall, too surprised to understand what was going on, until it landed on Red, covering him from wingtip to wingtip. He could no longer flap. And the weight forced him to go only one direction. Down.

"No!" Lis screamed and scrambled past me.

I caught her arm before she could get too far. But I needn't have worried about the Ice Men charging toward us. They'd stopped and were cheering as Red plummeted to the ground. On the cliff above, several Ice Men now stood and joined in the jubilation.

Too late I realized what had happened. The Ice Men hadn't intended to attack us. Instead, they'd likely witnessed Lis with Red during the battle with Swaine. Ever since then, they'd been waiting for the chance to lure the draco out of hiding. And with our trip up into the mountains, they'd taken advantage of the opportunity to feign an attack and draw Red down so they could capture him.

"No!" Lis cried again. She'd sensed the danger the Ice Men posed to Red, which was why she'd wanted Red to stay out of sight. But of course, Red loved Lis too much to listen.

From underneath the chain net, Red struggled to lift his wings and fly up, but he only made it a foot off the ground before falling back. As the Ice Men cautiously circled closer, Red breathed out his dangerous hot breath, but it was only a small burst. Without the ability to fill his lungs fully, he couldn't spit out enough fire to do any damage.

The Ice Men had been in the business of trapping and

training dracos for centuries. And they'd been hired by King Canute of Swaine in the last battle to aid in the fighting with the draco they already controlled. What would the Ice Men do to Red? Would they attempt to bend him to their will? Make him fight against Norvegia in the next battle? Or would they eliminate him altogether?

"Get out of here, Red!" Lis called, wriggling against my hold, clearly intending to race to Red's rescue.

I couldn't let her go. But neither could I stand idly by while her draco was chained and hauled away by the Ice Men. It wasn't fair to Red. But more importantly, I knew how much Red meant to Lis. And for her sake, I'd do anything to save the poor creature.

As I turned to Lis, she lifted her defiant face to mine. Her gaze was frantic, and tears streaked her cheeks. "Release me at once!"

I thrust her forward on the trail. "Go to the horses. I'll meet you there."

She shook her head even as she stumbled in the snow. "No, I'm not leaving. Not until Red is free."

"I'll take care of him." I was already stalking toward my closest opponent. With his attention on the draco, I could easily knock him out and several more before they realized I was attacking.

Lis

Ansgar had discarded his snowshoes and was barreling into the fray without hesitancy. The Ice Men weren't paying him any heed. They were focused on Red, attempting to communicate with him with shrieks and calls, a method oft employed by draco hunters that only worked to a degree. It didn't utilize the depth of trust that came from true bonding with a draco.

Red shrieked his distress at the same time that he was commanding me to get far away. But I couldn't leave him behind at the mercy of these men. Never. I cared about Red too much to let the Ice Men drag him away as their prisoner.

I'd known the peril to Red in the mountains, known the Ice Men would do everything they could to capture him. Somehow, they'd learned of his presence, even though Red had stayed out of sight. Or perhaps the Ice Men recognized me and had purposefully attacked me with the hope of drawing Red out of hiding.

Regardless, I wasn't about to run off and allow Ansgar or Red to fight the Ice Men alone.

But what could I do?

I glanced at my lone knife. I wasn't a trained fighter and wouldn't be able to fend off the experienced Ice Men. 'Twould be foolhardy of me to jump into the skirmish. And yet, I must do something.

Ansgar marched forward, slicing down men before they could even turn to discover what had happened. As one Ice Man after another fell to his blows, those surrounding Red began to pay attention to Ansgar's attack.

Some of the warriors, in the process of staking the chain net holding Red, left their posts and ran toward Ansgar, their pikes and swords out and ready for a fight.

Ansgar met them calmly, almost methodically. I'd heard about Ansgar's skills and bravery in battle, but

I'd yet to witness him in action. Now, as he thrust his sword first one way and then another, cutting down anyone who came near, my heart quavered with a strange new fear.

I didn't want to lose Ansgar. Even if I could never have him for myself. Even if all he'd ever be was my bodyguard. I'd rather have him in some capacity than none at all.

He spun, dodging a pike, swinging back around and disabling another opponent. With shouts at Ansgar's attack, the rest of the Ice Men rallied and rushed at him with their terrifying cries.

With at least a dozen Ice Men coming at him, how would Ansgar survive? Even with his renowned skills, he couldn't fight off all the men. He needed help, and he needed it now.

Red's distress echoed in my head, and I bolted toward him. I didn't give myself a chance to second-guess my decision. I had a tiny window of time to free him while the Ice Men were distracted. I had to at least try.

I darted along the rocky wall until I was well beyond the conflict. Then I broke away from the safety of the wall and tramped as quickly as I could through the snow toward Red in the middle of the trail.

Red made an effort to fly up, but with parts of the net already driven into the ground, he couldn't get the momentum he needed.

"Stay still," I whispered to Red, kneeling and jerking one of the stakes free and moving on to the next. If he made too much effort, he'd draw the attention of the Ice Men back to him and expose me.

Red gave a soft trill in response and seemed to

quiet himself, though I could sense his mounting agitation.

From the corner of my eye, I glimpsed Ansgar in an intricate balance, trying to anticipate who would attack him next, evading the sharp edges of weapons being thrust his way, all the while swinging his sword and knife.

I tugged up another stake and crawled toward a third. As I pulled it from the snowy ground and threw off part of the heavy chain net, several of the Ice Men spotted me and released cries of alarm.

"Move toward me, Red," I quietly commanded as I hurried to roll back the rest of the steel links.

Red tried to do as I instructed, but he was still too entrapped.

As more men became aware of what I was doing and started back to the net, Ansgar roared his anger and slashed down several more.

I was running out of time. Despite Ansgar's efforts, the men were careening toward me, their weapons outstretched, intent on stopping me even if they had to kill me to do so.

Go. Red's order reverberated through me as though he, too, sensed I wouldn't have enough time to free him.

I shoved at the iron links. "I'll lift it again, and when I do, push hard."

I didn't give Red the chance to protest. Inhaling a deep breath, I heaved against the net and threw it as hard as I could. In the same movement, Red pushed his head and one wing free.

An Ice Man raised his pike and aimed it at me. I scrambled backward, fear crowding up into my throat.

This was it. I was going to die.

Before the bulky warrior could throw it, he froze and fell to the ground, Ansgar's knife protruding from his back. More Ice Men thundered past their fallen comrade, their weapons ready to hurl. Ansgar wouldn't be able to stop each of them from turning on me. And though I continued to move away as fast as I could, I knew I wouldn't make it.

As the Ice Men aimed their pikes at me, Red began to lift into the air, flapping hard against the rest of the mesh holding him down. For several seconds, the heaviness seemed to weigh him to the ground, but as he gave a frantic thrust, the net fell away, and he soared upward.

Immediately, the Ice Men shifted from pursuing me to chasing after Red, thrusting their pikes at him.

I wasted no time putting more distance between myself and the Ice Men, knowing if they got their hands on me, they'd stop at nothing to lure Red into their net, using me as bait to capture him again.

Ansgar was already crossing toward me, swooping down to retrieve a pike from the outstretched hand of an Ice Man lying facedown, his blood staining the snow. Ansgar didn't slow his stride, even as he bent to pick up another pike. He moved with a purpose and authority that proved him to be the hero everyone talked about.

As one of the Ice Men shouted and started after me, Ansgar aimed the pike and threw it with such strength and speed that it impaled the man and threw him to the ground in one motion.

Overhead, Red ascended into the sky, and I breathed out my relief that he was free. "Go. Please," I whispered to him. "You're not safe here."

Ansgar tramped forward, each step certain and menacing, his bloody sword in one hand and the second pike at the ready.

The remaining Ice Men halted, watching Ansgar warily. With so many of their own already injured or dead, they must have realized they would meet the same fate erelong if they didn't proceed with more care.

Ansgar reached my side, and without taking his steely gaze from his opponents, he clasped my arm and lifted me to my feet. "I told you I'd take care of Red." His tone was low with anger.

Above, Red swirled, finally out of reach of danger. I could sense his anger too. And his need for revenge.

As before, Ansgar pushed me behind him into the shelter of his back, standing before me and facing the remainder of the Ice Men. With his feet apart and the blood-slickened weapons acting as a warning, the Ice Men didn't move.

Blood oozed from a cut on Ansgar's arm and one on his back. But if they pained him or if his previous leg wound bothered him, he didn't show it.

Ansgar glared at the men, and then he backed up from the scene of the fight, inching down the path, all the while keeping me securely behind him. As some of the injured Ice Men picked themselves up from the ground, I had no doubt they would regroup and attack again. I wanted to turn and run, but I pressed a hand to Ansgar's rigid back, drawing fortitude and courage from him.

I felt Red's presence drawing near, and I whispered a warning. But regardless of my opposition, he dove back into the canyon, his fury palpable. I wouldn't be able to stop him from unleashing his wrath. All I could do was use the opportunity to escape with Ansgar.

"Red's coming." I grabbed Ansgar's hand, spun, and tromped through the snow as fast as my legs would carry me. Ansgar hesitated but then let me pull him along, keeping one eye on the Ice Men behind us.

In the next instant, Red's shriek echoed against the cliffs. He flew low and breathed fire upon the remaining Ice Men.

We picked up our pace, slipping and sliding down the snowy trail, racing to get to our horses. Only when we reached our mounts did Ansgar release my hand. As he hoisted me into my saddle, his gaze raked over me, likely searching for injuries.

"I'm unharmed," I assured him through my labored breathing. And as far as I could tell, Red was no longer in danger either. He'd given us the time we needed to make our escape, and now I could feel him soaring away.

Ansgar pressed his lips together, as though to keep himself from rebuking me further. Then he climbed onto his horse, the spots of blood widening across his cloak.

"You're wounded and need doctoring."

"Not now." He kicked his mount forward, leaving me no choice but to follow.

Chapter 15

Lis

Ansgar rode as though we were being pursued by the devil himself. Even after darkness fell, he didn't slow our pace. He gave me no opportunity to converse, pushing hard league after league, hour after hour.

Eventually I realized we were riding along a river trail, but I didn't know where we were going, and I grew too cold to care.

When finally I didn't know how I'd last a moment longer, he slowed and pointed to a distant light on a hilltop. "We're almost there."

I could do nothing but nod and urge my horse after his, praying for a last ounce of fortitude to endure until the end.

When we drew nearer, I realized the light was shining from a stone fortress. As Ansgar led the way up a narrow road, the outline of a sturdy stone wall and turrets told me this was a place of importance but that it was also in a state of some disrepair.

Upon arriving near the gate, Ansgar called out,

"Tell your master I am a friend in need and that I request respite."

He stayed well cloaked and well out of reach of the light. He dared not mention his name or show his face. The longer he could hide his identity, the better.

Torchlight from within the gatehouse tower revealed the guard there. He didn't move to do Ansgar's bidding, had instead taken aim with an arrow. "The master sleeps and will not wish to be disturbed."

"Go to him with a message anon, and tell him a Brethren needs refuge for his son Torvald's sake."

The guard dropped his arrow, stared but a moment longer, then disappeared.

Though I'd never interacted with Torvald before, I knew who he was from our return voyage to Vordinberg last month. He was another of the Knights of Brethren. The question was whether he was a friend or foe.

Early during Ansgar's stay with Father and me on the farm, Ansgar had shared how Sigfrid, one of his faithful friends among the Brethren, had betrayed him. I could understand his wariness now. Could he ever trust any of the Brethren or their families again?

While we waited, I wanted to ask Ansgar why he'd come here, why he was taking such a risk. But a part of me already knew. He'd done it for me, to get me out of the cold and to find a haven away from the Ice Men who were likely following us. I hadn't complained during the past hours, had wanted to prove my strength and endurance. But I should have known Ansgar would guess my discomfort.

From the careful way he kept examining every inch of the fortress as well as glancing behind us, he was singularly focused on staying safe.

Red wasn't far away. He'd been trailing us all night. Even so, I warned him to stay hidden. I didn't want him to face the Ice Men and their traps again. Ultimately, I knew that if I wanted to protect Red, I had to stay out of trouble. No doubt Ansgar had come to the same conclusion.

I wanted to ask him about his wounds, scold him for going so long without tending to them. But as he slid a dark look my way, I held back my concerns. I had to stop caring so much about him.

All the many hours of our journeying away from Ulla's, I'd had time to reflect upon everything the ancient woman had spoken. I'd concluded that Ansgar would be much better off without me. Moreover, I couldn't give myself over to any man, not with the knowledge I'd inherited the firstborn-daughter curse and would someday bleed to death just as Blanche had.

'Twould be selfish of me to wed anyone when I had no future. All the more reason to put an end to my longings for Ansgar. I couldn't encourage affection when doing so would lead nowhere and end only in pain for him.

At the creaking open of the large iron gate, Ansgar sidled his mount closer to mine.

A large, thickly muscled man ducked under the rising gate. He motioned toward several guards to stay back, then hurried toward Ansgar, his heavy fur cloak falling open in his haste.

"Torvald?" Ansgar slid down from his mount but kept his face concealed by his hood.

Indeed, the man approaching us was Torvald. The young knight with his dark-brown hair and grayish-blue eyes was handsome but in a brooding way, with a severity about him that lent him a ruthless countenance.

"I believed you were dead." Torvald spoke in a whisper so the guards at the gatehouse couldn't hear him.

Ansgar held back, his hand upon the hilt of his sword. "I expected your father, not you."

"Rasmus dismissed me from the Brethren and sent me home."

"I suppose he also attempted to eliminate your life on your journey home."

Torvald shook his head gravely. "After your death, he could not murder any more Brethren or risk drawing suspicion. But I do not doubt my days are numbered, as are Kristoffer's and Gunnar's and Espen's."

"They were dismissed too?"

"All except Sigfrid."

The two men exchanged a long look, one filled with unspoken sorrow and understanding. At a distant howl, Ansgar glanced into the darkness by way of the river and then at me before addressing Torvald again. "I am in need of refuge—"

"Say no more." Torvald waved toward the now-open gate. "You will stay here as my guest."

Ansgar gave a slight bow of his head. "I beseech it for myself and . . . my wife."

I startled at his pronouncement. For one who prided himself on his honesty, I hadn't expected Ansgar to resort to such deceit. But after experiencing betrayal once, Ansgar was likely unwilling to reveal all the details of our mission until he was more certain he could trust Torvald.

Torvald's mouth hung open for several seconds as he stared between Ansgar and me.

Ansgar cleared his throat. "She is frozen, and I would be grateful if I might take her inside and help her warm up."

"Your wife—" Torvald stared at me. After hours of riding, I wasn't at my best. I must appear bedraggled and certainly not a woman worthy of Ansgar. "She is welcome here anytime, as are you, sire."

Again, Ansgar's attention shot to the dark river beyond, and the grooves in his forehead deepened with the telltale signs of worry.

Apparently sensing the same danger, Torvald motioned us through the gate. "Come, let us linger no longer."

Ansgar tugged at his hood again, attempting to hide his identity from the guards. He might be able to avoid their scrutiny for a short while, but how long before someone recognized him and realized he wasn't dead after all? It was even possible the Ice Men had realized who they were fighting. What if they spread the word that Ansgar was alive? It wouldn't take long for Rasmus's loyal guards to converge upon the place to flush us out.

Torvald led the way inside, passing through an outer bailey, a second gatehouse, and then into the heart of the fortress. Except for a few guards on duty, the inner bailey was silent and still. The thatched structures built against the wall were dark, those within yet asleep.

An imposing square keep of thick stone rose at the center, each corner topped with a tower. A light from an upper room must have been what we'd witnessed from afar, perhaps Torvald's chambers. From his attire and the rapidness with which he'd come to the gate, I surmised he'd already been awake at the early hour.

As we neared a side entrance of the keep, Ansgar stepped up to my horse and lifted a hand to aid my descent. I could hardly make my frozen limbs move, but somehow, I managed to slide down. However, as I touched the ground, my feet were too numb to work. I took a stumbling step only to have Ansgar catch me and sweep me up into his arms, carrying me as easily as a babe.

I didn't protest, though I knew I should. He didn't speak either, following Torvald as silently as possible into the dark castle. With each step, we wove our way deeper inside. I prayed this trust in Torvald wasn't misplaced, that Rasmus hadn't influenced this knight against Ansgar.

After watching the way Ansgar had battled the Ice Men, I knew he would fight again just as skillfully and fiercely if need be. But he was only human. His wounds proved it. And I trembled a little at the thought of him having to defend our lives over and over.

Finally, after winding through one passageway after another and climbing several flights of stairs, Torvald stopped in front of a door and beckoned to a manservant standing at the end of the hall. "We have need of provisions for our guests—a fire, warm water, and food and drink."

Ansgar needed no invitation to open the door and carry me into the room. He quickly moved into the shadows, away from the torchlight and away from scrutiny as two servants entered to do Torvald's bidding.

"You can put me down now," I whispered, but made no effort to free myself.

"I'll put you down when I'm ready to." His whispered retort was warm against my cheek.

I much preferred this belligerent and strong-willed attitude to the groveling one he'd taken upon himself since learning of my royal ties.

"If you're hoping to warm yourself with my nearness," I whispered, "I fear you'll be sorely disappointed."

"You'd be surprised at just how much your nearness heats me." As his nose brushed my cheek and then my hair, I could almost imagine we were at the farm, when our feelings for each other hadn't been hindered by anything other than Father's watchful eyes.

Was Ansgar admitting I still affected him no matter how much he tried to deny it? I could admit I turned into melted tallow at his slightest touch. At the soft exhalation of his breathing near my ear, I was suddenly attuned to his body—the scrape of his scruffy facial hair against my cheek, the hardness of his arms holding me, and the thud of his heartbeat so close to mine.

I leaned my head against his shoulder, my blood flowing warmer with each passing second. With the tilt of my head exposing my neck, he dipped down. In the next instant, his lips pressed against my throat.

I couldn't hold in a gasp of pleasure, the firm but hot kiss chasing away all thoughts but of his mouth and the need to share more kisses with him.

He immediately withdrew and straightened, as if somehow he'd gotten the exact response he'd wanted from me . . . and the servants.

Though they continued about their work, they cast down their gazes and hastened . . . rushing about to situate the pot of steaming water, drinks, and a platter of food.

Was Ansgar's kiss nothing but pretense, as it had been that day at the waterfall? This time to hasten the servants from the room? To hide our true purpose in being here? If the servants believed we were newly wed, they would likely refrain from interrupting, which would allow us greater privacy.

Standing just inside the door, Torvald peered into the hallway, clearly as embarrassed by our display as the servants. Was Ansgar's performance for Torvald too? To test his loyalty in some way?

My ire swelled quickly within. How dare Ansgar use me? Kiss me without thought to how it would undo me? How would he like it if I did the same?

Though my hands were numb and my fingers stiff, I lifted them to Ansgar's cheeks and drew his face back down. His eyes widened with surprise as he grasped my intention. I managed a half smile before giving him little choice and pressing my lips to his. I held nothing back, arching up and letting our mouths fuse. The touch was as explosive as in the past, nearly making the world and everything in it disappear. Except him. Always him.

He seemed to try to hold back his fervor, but within seconds, he was as lost to the kiss as I was. It was the place where we were meant to be, as if this was our destiny.

But it wasn't our destiny. We could never be together.

I broke free and laid my head against his shoulder, attempting to act as though the kiss hadn't just captured me body, soul, and spirit.

Ansgar held himself just as casually. I wouldn't have known the kiss had affected him if I hadn't felt the heavy rise and fall of his chest and heard the rapid beat of his heart.

As the servants finally made their way out of the room, Torvald lingered in the doorway.

Ansgar stepped from the shadows. "Instruct your servants not to come nigh the room again, that I have no wish to be disturbed."

He bowed his head. "Of course."

"And Torvald? I would keep this marriage private for as long as possible."

Torvald hesitated but then bowed again. Without saying more, he stepped into the hallway and closed the door.

As the door latched, I wiggled to free myself. "What do you think you're doing—"

He lifted a finger to my lip, silencing me. He gave a pointed look at the door, then bent in close to my ear. "Until I know if we can trust Torvald, we must maintain this ruse."

I glanced to the closed door and imagined Torvald or one of his servants on the other side, listening and attempting to discover the true nature of our visit.

"If he believes you are my wife and speaks of it to no one, then I shall know his heart still remains loyal to mine. But if word spreads amongst court that I have taken a wife, then I'll know he is not the man I once trusted."

The rigid set of Ansgar's jaw and the hard gleam in his eyes told me Torvald had yet to prove himself.

"And what if his servants spread gossip?"

"To them we are nothing more than travelers passing through."

"Will they not recognize you?"

"Not if I refrain from showing myself."

"Surely they will guess your identity."

"They believe Sir Ansgar to be dead. Even if he was alive, he would not have a wife."

I wiggled again to free myself from his hold, suddenly embarrassed that I'd kissed him so ardently.

He placed me on my feet and steadied me, even as I shook off his grip. "You could have figured out another way to test Torvald."

"I apologize. 'Twas the first thing that came to mind."

"I have no wish to be used in your ploys."

"And I have no wish to be used in yours." His gaze dropped to my lips, the reminder that I'd engaged him too.

I unhooked the clasps of my cloak. "I only did so because you initiated the pretense first."

He was silent, his eyes smoldering with something I couldn't name but that sent a rush of warmth into my belly. "Don't do that," I whispered.

"Do what?" he whispered back.

"Look at me like that."

"Like what?"

"Like you would kiss me again if you could."

"I would."

More warmth rolled through me. At this rate, I wouldn't need the fire or drink to restore my body's heat. His looks and words seemed to be doing the task well enough.

I had to put distance between us, had to get away from the strength of his magnetism before it dragged me right back into his arms. But before I could move, he did first. He stalked toward the large canopied bed and threw off his heavy cloak and chain-mail hauberk underneath.

I gasped anew, but this time at the blood drenching his shirt. Since arriving at the fortress, I'd become so preoccupied with fighting my attraction to him that I'd forgotten about his needs.

I was no better than a louse. A selfish louse.

Pushing aside all thoughts of our interactions from moments ago, I tossed aside my cloak and crossed to Ansgar. He was attempting to peel off his tunic, but some of the blood had already dried and the material stuck to his back.

"Here let me." I bumped his hand aside and took over.

"I'll be fine." His head drooped, as though he no longer had the strength to hold it up. "Go warm yourself by the fire."

"I'm fine too." I gently plied the linen away from the wounds.

"I'll manage." He started to pull back.

I took hold of his arm to hold him in place. "For once cease your stubbornness."

He hesitated.

"I intend to help you whether you welcome it or not."

"And now who is the stubborn one?"

"I'm not stubborn. I'm merely determined to get my way."

He released a scoffing laugh but didn't resist as I finished freeing him from his tunic. Blood coated his skin, still oozing from several cuts. Thankfully, they were only flesh wounds, the weapons not having penetrated too deeply.

"Come sit by the fire. I'll clean them and see if they need stitching."

Again, he hesitated.

Without giving him a choice, I guided him toward the fire, dragging a stool along. I pushed him onto it and focused on washing away the blood and cleansing his wounds. Then I retrieved my mother's medicinal pouch from my bag that the servants had unloaded from my saddle, thankful I had a few basic supplies for emergencies.

After stitching the wounds and applying a healing salve, I stepped away to examine my handiwork. Now that his back was clean and the three areas stitched and covered with the salve, I couldn't keep from admiring his magnificent torso and all the beautiful muscles on display.

He rested with his elbows on his knees and his head in his hands. "I should be tending you, helping you get warm, not sitting here letting you wait upon me."

"I'm warm enough now." Though my toes still ached, I'd regained feeling in them. "Besides, that's utter nonsense that you should be waiting upon me."

"'Tisn't nonsense—"

"Yes, it is entirely. And I've loathed the way you've treated me differently since you discovered the truth—"

He twisted me around so quickly that the motion cut off my words. Slanting a glance toward the door, his gaze warned me to say no more, that we didn't know who might be listening, and that I would put us both into grave danger if I told anyone I was the princess.

I nodded my understanding. Before I could pull away, he reached for my hips and drew me toward him. He peered up at me, the tight lines in his face attesting to the pain of my stitching and the wounds.

"Thank you for saving me today," I whispered.

"I was just going to thank you," he whispered back.

"For what?"

"You saved me too."

"I did? How?"

"From worse injury." The honey brown in his eyes glowed warm.

I wanted to trace the tiny scar above his eye but held myself back. I'd been forward enough with kissing him tonight, already having proven myself too much a fool. No matter what tug I might have toward Ansgar, I had to remember I would only hurt him if I persisted in loving him.

With a force of will I didn't know I possessed, I retreated a step, breaking our contact and making myself yawn. "You may be able to go days without sleep, but I cannot."

Before I could get lost in his eyes, I started toward the bed. I would have to remain at my strongest and most vigilant if I had any hope of rising above my own selfishness and doing what was best for both Ansgar and the kingdom.

Chapter 16

ANSGAR

I SLEPT FITFULLY ON A PALLET IN FRONT OF THE CHAMBER DOOR. I tried to tell myself I was restless because of my wounds. When that didn't work, I tried to tell myself I was restless because I was staying alert for any signs of treachery from Torvald.

But in the quiet moments when I rose to my elbow and glimpsed Lis asleep on the bed under piles of covers, I couldn't deny the longing to be more to her than just her bodyguard and servant.

"I've loathed the way you've treated me differently since you discovered the truth." Her words pulsed through me, as did the memory of the touch of her lips, a kiss that had reminded me all over again just how consuming my love for her was. Even if she hadn't confessed her feelings, she cared for me too. I'd felt it in the way she kissed me.

Could I truly give that up for the rest of my life? Or was there some way we could be together? Maybe not now. Not immediately, with all that was left to accomplish.

But was it possible that somehow, someway, we might be able to find a solution? Was I selfish to hope that Princess Elinor could remain the heir and that Maxim would be given permission to be the king by her side?

Stiff and achy, I sat up, letting my covers fall away. The frigid air of the chamber slapped my bare skin, and I arose to add more fuel to the fire.

The light breaking through the shutters indicated that the day was already well underway. The sounds from both within the castle and outside in the busy bailey made me feel as though I were at the royal castle in Vordinberg.

I'd had little news in the few weeks since I'd been forced from the capital city, and now I was eager to converse with Torvald and learn how King Ulrik fared. If only we could find a way to return the king to his right mind. If restored to wholeness, he would surely remember how much Princess Elinor adored him and what a good queen she would be. After all, she'd been raised for that very purpose: to rule Norvegia.

But Lis? She hadn't grown up with the same privileges and education. She didn't know the intricacies of court life or the intrigues of politics. And she wasn't familiar with all the manners and customs of the nobility.

Already she had a hard-enough time allowing me to serve her and treat her deferentially. If placed into the position of queen, she would have dozens of people serving her, calling her by her title, and making her the center of their world. How would she stand it?

Of course, if anyone could rise to the challenge, Lis could.

At a soft tapping in a pattern used by the Brethren, I shoved my blankets and pallet into the wardrobe. I'd already burned my bloody garments and any other evidence of my battle with the Ice Men. Now I grabbed a fresh tunic and stuffed my arms into it even as I opened the door a crack.

Torvald stood outside, carrying a tray with fresh food and hot beverages.

At the sight of me hastily dressing, he gave a slight bow. "If you're busy, I can return later."

Seeing that he was alone, I opened the door wider and motioned him in. "No, come. I'm eager to have words with you and hear the news of the king and court."

As he entered, he quickly closed the door. "No one yet knows you are Sir Ansgar, not even my father," he whispered. "And I would keep it that way for as long as possible."

"Who do they think I am?"

"A newly married nobleman who is madly in love with his bride." Torvald kept his back turned to Lis, too much a man of honor to look upon the marriage bed of another man's wife. He placed the tray on the stool I'd abandoned once Lis was asleep, and then he peered at me, his eyes full of questions and wariness.

He knew my position on marriage. He knew I'd never intended to take a bride. He knew I'd vowed to devote my life to protecting the king.

As much as I wanted to reassure him that I hadn't changed, I still had to proceed with caution until I knew whether Torvald was working for or against me.

I finished shrugging into my tunic.

"You love her." Torvald's low statement was definitive, without a hint of question.

"Yes." At the very least I could be honest with him about this.

From the intenseness of Torvald's gaze, I guessed he

was attempting to understand how my love for her had developed. "She's dangerous to love."

I reached for one of the hot mugs of ale, took a sip, and waited for him to say more.

He stared straight ahead into the flames. "Did her draco save you?"

"Lis saved me, and I recovered at her farm." I should have known Torvald would see what I had seen during the retreat to Vordinberg when Lis had ridden along. He'd obviously figured out that she and the draco belonged together. How many others had come to the same conclusion?

"The Ice Men," Torvald continued, "they are chasing her in order to seize her draco."

I'd sensed the Ice Men following us all day yesterday, and now they'd tracked us to Wahlburg Castle. Were they even now amassing outside the walls? "I shall help you fend them off."

"They are too weak to attack."

I nodded. Most of the Ice Men were already ensconced in their homes for the winter months. This group plaguing us would give up their hunt for Red erelong and return to the mountains before the traveling conditions worsened. "Then we have nothing to worry about."

Torvald's jaw flexed. "Sigfrid betrayed you, but I never will."

I took another sip of the brew. What could I say? I'd trusted Sigfrid too.

"I will aid you and your wife to safety." Torvald spoke in a low whisper. "Tell me what you desire, and I shall see it done."

Lis shuffled under the covers. She would soon be awake. As much as I wished we could stay indefinitely, I couldn't put myself into such a tempting situation and expect to remain a man of honor forever.

Not only had I fabricated the story of our marriage to test Torvald but also to stay close by Lis's side. I'd needed to remain in her room at all times to make sure she was never in jeopardy. But without chaperones or ladies-in-waiting, my presence as a single man wasn't appropriate or proper.

Under the dangerous circumstances, I'd justified all my actions. But my craving for her only intensified with every passing hour. And my resistance was weakening.

We would do best to be on our way soon. If Torvald believed he was sending us one direction, then we could start out that way, allowing everyone to persist in believing we were indeed newlyweds traveling to my home in the north.

"We shall leave at nightfall." I returned my attention to Torvald. With evidence that the Ice Men were on our trail, no one would question our leaving under the cover of darkness. "If you would be so kind as to provide provisions and ready our mounts, that is all I ask."

He studied my face for a moment longer, then nodded. "All I ask is that you allow me to aid you in saving the king."

From the sincerity in his expression, I guessed he wasn't serving Rasmus. Even so, my mission at hand was too precarious. I couldn't let anyone or anything interfere with bringing Lis before the Noble Council and the king to prove she was the rightful heir to the throne.

I picked up a handful of dried currants from the tray, my appetite having returned in full at the break of day. "Tell me all you know of what is transpiring with the king and his court."

"A majority of the Noble Council has finally voted to change the law so that royalty and nobility may marry commoners with the approval of the king."

Although I'd not long ago scoffed at such a law, I could no longer afford to do so. The new law would make it easier to persuade the king to accept Princess Elinor's decision to wed Maxim. If he approved of Maxim, then she could continue as the heir just as she'd always planned.

Even if the law was preposterous, I couldn't deny that many good and honorable men existed among the common stock—men like Maxim, who would sacrifice much for their country. Yes, Maxim would make a good king . . . if King Ulrik could only open his mind to see the truth.

I chewed the savory currants and waited for Torvald to continue with his news.

Torvald glanced to the door, as though he knew he wasn't safe even in his own home. Did he suspect Rasmus had influenced, perhaps bribed, his servants to act as spies? "Rasmus has continued to persuade the king to reject Princess Elinor as his heir. Without anyone else of royal blood who can take her place, the king has persisted in his belief that the Sword of the Magi will determine the worthiest man in all the land, whether commoner or nobility."

I studied him. His news confirmed what Nils had brought back from town. "And the chieftains, Sages, and Noble Council have agreed with Rasmus?"

"They worry that since they cannot find an additional heir of royal blood, King Canute will make another move to take Norvegia's throne. With such a threat, everyone agrees they must decide upon the next heir soon and so will allow the sword to do its choosing."

King Canute of Swaine was a distant cousin of King Ulrik, having a Norvegian princess in his bloodline. No one wanted a foreign king to take the throne. But would Canute ever respect the man who freed the sword—especially if he was of common blood? Or would a king of common stock only incite Canute to attack again and again until he won the throne for himself?

My gut rolled with unease. "While I would like to believe in the power of the sword, that it truly is blessed by God, I cannot also dismiss the notion that man can meddle where he shouldn't."

"Then we share the same concern. Rasmus has enough knowledge of the Sword of the Magi to share its secret with the one he chooses to be the next king."

"Gotfred."

Torvald nodded solemnly. "Gotfred continues to do whatever Rasmus demands. And Gotfred has ingratiated himself with the king. The king has even started calling him *my son.*"

"Then 'twould be an easy step for the king to approve of Gotfred becoming his heir."

"Much too easy."

While I'd come to accept the prospect of a commoner like Maxim ruling alongside Princess Elinor, I couldn't so easily accept the idea of Gotfred taking the throne, not when Rasmus would essentially rule through him.

My pulse tapped with a new sense of urgency. "If Rasmus intends for Gotfred to pull the sword free, then how much time do we have until that happens?"

"Rasmus dare not act right away," Torvald responded, "or he will come under suspicion for conspiring with Gotfred to free the sword. My guess is that Rasmus will wait until he can make the freeing look most natural."

"Perhaps in a skirmish?" I knew Rasmus well enough to understand that if he aimed to put Gotfred onto the throne, he would calculate every detail and leave nothing to chance.

"Perhaps Rasmus is waiting for someone to arrive to threaten the king." The light in Torvald's eyes spoke of his understanding of Rasmus's scheming.

I added my conjecture. "At just the right moment of threat, Gotfred will free the sword and use it to defend the king."

We were both silent, sorting the tangled net Rasmus had cast, so much like the net the Ice Men had thrown over Red. Was there any way to extricate all those caught within it, including us? Or were we doomed to accept Gotfred as the next king?

Did I yet have time to take Lis to Vordinberg and prove she was a royal princess? And if I did, would I find Rasmus simply waiting for a dissident like myself to return and cause trouble, thus providing Gotfred the opportunity to prove himself by pulling the sword loose?

"So the capital is now flooded with commoners seeking to have an opportunity with the sword?"

"I have not seen the capital for myself," Torvald whispered, "but I have heard that masses of men are arriving every day. The city is overrun with commoners awaiting a turn at liberating the sword before the worst of winter arrives and prevents travel."

With so many people converging upon the capital, perhaps Lis and I would be able to enter Vordinberg without detection. We would have to find a way to blend in, but I didn't know how I could do so, not with how recognizable I was. No matter the extent that the people loved me, I also couldn't forget I had a bounty upon my head. Many men—perhaps even men I'd once trusted—would be all too eager to turn me in for reward or recognition.

But what choice did I have? No matter my reservations for either my safety or Lis's, we had to go to Vordinberg with all haste. We needed to prove she was the princess and rightful heir to the throne before anyone, including Gotfred, could pull the sword free.

Chapter 17

Lis

I changed the dressing on Ansgar's wounds again, forcing him to sit upon the stool in front of the fire. By daylight, I could see all the scars across his back and rib cage, some newer—likely from the battle with Swaine last month.

I hurried through the ministrations, not wanting to cause him any more pain than necessary. But even as I finished, his shoulders were rigid and his hands clasped so tightly the veins bulged in his arms.

I stood back and examined him, wiping my hands onto a rag. "I'm sorry I don't have my father's soft touch and am causing you so much pain."

"If only it were pain your touch caused me." His voice was low and raw. "But 'tis far from it."

Warm pleasure cascaded through me. I couldn't deny I relished the chance to doctor Ansgar, but I understood now why my father had taken over the task. Even if innocent, so much touching was clearly affecting us both. As always.

I had to switch the subject and focus on something besides him. I spun away and packed the medicinal bag. "Tell me how you intend to disguise yourself."

We were leaving after darkness fell. With the lengthening shadows of late afternoon, I guessed we had less than an hour before our departure.

"You'll help me darken my hair coloring with charcoal, and we'll trade for peasant garb."

I paused and glanced at him over my shoulder. "And you think that will truly work? That with your girth and muscles you'll escape notice?"

He started to respond but then released a sigh. "I suppose you have a suggestion for me."

"While I don't want to persist in our charade of being husband and wife, it may help."

"You don't want to persist?" He twisted on the stool and grabbed my hand. "That's not true."

I attempted to pull free but not overly hard. "'Tis entirely true."

His fingers closed around mine, and his smile made an appearance, a sight that never failed to make my breath hitch. "You're enjoying this charade as much as I am."

I was, but I didn't want him to have the satisfaction of knowing it. "Yes, you've made my dreams come true, the dream to be a counterfeit wife in a counterfeit marriage."

He laughed then, the flecks dancing in his brown eyes.

I couldn't keep from smiling.

His fingers tightened, and something in his expression beckoned me to come nearer of my own volition—because I wanted to be with him and not because I was acting.

At a soft rhythmic tapping on the door, the carefree air between us vanished.

"'Tis Torvald," Ansgar whispered reeling me closer.

I didn't resist his tug. "You still don't trust him?"

"Not yet." He pulled me down onto his lap.

For a moment I was too startled by our proximity and his bare chest to do anything but sit primly.

He wrapped his arms around my waist.

Once again, as on the previous night, I was having difficulty separating our pretense from reality. Every small touch made me keenly aware of him, so much that I scooted to the edge of his knees.

Ansgar drew me back. "The goal is to convince him you like being with me. Not that you can't abide sitting on my lap."

"I can't abide it."

"If I kiss your neck, will you like it better?" His whisper contained a note of teasing.

I gently swatted his arm. "No kissing."

"Are you sure?" His eyes seemed to plead with me, but his smile crept back out.

The knock came again, just as distinct but louder.

"Come in," Ansgar called, and in the next move, he burrowed his face in the crook of my neck. The closeness took my breath away, and I grabbed on to his arms to keep from sliding off. As the door opened, I pressed a kiss to the top of Ansgar's head at the same moment Torvald entered.

Tougher and fiercer by daylight, the knight took in my position on Ansgar's lap before he ducked his head. "I beg your forgiveness for disturbing you, sire."

Ansgar expelled a sigh, likely for Torvald's benefit,

then pulled away. Even then, he didn't release me from his embrace.

Torvald closed the door but held the handle. "We have evidence the Ice Men are still lurking in the woods beyond the castle."

Ansgar glanced toward the window. The shutters were closed but allowed in a scant amount of light. "We shall outride them as we did on our way here."

"I propose we change your mounts and send out decoys at the same time you leave."

Ansgar's expression turned serious, and he shook his head. "No, I cannot put anyone else's life in danger from the Ice Men."

Torvald's attention shifted to the newly doctored wounds on Ansgar's back, the evidence the Ice Men were indeed brutal. "I offer myself. And one of my squires has also volunteered to ride with me. Although not overly small, he will pass at a distance as your wife."

Ansgar held Torvald's gaze for a long moment as though attempting to test the sincerity of the sacrifice.

"I should have gone with you when the king dismissed you." Torvald's tone turned ragged with remorse. "I have lived these many weeks with the guilt of your death upon my shoulders, and I would do now what I did not do then. Stand with a friend who has never been anything but true and good and brave."

Beneath me, I could feel Ansgar's muscles tense. I knew he wanted to trust Torvald, that he was likely fighting an inner debate on whether or not he could. "You need not hold yourself responsible. We all agreed you needed to stay and protect the king."

Torvald shook his head. "We should have realized

Rasmus would never allow us to stay."

Ansgar remained rigid several heartbeats longer, then relaxed and tugged me closer. "We never know the way everything will work out, only that Providence is weaving together all things for his purposes."

As he looked into my eyes, I realized he was using Ulla's prophetic words to describe the way we'd met. Somehow God had used Ansgar's flight from the capital and the betrayal by a friend to bring us together. Without Ansgar's presence at the farm, I might never have had the courage to leave my comfortable life. And without his presence as my protector, Father might never have had the courage to set me free to fulfill my destiny.

Torvald opened the door. "I will leave with my squire a quarter of an hour past dusk. Once the Ice Men are on our trail, then you will sneak out with your wife and go the opposite way." He made a move to leave.

"Wait."

Torvald closed the door and faced us, his expression unreadable.

Ansgar stood, lifting me to my feet and setting me gently beside him. "Lis is not my wife."

"I realize that."

"You do?"

He nodded. "You love her, that much is clear."

Ansgar didn't reject the statement. He never had. And I guessed he never would. Admitting he loved me in the short term was much easier than committing to loving me forever.

Did I want his commitment forever? Ansgar had

already stated he had no intention of taking our relationship further. And hadn't I resolved he was better off without me?

"What gave us away?" Ansgar asked.

"Though it is clear you are trying to be convincing, you have used much restraint and caution. Too much for a newly married man." Torvald's blunt words sent embarrassment tumbling inside me.

"And what else do you know about me?" Ansgar didn't seem mortified, only curious.

Torvald again met Ansgar's gaze directly. "You are not going home. I am wagering you are returning to Vordinberg, though I have not determined why."

"I may yet be able to save the kingdom from Rasmus's grip." He glanced at me. "God has provided a way, and now I am tasked with seeing his plan to completion."

"I would stand by your side in whatever the task, sire." The sincerity infusing Torvald's voice and expression left me with no doubt he would never betray Ansgar.

Ansgar slipped his hand into mine. "You have helped us greatly already."

"I intend to do more."

"Then I shall accept your aid of a decoy with a grateful heart."

Torvald bowed his head, and without another word, he exited, leaving us alone.

Ansgar stared at the closed door, his jaw flexing.

Silence settled in the darkening room, and I relished the pressure of Ansgar's hand within mine. "I believe his desire to help is genuine. Do you not?"

"I believe the same." He released me and reached

for his tunic. "But 'twill be a dangerous mission ahead, and I would not put his life at risk alongside mine."

His statement sent a shiver up my spine. He was right. We would have a dangerous mission, one in which he was putting his life at risk. With Rasmus's bounty upon his head, there was the very real possibility he would be captured and killed.

The more I cared about Ansgar, the less certain I was about bringing him along with me. Perhaps this was a mission I needed to accomplish on my own.

Chapter 18

ANSGAR

I kept my head down among the busy throng ascending the road to the royal castle in Vordinberg. With my arm draped around Lis, I allowed her to guide us. Attired in her simple homespun skirt and heavy cloak, she didn't attract any undue attention, especially with her hood drawn up to hide her pretty features.

After riding hard all night and half the day, we'd arrived at Vordinberg well past noon. Thankfully, we'd had no confrontations with the Ice Men. Torvald's effort to lead them away from us had succeeded. I prayed he and his squire had come out of the encounter with the warriors unscathed. I surmised that once the Ice Men learned of our deception, they would give up the chase and return to the mountains.

Red remained safe and had followed us toward Vordinberg. At Lis's command, he stayed in the hills outside the city. He could provide us with no assistance here, especially once we were inside the castle.

Lis glanced to the sky overhead as though checking for Red.

"What is it?" I asked in the gravelly voice I'd been using since we entered the city. Lis had darkened my hair with charcoal and added some to my face for good measure. I'd also traded for a ragged cloak to cover my chain mail. Adding a slouch and limp to my performance, I hadn't drawn undue attention.

If anyone was expecting Sir Ansgar, Grand Marshal of the Knights of Brethren, to return today, they hadn't discovered him. Having Lis by my side deterred suspicion as well, especially because she'd stuffed her bag inside her tunic, making her appear pregnant.

Lis leaned in and spoke so only I could hear. "Red has seen Torvald riding near to Vordinberg."

On the one hand, that was good news. Torvald had survived his clash with the Ice Men. On the other hand, it could also mean he'd come to betray me to Rasmus. I didn't want to believe that about him, not after the sincerity we'd shared before leaving at dark. With Rasmus's tightening grip over the people and land, I could only pray I hadn't misplaced my trust in Torvald.

I picked up my pace. "We must move faster."

Lis continued in her unhurried manner. "No, we'll do as we planned."

I took in a breath and tried to squelch my impatience. I couldn't forget that strategy off the battlefield was just as important as on and that I needed to stay true to our plan.

We'd had many hours to discuss the intricacies of how we would infiltrate the castle and how Lis would present herself to the king without Rasmus knowing who she was or what she was doing until it was too late.

I'd plotted with her how to enter through the

servants' quarters and detailed every step she should take as she made her way to the great hall. I'd even revealed several hiding places where she could tarry until I worked my way inside by joining the line of commoners awaiting a chance at freeing the sword.

Once she saw that I was close to the front, she was to make her way into the great hall, pretending to be a kitchen maid. We had to time our appearance so we were near the dais as the king came in for his evening meal but before the men were sent away for the night.

The closer we came to the castle, the more my muscles tightened with the need to hoist Lis into my arms and take her back to her father and the farm.

"I'll be alright." She spoke softly and squeezed my arm, as though she felt my turmoil.

Next to us several men jostled each other good-naturedly. The scent of ale was heavy in the air around them, and I guessed they'd spent the morn at a tavern before venturing to the castle. Others led their horses. Some had servants. Only a few men, like me, came with a woman.

The snow showers of the past couple of days had ceased, and today the sun had made its appearance, giving us a break from the unrelenting cold. Even so, my limbs were chilled, and I had no doubt Lis was faring worse.

I gently squeezed her in return, admiring her all the more for her unwavering determination to stay the course before us no matter how uncomfortable and no matter the risk to herself. Although we hadn't talked about Ulla's revelation about Princess Blanche's curse, Lis must be feeling some trepidation in returning to the royal house, even if she didn't show it. With every passing day, this amazing woman impressed me with her ingenuity, calmness under pressure, and strength of character.

At a commotion ahead, I drew her closer into the crook of my arm. The crowd began to part and make way for someone leaving the castle. As the pounding of horses drew nearer, I moved with Lis against the stone wall along the edge of the road. I allowed myself a glimpse of the retinue descending on the path toward us and then wished I hadn't.

Sigfrid rode proudly upon his steed at the forefront of several other Knights of Brethren and their squires. They were attired in their armor and heavily outfitted with weapons . . . as if they intended to do battle.

I slipped my hand to the hilt of my sword beneath my cloak. Were they coming for me? Had someone guessed my identity and alerted Rasmus after all?

My heart pounded in preparation for combat. I would fight Sigfrid again. And this time I wouldn't let him or his men gain the advantage.

"Who is it?" Lis had stiffened too, clearly sensing the change in my demeanor.

I leaned in so only she could hear. "Sigfrid."

"If you duck your head when he passes, he may suspect something," she whispered, a thread of panic in her voice. "But if you stand tall, he might recognize you even with your disguise."

Sigfrid and his men were fast approaching and hadn't yet slowed. Was it possible they were on another mission? That they didn't know I was among the crowd?

I quickly brought Lis around so that the roundness of her abdomen was clearly seen from the angle of Sigfrid's approach. I placed a hand on the swell, hoping to draw the attention away from myself.

As the group drew nearer, I waited for them to point at me and shout out my name. But the plodding of the horses didn't slow. When Sigfrid was but a sword's length away, I bent and pressed a kiss to Lis's cheek, praying I looked like a husband using the break in the flow of traffic to dote upon his pregnant wife.

She lifted a hand to my chest and leaned in, playing to perfection the role of a loving wife.

I tried to relax, tried to slouch, tried to keep my face hidden. But all the while, I was aware of every step of Sigfrid's horse and the other Brethren with him. As they passed, they left nothing but the scent of horseflesh and a draft of cold air. Still, I didn't move, bracing myself for them to stop abruptly and turn on me.

But on the road in front of us, the people moved again, pushing upward, their momentum sweeping us along. I captured Lis's hand and drew her with me, anxious to be on our way.

Lis swung our hands in a carefree manner and offered me a smile as though we were just another couple on a grand adventure. Her eyes remained guarded and tense, so I knew she was only pretending.

As we continued without a confrontation from Sigfrid, I breathed easier. I'd passed the test. Although I knew I should have been glad of it, a sliver of unease pricked me. The discomfort swelled until at last I realized why. If Sigfrid wasn't seeking me, then he was seeking someone else.

What if he'd learned Torvald was on his way to Vordinberg? Did he intend to ride out and attack Torvald the way he had me? If so, how would he explain away Torvald's death to the people? While Torvald hadn't garnered the same attention I had, he'd been beloved and respected for his service to the king. The people would surely grow alarmed when a second of the Knights of Brethren turned up murdered.

No, Rasmus wouldn't take such a chance. Besides, he might even be waiting for Torvald to return and cause a skirmish, giving Gotfred an excuse to remove the sword.

Sigfrid was leaving for a different reason. Clearly something urgent. But what? What would draw him away? Only someone who might pose a threat to Rasmus. If not one of the Brethren, I could think of no one else but Maxim and the Princess Elinor.

Maxim and Princess Elinor.

I nearly stumbled.

Lis grabbed my arm and steadied me, her eyes rounding with questions.

With the ever-growing crowd of people around us, I leaned in as I had earlier so our conversation couldn't be heard. "What if Sigfrid is hunting for Maxim and Princess Elinor?"

Lis took her time thinking about my pronouncement. "If your initial missive found them without too much delay, then the timing would be right."

"I concur. Now someone has betrayed them or at least spoken of seeing them nearby." My mind churned over the possibilities. "And Rasmus seeks to eliminate them before they can reach the king and plead their case to him."

"Should we go to their aid?"

"We don't know where they are."

"We could follow Sigfrid."

Even as we trudged up the path, my heart warred within me. If we abandoned our undertaking to present Lis as the rightful heir, we could assist Maxim and Princess

Elinor in their claim for the throne. Lis wouldn't need to reveal who she was. She could go back to living in anonymity in the country. And hopefully she would stay safe from the curse.

Before the thought could take root, I weeded it out. Whether or not Maxim and Princess Elinor became the next king and queen, Lis needed to do this today. Then Rasmus would know without a doubt he'd lost, that his scheming had come to naught.

I swallowed hard, pushing down my selfish desires so I could do the greatest good for Norvegia. "I believe we should continue with our plans." I paused, waiting for her to protest, to insist that we rescue Maxim and Princess Elinor.

After several steps, she seemed to swallow hard too, then spoke quietly but firmly. "I agree. But there is one thing I may yet do for them."

When she whispered a command, I prayed Red would find Maxim and Princess Elinor before Sigfrid did.

We rounded a bend in the path, and the massive gatehouse stood less than a hundred paces away. From what I could tell, the guards were allowing everyone to pass through, hardly giving anyone a second glance.

I held my breath as we strolled past the first set of guards. They were busy talking with each other and didn't seem to notice me among the many others. As we made our way through the gatehouse passageway to the other side, a second pair of guards waved us onward, again without paying attention, likely weary of the masses of people coming every day.

The sunshine bathed us as we entered the inner bailey. It was always a hectic place with traders and laborers coming and going—almost a tiny city unto itself. Now it had become even busier, crowded with the companions and family members waiting for their men to complete their turn with the sword.

My heart sank at the sight of the endless line of those hoping to become the next king. It snaked out the front door, down the stone steps, and through the yard. How would I ever make it to the front today?

"I need to go get in line."

Lis released me and took a step back. She laid a hand over her protruding abdomen like an expectant mother might do. "Good luck to you, husband."

If anyone was watching, she was giving them no cause to suspect we were there for any other reason but the sword. I needed to do the same. I placed my hand over hers on her abdomen. "If we become king and queen, perhaps God will bless us and our children with a good future."

Her beautiful green eyes were wide, windows to her soul. For the briefest of moments, I gained a glimpse inside. A clear and untainted love shone there. For me.

Swift and fierce desire clamped around my heart. Before I could talk myself out of it, I bent down and captured her mouth in a hard and hungry kiss, one I prayed wasn't my last but feared might be.

I ended the kiss before I was tempted to prolong it. I spun and moved away, acting the part of a limping man. As I took my place in line, I could feel the heat of her gaze upon me.

I forced myself not to look back at her. If I did, I knew I'd never be able to go through with all the sacrifices I must make this day. For her.

Chapter
19

Lis

We were running out of time.

I hopped off the keg of ale and tiptoed toward the open door of the buttery. I peered down the passageway that led to the great hall. With no one in sight, I picked up the jug of wine I planned to carry with me as Ansgar had instructed. Although maidservants didn't oft serve in the great hall, he assured me no one would question my presence there, at least not right away.

We'd agreed I would wait until he reached the great hall. But after hours of hiding, I'd seen no sign of him, and my heart was beginning to tap a rhythm of dread. Had something happened to him? Perhaps one of the guards had recognized him. Maybe he'd been arrested and thrown in the dungeons.

Bracing myself and pretending to be a serving girl, I again made my way to the arched door that led into the back corner of the great hall. Thankfully, I'd had the area to myself for most of my stay. Only within the past hour had several servants come and gone, preparing for the evening meal that would soon be served. The tantalizing scents of roasting meat and vegetables confirmed that I needed to act now before the men standing in line were sent away.

I paused in front of the first door. The clamor within the great hall had increased. More laughter and voices met me this time, another sign I needed to do something soon. Although I'd managed to sneak in through the various routes Ansgar had laid out for me, I had no guarantee I'd be able to do so undetected again on the morrow. And Ansgar had no guarantee he'd make it to the front of the line on the morrow either.

Besides, the longer we waited, the more chances Ansgar had of being discovered and hauled away—if he hadn't been already.

"Red?" I whispered. "Are you alright?" I paused and waited, but my communication seemed to go nowhere, as it had for the past hours.

If he was near, he couldn't hear me. I'd taken a risk in sending him away to find Maxim and Princess Elinor, if indeed they were in the area. If the Ice Men had traced my presence to the capital, then they would be hiding in the hills, ready to toss their heavy net over Red again the first chance they got.

"Please, Red. Find Princess Elinor." I closed my eyes in an attempt to concentrate on locating his presence. "She's my sister. My family." Although admitting such a thing seemed treasonous, I wanted Red to know the importance of this mission.

The truth was, I needed Elinor. For although I had bargained my firstborn daughter to Ulla in order to gain proof of my royal ties, I didn't want to be named the next heir to the throne of Norvegia. I wasn't meant to be queen. I had no aspirations for it, no knowledge of how to be and act like a queen, no skills that would qualify me.

I was a simple girl from the country. Yes, a part of me had always been restless, had perhaps known I was made for more. Even so, I had to return home and help Father take care of the farm. He wouldn't be able to do it alone. And I didn't want to leave him there all winter by himself.

Elinor was more suited to becoming the next queen of Norvegia. Much more suited. I would plead with the king to give her that right. But if the king and his council refused, then I would be left with no choice but to step in and do what was right and necessary. Maybe eventually I would find a way to transfer the throne to Elinor. At the very least, I would bequeath the throne to her offspring. With the curse upon myself, I couldn't take a chance of marrying and having children.

With a final whisper to Red, I opened my eyes, focused on the doorway, and moved forward.

I'd been preserved for such a time as this, to go before the king and his royal court to present myself, to save the royal bloodline from extinction, to keep the kingdom from falling further under the conniving control of Rasmus, to maintain integrity, justice, and goodness.

I let those thoughts roll through my head as I stepped into the great hall. One glance at the dais showed the king, his knights, and his closest advisors— including Rasmus—present.

I searched the lengthy line of commoners stretching through the room and out the double doors. Ansgar was still nowhere in sight. Perhaps his absence was for the best. He would remain safer this way.

Straightening my shoulders, I pressed onward. Though my insides quavered, I didn't let my steps waver. I wound around tables, past servers as well as many other people I couldn't identify. I didn't take my focus off the head table, zeroing in on the king where he now sat at the center.

He slouched in his chair. His hair was stringy and thin, his shoulders boney, and his frame skeletal. As if that weren't enough, his face was gaunt, eyes hollow, and skin jaundiced.

As he lifted his chalice to his lips and slurped a sip, much of it dribbled down his beard. His hands shook, causing more liquid to slosh over, staining the white linen tablecloth.

My stomach roiled. His condition was dreadful. Even on the ship voyage home to Vordinberg after he'd been injured, he hadn't looked so terrible. This man was nothing but a shell of his former hearty and robust self.

It was no wonder Ansgar had sought to uncover what was going on. And it was also no wonder he wanted so desperately to return. The king's condition was indeed grave. The hermit tonic was killing him.

No, *Rasmus* was murdering the king.

My pulse quickened with anger, and I lengthened my steps, no longer pretending to be a servant. The king's life depended upon me.

As I reached the dais, I stopped in front of the king, making sure he could see me from his hunched angle.

"Your Majesty, King Ulrik." I raised my voice so I could be heard above the din.

Behind the king and talking with a young knight, Rasmus paused and glanced my way.

"King Ulrik," I called again, louder and with as much authority as I could muster.

Thankfully, this time the king lifted his gaze. Though his eyes were hazy, he seemed to be trying to focus.

"Your Majesty, I am Princess Elisbet, the firstborn daughter of your sister, Princess Blanche. I present myself as the rightful heir to the throne of Norvegia."

Around me, the conversations began to fade away. I could feel the attention shifting my direction. The king seemed to sit up straighter. At the women's table, the queen fell silent, her face going pale. I would have known she was the queen even if she hadn't been wearing a crown upon her fair hair. Although her face was overly thin and dark circles shadowed her eyes, she was still a beautiful woman.

Rasmus's eyes narrowed upon me, his expression stoic. If I'd taken him by surprise, he quickly masked it.

I didn't give him the satisfaction of acknowledging his presence. Instead, I continued to direct my conversation to the king. "I do not aspire to rule, but when word of Princess Elinor's disinheritance reached me, I knew I could do nothing less than offer myself as the salvation of this land from dark forces seeking to invade."

An eerie silence descended, one that extended to the far corners of the room.

The king began to push back from the table and

attempt to stand. But he had so little strength that he only made it a short distance before he sank back into his chair.

The young knight I guessed to be Gotfred held out a hand, but the king's gaze was now intent and clear upon me. "Remarkable," he spoke, his voice weak and wobbly. "You are the identical image of my sister."

I bowed my head to acknowledge his statement. If only I'd been able to speak with him on the longboat voyage to Vordinberg during the retreat. Would he have recognized me then? Would we have eliminated all this turmoil? As it was, he'd been surrounded and too far away to notice me.

"Your Majesty, I urge caution." Rasmus bent in toward the king. "She could very well be an imposter. We have no proof she is who she claims."

Somehow, I sensed that each word he'd uttered was intended more for me than the king, as though he was setting a trap and beckoning me to walk into it. His intelligence and wisdom were renowned throughout the land. In addition, Ansgar had warned of Rasmus's ability to scheme. I needed to proceed with extreme caution.

I wished I had some irrefutable birthmark or other identifying sign that could prove who I was. But I had nothing except for the bangle Ulla had given me. I pushed up my sleeve and withdrew the jeweled armband. Then I held it up so everyone in the great hall could view it. "This belonged to Princess Blanche, my mother. As in the tradition of mothers to daughters, her mother bequeathed her the bangle at her coming-of-age ball."

The king pushed to his feet, almost as if the sight of

the bangle had given him a magical burst of energy. His eyes remained riveted to it. "That belonged to my mother."

"She gave it to her daughter, Blanche. And now, as Blanche's firstborn daughter, it is mine to wear."

Rasmus stepped next to the king into a position reserved for the king's closest of companions. The very sight of Rasmus placing himself beside the king sparked more ire inside me. Rasmus had clearly gained influence with the king that made him comfortable standing at his side, especially because the king didn't protest and instead took Rasmus's offer of his arm to lean on.

"What do you think, Rasmus?" the king asked, still staring at me.

"In this time when the future of this country hangs in the balance, we cannot be too careful. There are those who will go to great lengths of scheming to take the throne."

I wanted to blurt out that he was describing himself, but I wanted to snub him as long as possible. "I have no aspirations for myself. I only desire what is in the best interest of this kingdom."

The line of commoners making their way to the front had come to a standstill. The guard next to the pedestal table that held the long red cedarwood case containing the sword had halted the proceedings. I still saw no sign of Ansgar, and now I doubted he'd be able to make his way into the great hall—not past the guards or the men who'd been waiting for hours ahead of him.

Rasmus patted the king's hand and gently helped lower him into his chair. "Have no fear, Your Majesty.

I shall determine whether this maiden speaks the truth or whether she is an imposter. My intuition is never wrong."

"Good, Rasmus." The king sank into the cushions and leaned his head back as though he might fall asleep at a moment's notice.

Was this it? Had I lost my opportunity to influence the king? "Your Majesty, I ask that you and everyone who knew Princess Blanche look upon me and determine for yourselves what similarities I share with her."

The king closed his eyes, his features tightening with obvious pain. The hermit tonic was likely eating away at him from the inside out. If someone didn't put an end to this torture, he would soon die.

"Let me ask you this." Rasmus drew himself up. In his black robe and long dangling black hat, he had an air of regality, almost as if he already believed himself to be the ruler. "Why did you wait so long to come forward as the next heir?"

"I recently learned of the change in the law that would allow for a new king, one picked by the sword. But I also learned that you, as the highest of Royal Sages, might possibly share your secret for removing the sword with the man of your choosing. I couldn't stand idly by and allow that to happen."

"My secret for removing the sword?" Rasmus raised an eyebrow. "If such a secret exists, would I not have accomplished the feat by now?"

"I suspect you are waiting for the opportune moment."

"The real question is, who gave you the bangle? Certainly not Princess Blanche."

What should I say in response? I couldn't lie and tell everyone I'd had the bangle since birth, that Blanche had left it for me. Nothing good ever came from lying. No, I needed to speak the truth no matter the consequences. "When Princess Blanche ran away eighteen years ago, she went to the healing woman Ulla in the Snowden Mountains and gave her the bangle in exchange for help."

"You sought out Ulla?"

"For proof that I am Princess Blanche's daughter."

"And you bargained with her in exchange for the bangle?"

"Yes."

"So Princess Blanche did not give it to you?"

Rasmus's questions insinuated that my process of obtaining the bangle wasn't legitimate. How could I substantiate anything when I didn't even know for myself? I'd trusted Ulla. "Ulla saved it in order to give it to me."

Rasmus seemed to peer deep inside, seeing my doubts. "You're asking us to believe the word of a decrepit old woman who is nothing more than a witch?"

"She was of sound mind—"

"Who are you working for?"

"No one."

"Someone has put you up to this. Clearly, someone aspiring to the throne."

"I am here of my own volition to offer myself to the king as his subject and to do my duty as his heir." As I spoke, I willed the king to look at me again, to acknowledge that I was his niece, but his eyes were still pinched shut. Instead, I glanced at the queen, hoping she would offer me assurance that she recognized me and the bangle.

She nodded at me as though to encourage me. Before she could speak, Rasmus continued. "I see no way possible you could come into possession of the bangle without assistance. If you wish to save yourself, you must reveal who you are conspiring with."

How had Rasmus so swiftly turned my declaration into an accusation?

He nodded toward the Knights of Brethren sitting on each end of the head table. Four of them rose and made their way toward me. While none of them was as strong and intimidating as Ansgar, all wore their chain mail and were armed. No one would dare fight against them to save me, a stranger in their midst.

"Tell us who is responsible for your actions," Rasmus said again. "If you do not, you will give me no choice but to have my guards take you to the dungeons and hold you there until you confess the truth of your plotting."

I eyed the door. Could I make my escape? Or would doing so make me look even guiltier? I lifted my chin and glared at Rasmus. "I have spoken the truth. And I believe no one here would so easily dismiss an heir to the throne if they did not fear your retribution."

"Quite the opposite. Everyone here is happy that, with the king's weakened condition, we have wisemen who can continue to advise him." Rasmus laid a hand boldly on the king's shoulder. From the tilt of the king's head and his open mouth, he'd obviously fallen asleep and was no longer concerned about the matter at hand. I wouldn't find any defense from him.

The four knights drew closer. Would they really

drag me away to the dungeons? Was I to fail even before I had truly begun?

Watching the knights with worried eyes, the queen stood abruptly, wringing her jeweled hands. "We do appreciate your wisdom, Rasmus. But I should think we need to investigate this possibility since she looks so much like Princess Blanche."

I met the queen's gaze again and hoped she could see my gratitude. Before she could say more, a commotion at the entrance of the great hall drew my attention as well as every eye in the room.

Relief swept through me. A man I would recognize anywhere tossed off a guard who attempted to halt him. Ansgar. He was alive and well. Perhaps he'd been delayed farther back in the line. And perhaps as gossip had passed through the commoners and reached him, he'd charged into the hall.

Whatever the case, he was here now, and hopefully he could help free me from Rasmus's net, one I'd believed I could avoid but that now had me ensnared.

Several guards were chasing after Ansgar, and some of the men standing in line were grumbling and calling at him to wait his turn.

As another of the guards tried to grab Ansgar, he spun and threw a punch that knocked the man backward into his companions. Ansgar was still wearing his cloak and hadn't shed his disguise, but as he neared the front of the great hall, he let his hood fall away.

Even with the charcoal-darkened hair, his identity was plain to see. Gasps and murmurs echoed in the room, and the men in line who had just been complaining now stepped aside to give Ansgar leeway, their eyes widening and their faces filling with admiration.

Whispers of "Sir Ansgar" rippled through the crowd.

The guards ceased their efforts to capture Ansgar, likely having no wish to face him in combat. Or perhaps they admired him and wouldn't stand in his way.

Ansgar now strode unhindered to the front of the great hall. As he stopped near the dais, he took in the four knights who had encircled me. "You will accept Princess Elisbet as the heir to the throne, or you will answer to me."

My chest swelled with admiration for this brave man who stood for what was right no matter the cost to himself. Confidence radiated from him, and he held himself with the bearing of a leader, a man used to being obeyed without question.

He looked next at Rasmus. "You've lost, Rasmus. Accept defeat and step aside so that the rightful heir can take her place."

Rasmus stood unruffled. His lips twitched into what could only be classified as the beginning of a smile. What did the Royal Sage have to smile about at this moment?

"We have our answer to who is behind this threat to the king," Rasmus said. "Sir Ansgar. I hadn't expected to see you again. But since you were plotting to overtake the king once before, I should have guessed you'd find another way."

Dread pricked my spine. Ansgar had walked right into Rasmus's trap. He would be ensnared just as easily as I had been.

Chapter 20

Ansgar

I'D FIGHT TO THE DEATH BEFORE I LET ANY OF THE KNIGHTS OF Brethren take Lis away to the dungeons. In fact, if one of them so much as laid a hand on her, I'd attack. Although these Brethren were new since my dismissal, their faces were familiar. From the wariness upon their countenances, I knew they didn't want to fight me, perhaps even feared it. They had likely watched me in battle or at the very least heard tales of my deeds.

They ought to fear me. Because at the moment, I wanted to lash out at someone or something. Not only because of the danger Lis was in but also because of the demise of the king.

Upon charging into the hall and getting my first glimpse of him slumped and asleep at the head table, frustration stabbed my chest. He was worse than I'd expected. And my guilt reared up along with the memories of my father after I'd pulled him from the river. I'd failed once, and I couldn't fail again. Not now.

With one eye on Rasmus and one on the Brethren, I

projected my voice to expose Rasmus once and for all. "If anyone has been plotting, it's you, Your Excellency. Not only are you murdering the king with the hermit tonic, but you schemed to kill me by dismissing me and sending fellow knights to waylay me. But Providence protected me, allowing me to return and foil your plans."

At Ansgar's bold declarations, the murmuring within the hall began again, this time with an angry rumble.

Rasmus's expression remained unchanging. "I sent you away because you are a threat to the king. Now, with your intention to foist an imposter upon the throne, it's clear you are still just as threatening."

"She's not an imposter. She has every right to the throne, more so than anyone you might attempt to put there."

"As everyone can see, I am not putting anyone on the throne. We are allowing the sword to choose the man who is most worthy. If anyone is interfering, it is the two of you by preventing these men from having their chance." Rasmus waved his arm toward the line of men.

I'd been in the long passageway approaching the hall, still trying to stay unnoticed but growing more anxious as the hour grew late, when I gleaned the news that a maiden claiming to be a princess had entered the great hall. I'd wasted no time in breaking from my rank and pushing forward, all too ready to begin this confrontation with Rasmus.

"You have given these men false hope," I continued in a voice loud enough for every man to hear, "for you have no intention of allowing any of them a chance to become king."

"False hope?" Rasmus's tone was filled with contempt. "You are the one offering false hope. If you have your way, you will take control of the throne for yourself, using this strange maiden as your means to do so."

I turned and faced commoners and nobility alike. "Let it be known that I, Sir Ansgar, have never aspired to the throne in the past, nor do I now, nor will I ever do so in the future. My greatest duty and desire is to protect the king and to end this ailment that has befallen him so that he might rule as he ought."

My words were met with a chorus of cheers, clapping, and whistles.

Rasmus gave a slight nod at Gotfred, who was standing dutifully by the king's side. Gotfred nodded back and then began to make his way off the dais.

Was this some kind of sign? Had Rasmus just given Gotfred the signal to pull the sword free?

My pulse tapped more rapidly. I couldn't allow Gotfred to get near the Sword of the Magi. If he released it from the case, what could any of us do to argue against Rasmus?

I reached to my belt to unsheathe my sword, but upon feeling the empty place where it was always encased, I stopped. No man had been permitted to enter the keep with his weapons. To proceed, we'd had to shed them at the door.

My fists were all I had, and I would use them just as I already had in making my way inside the great hall. I started toward the pedestal holding the sword.

"Arrest the woman."

At Rasmus's command, I stumbled to a halt.

He motioned to the Knights of Brethren still circling Lis. "Arrest her and use whatever means necessary to extract the truth of her connection to Sir Ansgar."

My blood ran cold. Rasmus wasn't so evil that he'd

torture Lis until she confessed what he wanted her to, was he? I prayed his words were an empty threat meant to frighten us.

Lis lifted her chin and leveled a steady look at Rasmus. "Sir Ansgar is a noble and good man. That is the only truth you will ever extract from me."

"Sir Ansgar has ingratiated himself to the king from the moment he entered this court." Rasmus spoke the words as if he truly believed they were true. "He has not stopped seeking the king's favor. And he will not stop until the king has declared him the next heir."

"You are the one who will not stop until you have control over the kingdom." From the corner of my vision, I could see Gotfred drawing closer to the pedestal table.

I had to find a way to keep Lis safe. But how could I do so while Gotfred went after the sword? Surely, Rasmus had intentionally placed me in this dilemma. I could save Lis or save the kingdom. Had he already seen the depths of my feelings for her and guessed which one I would choose?

From the glimmer in Rasmus's eyes, I suspected he was waiting for me to charge toward the Knights of Brethren to engage them in battle, giving Gotfred the excuse he needed to reach for the sword, doing so in a moment when he could claim he was defending the king from those who threatened him.

This was exactly the situation I'd expected Rasmus was waiting for. But he couldn't have known I'd come, not when he thought I was dead. Had he been waiting instead for Torvald or one of my other friends to come back and protest?

I glanced between Gotfred and Lis.

"Arrest her," Rasmus said again, his order ringing

against the walls and into the vaulted ceiling, giving the knights no other option but to obey.

They withdrew their swords and inched closer to Lis, all the while watching me carefully.

My muscles tightened. I'd failed my father. I'd failed the king. But I couldn't—wouldn't—fail Lis.

She had her eyes upon Gotfred. "Stop him, Ansgar."

I knew what she was saying. Regardless of what would happen to her, she wanted me to prevent Gotfred from withdrawing the sword from the case and to save the king and the kingdom from further ruination.

If I didn't start the skirmish Rasmus was looking for, then Gotfred would have no reason to pull the sword free. But if I attempted to fight the Brethren, then I would all but hand Gotfred the Sword of the Magi and the kingdom of Norvegia.

"Do what is best for the king and the kingdom." She spoke again with authority, reminding me that she was indeed worthy of being the next queen and that my destiny was entwined with hers. I'd been given the task of protecting her above everything else. *She* was best for the king and the kingdom, and I would fight for her no matter what happened.

Without further hesitation, I charged toward the nearest knight. My first need was in securing a weapon. I rammed my shoulder into his gut, sending him backward. In the same moment, I slammed his arm and wrist against my knee with enough force to break a bone. With a cry, he released his sword.

I caught up the weapon before it hit the floor and swung it toward one of the other knights lunging for me. I drew the blade through the unprotected area of his legs, slicing deep enough to debilitate him but not cause permanent damage. I didn't want to bring harm to these men who were Rasmus's pawns, obeying him out of fear and not respect.

"Make haste and alert the rest of the knights," Rasmus called above the commotion. "They must defend the king from these imposters."

Grabbing a second sword, I fought the remaining two Knights of Brethren and was thankful Lis had the sense of mind to race away while these soldiers were distracted . . . Except, from my periphery, I caught a glimpse of her running toward Gotfred, who had almost reached the pedestal table and the sleek case holding the sword.

His back was toward Lis, and he wasn't paying attention to her. Even so, she didn't have the ability or means to stop him.

"Lis! No!" My warning was cut short as a blade swiped into my arm through my flesh. The sting of the wound brought my full attention back to the fight at hand.

Fresh urgency spurted through me. I needed to quickly eliminate my opponents so I could charge over and engage Gotfred.

At the clank of armor and approach of heavy footsteps, I could see that at least a dozen more knights, outfitted with heavy plate armor and carrying all manner of weapons, were entering the side door of the great hall. Rasmus had obviously been keeping men-at-arms in the wings in preparation for something like this.

I pulled in a steadying breath. I couldn't lose my composure. I had to attack the new forces with a calculated approach, the same way I'd always handled my opponents in battle. But even as I readied myself and took careful aim at first one man and then the next, the edge of panic pricked me.

I needed to protect Lis from Gotfred. How could I do so if I was fending off a dozen knights bent on killing me?

With Lis in such danger, I couldn't keep my focus as concentrated as it needed to be. One of the knights slashed at my backside at the same time another nearly missed my face.

Lis had reached Gotfred and was attempting to wrest him away from the Sword of the Magi. Gotfred made a halfhearted effort to dislodge her before finally growing frustrated and throwing her. She stumbled backward into the men in line, who caught and steadied her.

I had to get to her. With a burst of determination, I fought my way through several of the newly arrived knights blocking my path.

"No!" Lis shouted as she propelled herself toward Gotfred again. Gotfred, in the process of reaching for the Sword of the Magi, slit a knife through the flesh of his palm and then wrapped his bloody hand around the sword's handle.

After thousands of men had already tried to free the sacred weapon, I wanted to halt and watch it coming to life—even if Rasmus had given Gotfred the secret for how to command it. But I couldn't take my attention away from the knights intent upon my demise if I had any hope of protecting Lis.

"No!" Lis cried again. She pounded against Gotfred's back as he stood in front of the sword and the case.

He didn't budge, didn't seem to even notice she was there. Instead, he remained rigid, took a deep breath, and then yanked upward.

The sting of a sword pierced through my cloak and into my arm. In the next instant, the hilt of another sword came down upon my hand. The pain reverberated through my arm, up to my shoulder, and rang in my head. I scrambled to keep hold of my weapon, but it clattered to the ground. Before I could lunge for it, one of the knights kicked it out of my reach.

I lashed out with my second sword, all the while inching toward Lis. I didn't want to bring the danger in her direction, but I also wanted to be close enough that I could come to her aid if she needed it.

At her cry of frustration, I glanced her way in time to see Gotfred throwing her off with a force that sent her tumbling to the floor.

At another jab in my arm, I sucked in a breath at the sharpness of the cut, guessing I would need stitching for this injury. In fact, from the gush of warm liquid flowing toward my wrist, I would need to staunch the flow or I'd grow weak.

For several seconds, I parried heavy blows coming at me, thrusting and swiping at my opponents. But as Gotfred tried again to lift the sword from the case, my attention strayed for a second too long. And before I knew what had happened, my second sword slipped from my hand.

Frustration coursed through me at my failures. I was losing this fight because I was too worried and distracted by Lis and what was happening with Gotfred.

At least I could take some comfort that he was having trouble liberating the sword. Whatever tricks or tips Rasmus had given him weren't producing results.

"Forfeit the fight, Rasmus!" I ducked and then spun to avoid a blade. I had to goad Rasmus and provoke him into saying something incriminating.

I swung a punch into one man's nose, sending him reeling, while at the same time I lunged for a sword, trying to confiscate another weapon but failing. "Gotfred can't do your bidding. He's too weak."

Rasmus was openly watching Gotfred's attempts to loosen the Sword of the Magi. Although the Royal Sage's features remained placid, his eyes had narrowed.

My breathing was labored from my exertion. A quick count told me at least eight knights were yet in pursuit, still circling cautiously around me.

"You probably need to give Gotfred clearer instructions," I called to Rasmus. "Go on, tell him what he's doing wrong. Then perhaps he might succeed at doing your bidding."

Gotfred glanced toward Rasmus, as though waiting for the Royal Sage to reveal more.

Rasmus pressed his lips together, likely to keep from saying anything. But something dangerous radiated from his eyes. "The man who brings me Sir Ansgar's head will receive double the bounty."

"I forbid it!" Lis had regained her footing and now strode toward the dais, each step firm and determined. "As the rightful heir, I forbid anyone from following Rasmus's commands from this day forth. If you do so, you will be cast from this kingdom."

Her words resounded throughout the great hall. She ascended the dais and stood at the center, in front of the thrones, peering out over the faces of nobility and commoner alike. She held herself as regally as if she'd been born to stand in that very spot at that very moment.

I had the urge to bend my knee and pay her homage. But I had to stay alert even though the knights surrounding me one by one lowered their weapons.

I used the moment of respite to rip off a piece of my tunic and tie it around the cut on my arm.

"This woman is an imposter." Rasmus lifted his voice, clearly trying to sound authoritative. "I command you to sever her head along with Sir Ansgar's."

The knights glanced at one another but made no move to resume their fighting.

"Do it now, or you and your families will suffer the consequences of treason—"

"Who will you follow?" Lis interrupted Rasmus. "A twisted man full of evil ambition who seeks to control you through manipulation? Or a valiant man who wants nothing but the good of this kingdom?" She waved a hand first at Rasmus and then me.

Rasmus again nodded at Gotfred behind me. At the widening of Lis's eyes and the panic in them, I darted sideways only to narrowly avoid Gotfred's knife slicing into me. He flew toward me again before I had time to catch my balance.

My momentum took me toward the sword display. Before I could halt myself, I hit the table. As it wobbled, I grabbed the edge along with the cedar case to keep the ancient display from falling. My fingers brushed the round pommel encrusted with glittering jewels. The thick, stout blade resting against a crimson velvet cushion was shorter than a regular sword and contained an engraving in an ancient language I couldn't read.

The relic was magnificent, believed to have been given to the Christ child by the three wisemen. While I didn't know if the tales of its power were true, I respected the traditions and tales of Norvegia enough that I didn't want to see this special item desecrated.

As the case began to slip from my blood-slickened fingers, I took hold of the pommel more firmly.

"Ansgar, watch your back!" Lis's warning rang out.

I spun to find Gotfred lunging toward me, his knife poised as if he had intended to thrust it into my neck.

I rapidly sidestepped. As I did so, gasps and cries rose around the room. The sounds were so alarming, I couldn't keep from scanning my surroundings. Was there a new threat? And if so, what?

To my utter surprise, the knights I'd just been fighting lowered themselves to their knees, placing their swords on the floor in a sign of surrender. The noblemen at the closest tables also knelt and bowed their heads . . .

Toward me.

Gotfred had frozen and was gaping at my outstretched arm.

Confused, I glanced down. I was holding the Sword of the Magi in my bloody hand.

I took a step back, as if that could somehow distance me from the relic. But the warmth of the pommel radiated through my hand and up into my arm.

What had I done? I hadn't meant to take it out of the case.

With my heartbeat pulsing hard, I spun and placed the sword as reverently as I could in its resting place. Where it belonged.

Chapter 21

Lis

I stared at Ansgar along with every other person in the room. Amazement coursed through me.

Ansgar had pulled the sword free from its case. In fact, he'd done it so effortlessly, he hadn't realized he'd accomplished the feat.

As he set it back into the container, his hand shook. When he spun around to the sea of people now kneeling and bowing their heads, his eyes widened and filled with what I could only describe as panic.

"I have no wish to become this land's next king." His commanding voice rang out. "I only desire to serve the true and rightful king, His Royal Majesty King Ulrik, and see him restored to his former glory."

Rasmus made his way past me and descended the stairs of the dais. "Gotfred loosened it. Ansgar wouldn't have freed it if not for Gotfred's previous attempts."

Several noblemen rose to their feet. One of them, a tall man with graying hair, spoke first. "We all witnessed Sir Gotfred undertake the feat to no avail."

Rasmus passed the nobleman without a word and continued toward the cedar box. "Gotfred shall be given a fair chance to prove he is the one the sword chose."

Gotfred hadn't moved since Ansgar had freed the sword. Now, Rasmus clutched a fist of the young man's sleeve and dragged him toward the pedestal table. Before anyone could protest, Rasmus forced Gotfred's hand upon the sword, whispered something to him, then stood back.

Gotfred drew in a deep breath, clutched the handle, and pulled.

From where I stood upon the dais, I had a clear view of the knight's face. His muscles tightened with his exertion until the veins in his temple protruded. After a long moment of struggle, he expelled a breath, let his shoulders slump, and dropped his hands from the sword.

It remained in the case, unyielding.

"Try again!" Rasmus grabbed Gotfred's hand, unsheathed a dagger at his belt, and sliced the young knight's flesh next to the cut already there.

Did Rasmus believe the shedding of blood would free the sword?

With blood now dripping from Gotfred's hand onto the tile floor, Rasmus pushed the knight closer to the table. "Do not stop until you free it."

Murmurs of protest arose within the great hall as more people began to stand to their feet. They had acknowledged Ansgar as the worthiest man to be king, just as the sword dictated. And now they were dissatisfied with Rasmus's attempt to overturn the miracle.

For it truly was a miracle. After weeks of failure by everyone who had taken up the challenge, the sword had finally determined who was worthiest to wield it.

Indeed, Ansgar was the worthiest man in the kingdom. Even now, he shook his head and took another step away from the sword, his humility and honesty preventing him from accepting the honor.

I tossed aside my reverie. I couldn't stand gawking. I needed to act decisively to make sure Ansgar accepted his destiny.

Gotfred grunted and strained, throwing his whole body into the efforts to remove the sword.

"Cease your futile endeavor," I called. "Everyone here has witnessed the truth, that Sir Ansgar is the only one who can free the sword."

Rasmus focused on Gotfred, ignoring everyone along with the complaints increasing by the moment.

I lifted my voice above the clamoring. "Now that Gotfred has had a second chance, we shall give Sir Ansgar another opportunity."

My suggestion was met with a chorus of cheers and agreement.

Gotfred sucked in a final breath, heaved against the sword, but then let go of it and stumbled backward, knocking into Rasmus.

"We want Sir Ansgar!" someone shouted.

A chant rapidly filled the air. "Sir Ansgar! Sir Ansgar!"

Ansgar remained several steps away from the pedestal table, his shoulders stiff, his expression severe.

If Rasmus was disturbed by the change in events, he'd composed himself and now stood as unruffled and undisturbed as though he hadn't just shown everyone his subversive efforts to help Gotfred.

Whether or not Ansgar wanted to become king, he needed to liberate the sword again. He had no choice. If he didn't, we would never have the evidence to convict Rasmus of wrongdoing.

Through the escalating chanting and hysteria in the great hall, my gaze connected with Ansgar's. The gravity in his eyes told me he'd come to the same conclusion.

He bowed his head in deference to me and then raised his arm in an effort to bring about silence.

Within seconds, a hush fell over the room, now crowded along the edges and in the back with men shoving their way inside, hoping to glimpse the miracle again.

When silence had completely descended, Ansgar spoke, his voice carrying throughout the hall. "I humbly ask that the sword be cleaned and that several other men test its security within the case before I touch it."

Ansgar had obviously recognized that blood had something to do with the miracle the same way I had. His own blood from a wound on his arm still coated his hand. While several noblemen came forward to fulfill his request, he rubbed his hands on his tunic, wiping away every trace of the blood, both his own and Gotfred's.

The great hall remained quiet as the tall, graying nobleman finished cleaning the sword, then bid several companions from his table to step forward and attempt to free the weapon. With great solemnity, each of the men took a turn, tugging heartily.

When the last stepped away red faced from his exertion, I spoke before anyone else could. "So that no one may ever question the sword's choosing, I beseech making the removal even harder. We shall blindfold Sir Ansgar and require him to use only one hand. The arm weak from injury and loss of blood."

My request was met with a low murmuring. But Ansgar bowed toward me in acceptance of the additional challenge.

A servant darted forward with a scarf, handing it to the tall nobleman who then tied it around Ansgar's face, covering his eyes. Once the blindfold was in place and Ansgar's strong arm was secured behind his back, the nobleman guided Ansgar to the table and the case.

The room fell silent again.

My heartbeat was already tapping hard and now thudded with more force. Could Ansgar do it again? Was he truly the one God had marked for kingship? If so, then I could leave Vordinberg and return to my place on the farm with my father, away from the curse. I'd live out the rest of my days—however many that might be—in peace, knowing I'd done my part but was no longer needed.

Ansgar lifted his hand so it hovered above the sword.

I held my breath and guessed every other person in the room was doing the same.

He hesitated, then lowered his fingers, grazing the pommel.

I could only imagine the thoughts going through his head, especially the resistance to the prospect of becoming the next king. If only everyone in this room could know his integrity the way I did, they would surely have no doubt he would make a good king even if he didn't free the sword again.

Blowing out a breath, Ansgar let his fingers settle around the grip.

Immediately, without even the slightest tug, the sword came free. Ansgar held it in place against the cushion, but it was too late. Those around him like me had witnessed the movement, and exclamations rose into the air.

With a bow of his head, Ansgar remained unmoving for several heartbeats. Then, as though resigning himself to the fate that had befallen him, he picked up the sword as easily as any other weapon he'd ever held.

At the sight of the Sword of the Magi once again in Ansgar's hand, the crowd erupted into bedlam with shouting and cheers of, "Long live King Ansgar."

Swiping off his blindfold, Ansgar shook his head. "No!"

The cries only grew louder.

Ansgar strode to the nearest table. With one lithe move, he hopped up, straightened, and held up a hand.

At the sight of him, feet spread with an aura of authority, his body radiating strength, my pulse ached with longing for this man who had become a part of me. I was so proud of him, and my love for him nearly overwhelmed me. But in the same instant, pain sliced through me. I couldn't hold on to him.

As hard as it would be, I needed to allow him to have a prosperous future without me. He deserved to have a queen by his side who was healthy and who could give him a lifetime of happiness. Not one fated to die of a curse.

The room began to quiet, and when Ansgar had everyone's attention, he pointed to King Ulrik. The king was still slumped in his chair, his head tilted to one side, his eyes closed in slumber. The queen had moved to his side and was holding his hand. Perhaps she'd tried to awaken him to alert him to all that was happening but had failed.

"There is our king," Ansgar said, his voice ringing with finality, "and we will respect and honor him for as long as he has breath."

"Long live King Ulrik," Rasmus spoke into the quiet. "He is still very much king and has the final say in all decisions, including approving the heir to the throne."

As long as the king languished from the hermit tonic, he would remain under Rasmus's control and wouldn't approve of Ansgar becoming king, no matter how much the people might want it.

The tall, graying nobleman conferred with several men standing beside him then bowed his head toward Sir Ansgar. "We believe the king will be more likely to accept you as the next heir to the throne if you would consider a marriage alliance with Princess Elisbet, since she is part of the Oldenberg bloodline."

I started to shake my head, but one glance from Ansgar halted me. His eyes challenged me the same way mine had him only moments ago. He hadn't wanted to free the sword, but he'd done so because of his willingness to sacrifice himself for the greater good of the kingdom. Could I do the same?

A part of me wanted to take this offer to marry Sir Ansgar. I couldn't imagine anything I'd rather do more than spend the rest of my life with him. The very prospect filled me with such a bittersweet longing that my chest ached with it.

But another part of me shouted the warning of the inevitable heartache I would bring to anyone bound to me. In addition, we had to avoid Ulla's bargain, couldn't risk having a daughter we might end up losing.

As if seeing the protest in my eyes, Ansgar gave a firm nod, as though to convince me that we must move forward with the arrangement regardless of the inhibitions we might have.

"We have no proof this maiden is who she claims." Rasmus returned to the argument from earlier.

"I believe we can assist the Princess Elisbet and Sir Ansgar on both accounts." A man's voice came from a side entrance. A vaguely familiar voice.

I strained to see past the swell of people now filling the great hall. As the crowd parted to make way for the newcomer, I glimpsed the undisguised frustration on Rasmus's face before he had the chance to hide his emotions. With that slight glimpse, I knew who had arrived . . .

Maxim and Elinor.

Chapter 22

Ansgar

I WANTED TO LAY ASIDE THE SWORD OF THE MAGI. THOUGH IT FIT in my hand as though made just for me and was lighter than any sword I'd ever held, the burden of responsibility that came with it was too heavy to bear.

I fingered the jewels in the pommel again. Was I dreaming? Might I awaken to find myself on the farm with Lis and her father, lying in front of the hearth, injured and feverish?

Though I wished I truly were dreaming, the throbbing of my wounds kept me grounded in reality. I couldn't deny I was in the great hall of the king. And everything I was doing had one purpose: to preserve the royal line, including the king and Lis as the future heir.

The press of bodies all around made the air warm and sour. Every man I'd stood in line with over the past hours now crowded into the great hall, their eager faces revering me, their eyes filled with hope. Nowhere did I see animosity or disappointment that they'd failed where I had succeeded. Rather, they seemed to accept without question that I was the chosen one.

Why couldn't I accept it as easily?

As the crowd parted, four knights in chain mail pushed forward, their strength and boldness evident in each step. At the sight of the familiar faces, my pulse kicked with a burst of fresh energy.

Gunnar, Torvald, Kristoffer, and Espen strode forward, their weapons drawn and their faces etched with determination.

I jumped from the table and started toward them, intending to warmly greet them. But as they neared, they didn't give me the chance to embrace them. Instead, they dropped to one knee, bowing their heads and holding out their swords in a symbol of complete subservience and servitude, the kind of homage paid to a great man.

I wasn't that man. Surely they knew it. They need only look at the king's wasted body in his place at the head table to recognize I'd failed to do my duty.

Nonetheless, at the moment I had to ignore my own insecurities and accept their display of support. We would have time later to sort out the truth of the future.

As I laid a hand of blessing over each of their outstretched swords, as was the custom, I caught sight of Maxim and Princess Elinor standing a dozen paces back, a burly guard with a gray beard beside them. They patiently allowed me to perform this ritual with my knights, all the while studying the Sword of the Magi in my hand with keen interest.

With dark shoulder-length hair and blue eyes, Maxim had a brooding, scholarly aura. While he was well built and muscular, he'd proven his weapon of choice was his mind, not his fists. I hadn't known him long because his homecoming weeks ago had been cut short by Rasmus's scheming, but I knew enough to realize I wanted him as a friend and not a foe.

Beside him stood Princess Elinor. For as swarthy and dark as Maxim was, she was the opposite, fair in every aspect from her pale skin to her golden hair to her bright-green eyes.

I could see the family resemblance to Lis in not only the coloring but also the elegant features, the curve of their chins, the beautiful angle of their eyes, and the gracefulness of their bearings.

She was looking at the king now, her eyes widening and filling with horror. I'd been discouraged by my first glimpse of the king's deterioration after my time away. How much more dismayed must Elinor be to see the man she'd loved like a father?

I'd not only let down the king, but I'd also failed his family. I didn't deserve any of these accolades, none of this respect. But again, what could I do but continue pressing onward with whatever strategy I could find to defeat Rasmus once and for all?

My companions rose to their feet and positioned themselves on either side of me. The fierceness in their stance would hold off anyone who might try to come after me, at least for now.

Lis stepped down from the dais and crossed to stand beside me too. Although my knights hadn't been present to hear her declaration of being the king's next heir, they bowed their heads toward her, obviously having learned from Maxim and Elinor of Elisbet's rightful claim to the throne.

With Elinor's hand tucked into the crook of Maxim's arm, the two crossed the distance toward us. Before I could stop her, Elinor lowered herself to her knees before us. "I pledge my fealty and service to Sir Ansgar and Princess Elisbet as the rightful heirs to the throne of Norvegia."

Maxim knelt beside Elinor. "I pledge my fealty and my service to Sir Ansgar and Princess Elisbet as the rightful heirs to the throne of Norvegia." His voice rang out, decisive and dignified.

I wanted to yank both of them up, kneel before them, and pledge them my life. But with each passing moment, the affairs were growing more complicated.

"All of this pledging of service and fealty is very touching." Rasmus stood off to the side, and his tone hinted at derision. "If only it meant something."

Maxim rose and offered a hand to Elinor, assisting her to her feet. Once standing, he laced his fingers through hers. She peered up at him, love glowing from her eyes. He met her gaze only briefly, but it was enough to see that his passion and love for Elinor ran deeply.

For a second, I felt a stab of envy. Amidst all their troubles, somehow Maxim and Elinor had defied convention so they could be together. If only I could do the same with Lis. If only we had the freedom to do whatever we wished. But we were both bound to fulfill the destiny set before us, whatever it might entail.

Rasmus took several steps closer, his presence always intimidating, especially when his eyes narrowed in calculation. "This maiden, Elisbet, has no proof she is the princess, and without sufficient evidence, she cannot be named an heir."

Maxim met Rasmus's gaze with a calculated look of his own. "From the moment I met Lis weeks ago, I knew within seconds her true identity. I testify to the people this day that she is the lost daughter of Princess Blanche.

If you cannot recognize and piece together the clues of her past to come to the same conclusion, then you are no longer worthy of being a Royal Sage."

I wanted to reach out and gratefully clap Maxim across the back for his skillful ability to wield his words. He had sharpened his wit the way a knight sharpened his sword.

"Maxim is correct." Lis lifted her chin in her usual way, regal and authoritative, a trait she'd inherited, certainly not one she'd learned. "But even without Maxim's confirmation, I have proof enough with my bangle."

"Bangle?" Elinor broke away from Maxim. "What bangle?"

Lis tugged up her sleeve as she'd done earlier. "'Tis a bangle given to me by the healer woman Ulla, one that Princess Blanche paid in an effort to find healing."

I could see the questions in Elinor's eyes, questions about her mother that she'd likely asked her whole life and never had answered. Now wasn't the time or the place for such a discussion, but I prayed the sisters would have many days in the future to regain all they'd lost.

As Lis tugged her sleeve higher over the band studded with jewels, Elinor gasped and reached out for Maxim's arm as though to steady herself.

"I see you recognize the bangle." Lis had stilled and was watching Elinor intently.

"She recognizes it," Maxim interjected as he tugged up Elinor's sleeve, "because she has the other half to it."

The bangle at Elinor's wrist had been given to her the night of her coming-of-age ball by Queen Inge. But as Maxim pushed the sleeve up, another bangle circled Elinor's arm, this one above her elbow. He helped her to remove it and then lifted it for all to see. "This bangle belonged to Princess Blanche, and the one Princess Elisbet has is a matching piece that fits with it."

Lis slid off the bangle Ulla had given her. Once it was free, she held it out to Maxim. He took it and fused it with Elinor's, forming a larger and more beautiful set. "If this isn't proof enough of Princess Elisbet's heritage, then I ask everyone in the room to gaze upon the portrait of Princess Blanche that has graced the wall of Princess Elinor's chamber for almost all of her eighteen years."

Two servants came forward carrying a large, framed picture draped in a velvet cloth. As they reached the front of the great hall, they positioned the portrait between them, and Maxim tugged the cloth away. An image of the former princess greeted them. And Maxim was correct. The likeness between Lis and Blanche was undeniable, especially the reddish-gold coloring of their hair. From the nods and murmurs of agreement, everyone else present was coming to the same conclusion.

"Princess Elisbet is the rightful heir to the throne of Norvegia." Maxim's confident voice carried across the room.

"If she is the heir," Rasmus cut in, "that still doesn't solve the problem that the king must not only accept and approve her as such, but he must also approve Sir Ansgar becoming the next king beside her."

Maxim's gaze flitted between Lis and me. What did his keen eyes notice? Could he see that I loved her and would marry her without hesitation . . . if Lis would have me? But when the lords had suggested the union, Lis had hesitated. I'd witnessed the wariness in her eyes, and the truth . . . She didn't want to wed me.

I cleared my throat. "Some of the members of the Noble Council have suggested that Princess Elisbet and I marry since the law has already been changed to allow royalty to marry a commoner—"

"With the king's approval," Rasmus said. "The king must approve, and he will never agree to Sir Ansgar, not after his questionable loyalty and his dismissal from the Knights of Brethren."

Maxim studied me but a moment longer before he shifted to face Rasmus. Both of them maintained a calmness I didn't understand—one that was unnerving, even intimidating.

"Word reached me that the king is ailing." Even though Maxim didn't say so, I knew he was referencing my message to him. He'd received it, and he'd returned to Vordinberg with all haste because of it.

"You have heard right. The king is ailing." Rasmus cast his sights upon the king, his brows slanting as though he was concerned.

I wanted to reach out, grab the Royal Sage, and force him to admit that somehow, someway, he'd been secretly administering the hermit tonic to the king. But a show of force wouldn't accomplish what a show of wits could. For that, I needed Maxim.

Maxim followed Rasmus's gaze to the king. "I have no doubt you have tried everything within your great wealth of knowledge to find a cure for his ailment." The statement was quiet, one that baited Rasmus.

Rasmus didn't respond at once, as though he sensed the battle he was fighting with Maxim and needed to plan his next move carefully. "I have done little else but seek a remedy for his Royal Majesty. Alas, I have exhausted every solution."

Maxim waited several moments as though purposefully allowing a thread of tension to pull tighter.

"Since you have exhausted your solutions, I have no doubt you will gladly give me the opportunity to test my solution."

"I would if there were any solutions left." Rasmus's tone remained unruffled. "But we Royal Sages have labored tirelessly for weeks. We dare not take a chance on the solution of a mere Sagacite."

Maxim had trained and been educated for the past ten years as a Sagacite. From everything I'd learned, he'd been planning to enter the Studium Generale in Vordinberg to become an Erudite and further his training as a wiseman with the hope of ascending to the rank of a Sage. His plans had come to naught when he'd been accused, like me, of plotting against the king and had to run for his life.

Nevertheless, even as a Sagacite, Maxim's intelligence was renowned. He'd proven himself when he opened the case containing the Sword of the Magi. Even more, he'd proven his loyalty, trustworthiness, and honor to me when he broke away from Rasmus's control and saved the king in battle.

That was all I needed to trust him again. "I propose we allow Maxim an opportunity to test his solution on the king. If we do so, we may yet have a chance to save his Royal Majesty. If we do naught, he will surely die."

From the nods around me, I surmised I could say anything and win support. With the Sword of the Magi in my hand, who would dare oppose me? Who would want to? For the first time, I understood the depth of the power and glory I had obtained by freeing the sword. I was unstoppable. I could do anything.

Maxim watched me, almost as though he could read my thoughts. He clearly knew of my power, that my word would hold great sway. The question was, would I treasure this power that had been given to me and use it for the greater good of others, or would I use it to further my own ambitions?

I was only human. And if I became king someday, I would face this temptation many times over—the temptation to wield my authority to better myself instead of my country.

"When I was Grand Marshal," I said in answer to Maxim's unasked questions, "I always consulted my fellow Knights of Brethren before making important decisions. Henceforth, I shall do the same. I'll ask my most trusted knights to always speak the truth, even if it's a truth that will sting when it's given."

Maxim nodded, his eyes lighting with his approval of my plan.

"I have only four of my most trusted knights left. They have proven themselves to be loyal and true to me. They will advise me, and eventually we will rebuild the Knights of Brethren with other knights just as trustworthy."

I looked at Torvald, letting him know I understood the risk he'd taken in rallying Kristoffer, Gunnar, and Espen to Vordinberg to aid me. I guessed they'd single-handedly helped to usher Maxim and Elinor into the great hall, casting aside opposition and keeping them safe.

"What think you?" I asked the four. "Shall we allow Maxim the opportunity to try his solution on the king?"

"I believe it is a very sound proposition." Kristoffer was the first to speak, his intelligent eyes assuring me I was doing the right thing.

Torvald nodded, his expression serious. "You speak wisely, Your Highness."

I wanted to oppose the title given to royalty, to a

prince, but how could I, especially at this moment?

Gunnar bowed his head. "I think Maxim should do so as soon as possible."

"I agree," Espen said loudly and forcefully.

I could feel Lis watching the entire interaction, having stepped back a pace. Even if she opposed the idea of an arranged marriage between us, I wanted her to have as much say in the kingdom as I did. She was, after all, the true heir.

"In addition to my knights"—I turned to Lis—"I shall also always consult the Princess Elisbet. She is loyal and true to this country and will put the people's needs above her own." She'd come back to the royal city at great risk to herself and had subjected herself to the possibility of the bleeding curse. "What think you, Princess? Should Maxim be given the chance to help the king?"

Lis seemed to be analyzing Rasmus. "I believe that if Rasmus truly loves the king and has his best interest at heart, he will seek out any means possible to save him, including Maxim's solution. Unless, of course, he has ulterior motives, such as keeping the king weak and under his control."

Inwardly, I smiled at Lis's directness. Outwardly, I raised the Sword of the Magi in a show of authority. "Let it be known, everyone is in agreement that the king should be taken out of Rasmus's care. With the suspicion cast against him, I hereby declare that Rasmus shall be removed from the royal residence and not allowed to return."

At the nods of approval from the men on the Noble Council as well as others among the courtiers, I allowed an inner knot to unravel. Rasmus had fallen out of favor, perhaps had never garnered devotion from the people.

How could he, when he sought to rule through fear and intimidation rather than faithfulness and goodness?

Once we found evidence Rasmus had been poisoning the king, I would put him on trial for treason. But for the time being, I would do my best to move forward with caution. Rasmus was still too powerful and too intelligent, and I couldn't accuse him of wrongdoing until I had enough proof.

I bowed my head toward Queen Inge. "Let us move the king to his chambers and begin the process of attempting to revive him."

As my declaration echoed throughout the great hall, the servants hustled forward. I could only pray we weren't too late to save the king.

Chapter 23

Lis

I'd gained a sister. Even if nothing else turned out the way I wanted it to, I could be happy in this one outcome.

I stood in the shadows of the king's chamber and allowed Elinor and the queen time alone with the king. I'd wanted to leave altogether, but Elinor had asked me to remain.

The queen sat on the edge of the bed, holding her husband's hand, and Elinor perched on a chair drawn close.

The king reached up and stroked Elinor's cheek. "You know I did not mean anything I might have said. You have remained faithful, and I was wrong to disinherit you."

Elinor bent down and pressed a kiss against the king's sunken cheek. "I was always hesitant about taking my place as Norvegia's ruler, and now I know why. Because Elisbet is the one who should reign someday, not me."

Maxim had spent the past twenty-four hours at the king's bedside, giving him sips of a special medicinal remedy he and Elinor had concocted before leaving St. Olaf's Abbey. They'd been staying at the remote northern abbey since fleeing from the battle against King Canute of Swaine. After receiving Ansgar's urgent message regarding the king's deterioration, Maxim and Elinor had utilized the help of all the brothers at the abbey in locating a solution to combat the hermit tonic. They'd scoured every ancient text held in the abbey's library until finally they'd located a formula.

Elinor and Maxim had left St. Olaf's the next day, but the journey had been arduous, since the northern lands were blanketed in heavy layers of fresh snow. With the aid of a sleigh drawn by reindeer, they made it to the coast. Even though the sea was tumultuous, they located a captain willing to sail them part of the way to Vordinberg.

As they traversed the last of the distance overland, apparently spies sent word to Rasmus about their approach. Upon their nearing the capital, Sigfrid went out to arrest them. Thankfully, Red found Elinor. He recognized her as my sister and came to her rescue, surprising Sigfrid and his men. Red injured and scattered the knights so they weren't able to capture Maxim and Elinor. Upon returning to the castle, Sigfrid had been promptly arrested and put in the dungeons along with the other Knights of Brethren who had conspired with Rasmus.

Maxim had explained that Rasmus had indeed learned the secret of the sword through reading the ancient cuneiform scripts that spoke of the original wisemen who'd brought the sword to the Christ child as a gift. The legends all attested to the sword being set free with the shedding of blood.

Maxim had assumed, like Rasmus, that the bloodshed was a literal spilling of blood by the person handling the sword, that the components in the blood would mingle with the magnetic field holding the sword in place and set it free.

But after learning of Gotfred's failure and Ansgar's easy success, Maxim had concluded that while the shedding of blood had been necessary, so had the need for sacrifice. Ansgar had spilled his blood in sacrifice, and that's what made the difference.

And now, Maxim and Elinor's medicine had accomplished wonders. The king seemed to be returning to his right mind more with every passing hour. He was still tired and weak, but he was better. I need not worry about whether I was the future ruler. He would rise up and reign again for many long days. Besides, he'd most certainly ask Elinor to be his heir. He was even now working at persuading her.

"Maxim has more than proven his loyalty to me," the king said in a raspy voice. "You are both worthy of being my heirs."

"But no one can deny that the sword has chosen Sir Ansgar to be the next king."

"He has proven himself too. But you are the daughter of my heart, and I would give you the crown if you would but ask."

"Thank you, Your Majesty." Elinor bowed her head. "You have been good to me these many years just like a father."

The sight of the queen and king with Elinor pricked my heart. I wasn't jealous of what they had, for I'd grown up in a loving family too. It simply reminded me of how inadequate I was, that I hadn't been raised for this kind of life.

"The truth is," Elinor continued, "I have aspirations to become a wisewoman and join Maxim as a Sage one day. After these past weeks of studying with him, I am convinced that is where my gifts lie. But Elisbet, she is a natural leader and will do well with Sir Ansgar."

Elinor believed I was a natural leader? Thought I would do better?

We'd spent many hours together over the past night while waiting for Maxim to finish administering the medicine to the king. I'd been glad for the time to get to know her better, to share our stories about our separate childhoods and what life had been like for each of us.

She'd wanted to hear all about my discoveries of our mother, the ailment that had led her to run away, my visit to Ulla, and the curse that now plagued me. How could Elinor tell the king I would do well with Ansgar when she knew the truth about my curse and the possibility that I would start bleeding to death someday just as our mother had?

Elinor squeezed the king's hand as though to assure him of her sincerity. "Everyone has given their approval of Princess Elisbet marrying Sir Ansgar. They need only your consent."

"Your Royal Highness." I stepped out of the shadows of the room. "I must object."

The queen, king, and Elinor shifted their gazes toward me. I moved into the glow of candlelight. Attired in one of Elinor's lovely gowns, I couldn't walk as quickly as I was accustomed to. The tightness of the bodice, the low belt, the long train—all constricted me. As the servants had assisted with my grooming, Elinor had assured me I would grow accustomed to the style. But at the moment, I only felt all the more awkward.

Elinor rose and glided toward me with outstretched hands and a lovely smile. "You cannot object to your birthright."

"I must." I'd already been presented to the king a short while ago, and now I bowed again. "I'm sorry, Your Majesty. But surely you know I have the curse of the firstborn daughter, the same as Princess Blanche."

"Yes," the king replied weakly. "Maxim informed me of all that happened to my sister and her child."

"Then you will understand I am not suited to inherit the throne."

"Maxim said we cannot know for certain if my sister's disease has been passed to you."

"But if it has, then I will surely die at a young age."

"Maxim will find a way to save you."

I paused, unwilling to contradict the king any further. Instead, I bowed my head to show my deference.

Elinor squeezed my hands before releasing them. "If anyone can locate a remedy, Maxim has the capability. But in the meantime, we cannot borrow trouble from tomorrow. Instead, we must live for today."

I sensed this was another quote she was reciting. Between Maxim and Elinor, I suspected they could fill a hundred volumes with the sayings they'd memorized.

The king held out a wobbly hand toward me. "Come here, my dear child."

I tried to glide the way Elinor had, praying I wouldn't trip. When I reached the king's side, I took his outstretched hand, bent, and placed a kiss upon it.

As I straightened, he studied my face, his eyes clouding with tears. "God has spared me so I might look upon you and see my sister again. After so many years, you are a gift."

"Thank you, Your Majesty." Somehow his words comforted me in my insecurity.

"If Elinor wishes for you to inherit the throne, then you must do it." Though his voice remained weak, something in his tone echoed with the authority of the strong and decisive king he'd once been. He was giving me little choice in this matter. How could I protest, though everything within me insisted I do so?

"I do wish it," Elinor said, now standing beside me.

The king expelled a tired breath, his face still ashen and tight.

The queen smoothed a hand over his forehead. "You should rest now, my love."

He gave her a small, sad smile. "I shall have time to rest for all eternity. Before I go, I must ensure the kingdom does not fall into evil hands again."

"You are not going anywhere yet, Your Majesty." Elinor spoke quickly. "You will get better erelong."

"Call Sir Ansgar, the priest, and witnesses anon." The king closed his eyes. "I would see Elisbet and Sir Ansgar wed before the day is spent."

"So soon?" My protest spilled out before I could contain it.

The king's eyes opened and fixed upon me. "Maxim has assured me there is a heart match between you and Sir Ansgar. He is not wrong, is he?"

How had Maxim learned of my feelings for Ansgar? Had Ansgar spoken to Maxim? I didn't understand how that was possible, since Ansgar had been busy making sure Rasmus was escorted out of the royal residence as well as having meetings with his knights and other important people.

"Maxim said the love between you and Ansgar is strong, but if he is mistaken, I would like to know it now." The king's gaze was lucid and clear, and it demanded honesty.

I swallowed my denial. I did love Ansgar. I loved him more than I'd ever loved anyone. "Maxim is not wrong. But—"

"Then we shall have a wedding here at my bedside as soon as it can be arranged." The king closed his eyes, the matter settled.

I waited, willed his eyes to open again, needing to make my case against the marriage. But the king seemed to have fallen asleep or, at the very least, was resting soundly now that the future of his kingdom was secured.

"Come." Elinor took hold of my hand and guided me toward the door. "We shall go prepare you for the wedding."

I stumbled after her. "How did Maxim know of my love for Ansgar?"

"Maxim has cultivated the ability to read the expressions and body language of people. However, even I, without such an ability, could see the attraction you and Ansgar share."

I should have known it would be evident to everyone. "I cannot marry him, Elinor. How can I, when I love him too much to lose him?" As soon as the question was out, I realized that mingled with my fear of hurting Ansgar, I was also afraid of getting hurt myself.

She tugged me into a smaller sitting room before pausing to look at me. I was amazed that this beautiful, kindhearted, and intelligent woman was my sister. Her eyes regarded me without pity, only understanding. "I have just been reunited with the sister I have always longed for. Should I withhold my love because I fear losing you once more? Or should I love you with all my being for the time Providence gives us?"

I wanted her to love me and for us both to cherish the days we would have together before Providence brought the time to an end. I didn't want to squander a single day.

As if reading the answer in my eyes, she nodded. "That is what I plan to do. To love you with every ounce that is within me for as long as God wills it."

A lump formed in my throat. I didn't deserve this woman's kindness or love. But I would do what I could to be worthy of it. I also understood I would love her likewise, for as long as God willed it.

But could I do the same with Ansgar?

Elinor smiled and tugged me again. "'Tis a good thing the king is demanding this wedding or else the two of you might persist in your self-sacrificing to your own detriment."

I followed her, but my heart tapped a strange rhythm of trepidation. Could I really go through with marrying Ansgar?

Chapter 24

Ansgar

I KNELT BESIDE THE KING'S BED, MY HEAD BOWED, MY PRAYERS FOR him rising to heaven. The room was quiet with only the soft, even rhythm of his breathing. My closest knights waited for me near the door, as did members of the Noble Council. The queen sat in a chair on the opposite side of the bed. And servants hovered on the perimeter of the chamber, ready to do either my bidding or the king's.

His breathing abruptly changed, and he shifted in wakefulness. "Sir Ansgar?"

I lifted my head to find his eyes open and upon me. "Your Majesty."

"It is good to see you." His greeting was hardly above a whisper.

The despair in my chest tightened, as it had since I'd arrived in his chamber to answer his summons only to find him in so weak a state. He was worse than I'd believed possible. Not even the covers could conceal his emaciated condition. "'Tis I who am heartily glad to see you, Your Majesty."

"You saved me, Ansgar." For the first time in weeks, his eyes were clear and free from the haze that had been confusing him. "Thank you."

"If only I had been able to do so sooner."

"I'm told you did everything within your power to come to my aid."

"I should have found a way to protect you."

"You could have if I had not so blindly trusted Rasmus."

Over the preceding hours, I'd learned Rasmus had fooled the king into drinking the hermit tonic, believing it would heal him of his battle wounds quicker. Although we still didn't have proof, I'd appointed servants to scour the castle until they uncovered evidence.

"I own freely," the king spoke haltingly, "I took what I thought would be the easy and selfish way of finding relief instead of doing the hard work necessary to heal."

I suspected there was a part of each of us that longed for the easy way. I wanted to keep on protesting that I wasn't willing to become the next king. But was it possible I was simply looking for an easier path for my life?

"I could not think of a better man than you, Ansgar, to pull the sword free. You are worthy, and I am sorry I ever doubted it."

"I am far from perfect, Your Majesty."

"As you can see, I am far from perfect too. But the kingship does not require perfection. Rather it requires that we step upon our mistakes, allowing them to take us higher and make us stronger."

The king's words settled over me. For so long, I'd been avoiding standing upon the mistake I'd made with my father. I'd allowed it to define me and fill me with insecurity and unworthiness. Was it time to finally step upon it, learn from what happened and allow it to make me stronger instead of weaker?

The king was silent, as if giving me the time I needed to make peace with my mistakes. I bowed my head and prayed I could.

After a moment, he shifted and spoke again. "I have summoned you here to my chamber to wed Princess Elisbet."

"What?" My head jerked up to find that once again his eyes were clear and lucid.

"I have given my approval of the marriage, and I would see it done today, here, now, as soon as possible."

"Your Majesty, as much as I care for Princess Elisbet, I will not force her hand in marriage." Every time I'd glimpsed Lis over the past hours, she'd all but gone out of her way to avoid me. If she didn't want to wed me, I could not push forward with it.

"She has agreed to it," the king said, "and will be here soon."

More likely she was coerced into it or felt obligated to go through with it.

As if I'd spoken aloud, the king gripped my hand. "I have never seen you back down from a challenge, Ansgar. If you want her to be yours, then hold nothing back in winning her."

Even as the king spoke, the door to the chamber opened. Princess Elinor poked her head inside the room.

I quickly rose to my feet and bowed to the princess.

She stepped inside and waited for someone else. A second later, Lis entered. My heart tumbled to a halt at the sight of her in a magnificent gown of a rich green that made her eyes large and luminous as she peered into the room. Layer upon layer of velvety swirls decorated the skirt. The bodice was also made of velvet and sculpted her lovely form. Someone had styled her hair so it hung in all its unfettered glory, long and silky, nearly to her waist with matching ribbons woven throughout.

My mouth and throat went dry at the sight of her beauty and splendor. She was a queen. If anyone had a doubt about her royalty, he would surely put it to rest now.

As her gaze landed upon me, she hesitated. Then squaring her shoulders and pressing her lips together, she marched forward, clearly forcing herself to go through with this obligation.

Frustration swelled in my chest. This wasn't how I wanted to start a married life with Lis. The king's words from moments ago echoed in my mind: *"I have never seen you back down from a challenge, Ansgar. If you want her to be yours, then hold nothing back in winning her."*

As she stepped to my side, I wanted to sweep her up into my arms and kiss her until all her hesitations fell away and she agreed to marry me eagerly and willingly. But I couldn't do that here. Not with everyone looking on.

"I propose a challenge," I whispered.

"What kind of challenge?" she whispered back.

"Give me three reasons why we should not be wed. If I cannot answer each of the three to your satisfaction, then I shall do whatever is necessary to release you from your obligation to me." Even if that meant I had to misuse my newly gained power. Though I'd vowed I wouldn't abuse the glory of the sword, I would do it this once to free her . . . if I couldn't convince her otherwise.

She glanced around the large chamber. All eyes—and all ears—were upon us, interest upon every countenance.

With a sigh, she gathered her skirt and hastened to

the door. When she reached it, she stopped and glared at me over her shoulder. "Well, are you coming or not?"

I didn't care if I looked like a puppy on a leash. I jumped to follow her, ignoring the knowing grins of my knights. As I entered the smaller chamber, I prayed I could convince her of my sincerity.

With her back facing me, she spoke. "Question number one: You once told me you did not wish to get married. And I spoke of the same. Why have you changed your mind?"

I crossed and stood behind her. Less than a hand span separated us. I didn't touch her. But I bent in so I could speak words meant for her alone. "Answer number one: I have fallen so deeply in love with you that I cannot climb out, no matter how hard I've tried. I have finally concluded I cannot live or breathe at the prospect of a future without you in it."

She drew in a sharp breath at my declaration and held herself motionless. Her hair had shifted away from her neck just enough that I could see her pulse pounding hard. It beckoned to me. How could I do anything less than answer the call?

I closed the distance so my chest grazed her back. In the same motion, I gently swept aside her hair, giving myself access to her neck. I let my fingers barely graze the spot.

She didn't move, as though determined not to give in to my touch.

I bent in and whispered in her ear, "Next question."

She took in a shaky breath. "Question number two: You gave your word to my father to be my guardian and protector. Will you now break your word to him?"

I brushed more of her hair away, then gave way to my

longing for her. I leaned in and pressed my lips to her neck.

Her gasp this time was louder. And rather than pull away, she reclined against me, angling her head to give me room to kiss her again.

I didn't. Instead, I whispered my answer against her neck. "Answer number two: I will never stop guarding or protecting you. You will always be my first priority, above everyone else. And our marriage will allow me to carry out my vow to your father more thoroughly and completely."

I could feel her weakening against me. I slipped my arms around her waist, drew her even closer, and held her securely, the way I planned to for the rest of my life.

"Question number three," she said softly, the tension dissipating from her tone. "I could very well die within a few years. Knowing my curse, why would you willingly subject yourself to a future of pain and misery?"

At the merest thought of her death, pain and misery crowded into my heart. It was but a foretaste of the heartache to come. "Answer number three: I loathe the thought of losing you in the future and intend to do everything I can to fight for your life. But I also loathe the thought of never having the chance to spend any time with you. I would take whatever time God gives us and cherish it forever."

"And what of the child Ulla requested?"

"We bargained with her once. If we need to, we shall bargain again."

She folded her arms across mine, hugging them closer.

"Did I win the challenge?" I burrowed my face into her hair. "Because if I didn't, then I shall have to convince you some other way."

Chapter 25

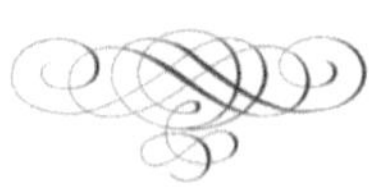

Lis

He was doing it again, just as he always did. Weakening my resolve and making me unable to resist him.

The simple truth was that I didn't want to resist any longer.

"Did I?" His voice was a low rumble that made my insides tumble and twist.

"Did you what?" I knew what he was asking, but I loved teasing him.

"Did I win the challenge?"

"No."

He released and spun me in the same motion until I was facing him. His serious eyes gauged my reaction, tested my answer.

I let myself feast upon him as I hadn't been able to do since leaving Torvald's. I took in his neatly combed hair, still damp from a bath. His tunic and doublet were of rich linen, and an equally elegant surcoat reached to midthigh over his leggings. Even so, his face was scruffy with stubble, lending him a dangerous appeal.

"You must do a little more convincing." I tried to speak in a haughty tone.

His brows rose. "Must I now?"

"Yes, you must."

"What must I do?" His arms snaked around me.

Sweet anticipation stretched my nerves. "I would like to test your worthiness for myself."

"Very well."

"Yes, very well."

"Tell me how I can prove my worthiness." His voice turned husky, and the gold flecks in his brown eyes darkened.

"Like this." I lifted up, wrapped my arms around his neck, and pressed my lips to his. He met me in turn, his ardor and passion everything I remembered and everything I wanted.

At several whistles and calls, I broke from Ansgar, flushing at the sight of his knights watching us from the doorway leading to the king's bedchamber.

Ansgar grinned at them, clearly pleased with himself.

Torvald pushed through the others and bowed. "The king would like the wedding to commence as soon as possible."

Ansgar's smile dropped away, replaced by a solemnity that told me the king wasn't faring well. Although Maxim and Elinor's medicine had brought clarity back to the king's reasoning, the damage done to his body might be irreparable. I prayed it was not so. I'd even sent out an order that everyone in the kingdom should offer a prayer for the king this day.

Ansgar reached for my hand and laced his fingers through mine. "Shall we, then?"

"Before we do, I want you to know one thing."

"And what is that?"

"I love you too."

He lifted my hand and kissed it, his eyes speaking volumes about how much my declaration moved him.

The door from the hallway swung open with such force it slammed against the wall.

In one swift move, Ansgar shoved me behind him and unsheathed the Sword of the Magi. Maxim burst through the door, his black tunic flying, his long, dark hair mussed. He came to an abrupt halt at the sight of Ansgar and the sword.

Maxim bowed his head. "Your Royal Highnesses, I beg your forgiveness for intruding. I was in a hurry to reach you and share the information I have just discovered." For a man who'd learned to hide his every emotion and thought, Maxim's eyes radiated with an uncharacteristic glimmer.

I stepped out from behind Ansgar.

He replaced his sword. "You have done well to heal the king's mind. I pray that now you have invented a means for healing his body."

Maxim gave us one of his rare smiles, one that sent a shiver of anticipation through me. "I've scoured through many scripts on healing methods. And I have learned of an ancient relic, a sacred chalice used by Christ himself." His voice dropped to a whisper, and he stepped closer. "It is believed to bring healing to those most in need, but we must tell no one else of such a possibility lest it fall into the wrong hands."

"Where is this sacred chalice?" Ansgar poised as though he would leave in an instant to ride to the far corners of the earth to retrieve it.

"It is here in Norvegia. The last records we have indicate it was locked away in the cathedral in Karlstad for safekeeping. I cannot say for sure that it is still there. But if not at the cathedral, surely the priests there will have some idea where it was placed next."

Ansgar made to move toward the door, but Torvald stepped into the room farther. "I shall go, Your Highness. You have more important matters at hand this day." He gave a nod toward me.

Ansgar hesitated.

"The king's life is more important," I said, knowing I was giving voice to Ansgar's thoughts along with mine.

"I shall ride with Torvald," Gunnar declared, swaggering into the chamber.

Ansgar stared between the two for several heartbeats before he gave them a curt nod. "Tell no one of your mission. But accomplish it with all haste."

Torvald and Gunnar wasted no time in jogging off. Ansgar watched them disappear before he turned to me and reached for my hand once more. "Let us pray they find the sacred chalice before it's too late."

"I have much to learn about the chalice," Maxim said, "but I pray it may also be the solution to Princess Elisbet's curse."

Ansgar's fingers tightened within mine at the same time a blossom of hope sprang to life inside me. Might I yet find a way out from underneath the curse and have a lifetime to spend with the man I loved?

His eyes brimmed with determination. "We shall find the chalice. In fact, we'll leave no stone in Norvegia unturned until we do."

Maxim nodded. "I shall keep studying the scripts

until I uncover more about the sacred chalice and its secrets. But I wanted to bring you this news today so you would not allow the cloud of Elisbet's curse to steal the joy of your union."

"Thank you, Maxim." Ansgar clasped his free hand on Maxim's arm. "I need you, and this kingdom needs you. I pray you'll stand beside me, both now and for many days to come."

"I would consider it a great honor, Your Highness." Maxim's countenance held only respect.

Even with the news of the sacred chalice to give us hope, I was learning much about letting go of my insecurities and not allowing my feelings to determine how I lived. I would move forth in faith, doing the right thing, sacrificing of myself, and trusting the future into God's hands.

Elinor stepped past Ansgar's knights into the small chamber. At the sight of Maxim, her eyes lit. His gaze shot to her, and he drank her in like a man dying of thirst.

I squelched a smile and prayed Ansgar and I would have a marriage filled with as much love as theirs.

"The king is growing tired," Elinor whispered. "He requests that the wedding take place now."

Hand in hand, Ansgar and I entered the king's chamber and took our place by his bedside where he could witness our union. More important people—nobility, courtiers, and those I still had yet to meet—filed into the room and stood on the fringes to witness the ceremony too. A priest led us through our vows, and within minutes he pronounced us man and wife.

As Ansgar and I knelt together beside the king's bed, we bent our heads. The king placed a hand first on

Ansgar's head and then mine. "I name Ansgar and Elisbet as my heirs to the throne of Norvegia. They will be the future king and queen of this beloved country. What God has entwined, let no man put asunder. Amen."

"Amen," I whispered at the same time as Ansgar.

We each kissed the king's outstretched hand before rising. Then, after facing each other, Ansgar lifted a hand to my cheek, brushed back a strand of hair, and bent down and kissed me with the kind of kiss I knew I would never tire of for as long as we both lived.

Chapter 26

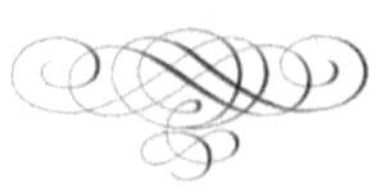

Lis

Two months later . . .

THE MOMENT WE WALKED INTO OUR PRIVATE CHAMBERS, ANSGAR snagged me and pulled me down onto his lap in his usual spot in front of the hearth fire.

"Lest you have forgotten"—I nodded at the cushioned chair beside his—"I do have my own chair."

"You have no need of a chair." He slid a hand up into my hair, twisting and combing his fingers therein until they were lost. "Not when I am here."

The bitter winter wind rattled the shutters, now boarded closed against the snow that blanketed Vordinberg and Norvegia. The darkness of the night had fallen, but the glow of the sconces around the chamber as well as the hearth fire provided enough light for me to see every handsome line of Ansgar's face. And his warm, hungry eyes.

"I don't want you to go away again." He brought his other hand up to my face and gently traced my cheek down to my chin.

I shivered, but not from the cold dampness that permeated the room. Still attired in my heavy fur cloak and hat, I had yet to warm my frozen limbs. Now, with him, I would be warm in no time. "I was gone but five days."

"'Twas five days too long."

It had felt like an eternity to me, but I missed my father. The two months we'd been apart since my leaving the farm with Ansgar had been an adjustment.

"Did you convince him to move to Vordinberg for the rest of the winter?" Ansgar caressed my other cheek, likely red and wind chafed.

"No, he's stubborn and refuses to consider moving." I'd gone to visit him the previous month as well, and he'd insisted on staying at the farm then, just as he had during this visit. "At least he'll have companionship now."

An older guard and his wife had offered to go along and provide Father with not only protection over the winter but friendship. Father had gladly welcomed them, and when I departed, Father had kissed my cheek and thanked me for my thoughtfulness.

"And Red?" Ansgar dropped his voice to a whisper. Though we were alone, the servants always hovered nearby, ready to do our bidding. I'd done my best to keep my communication with the draco to a minimum so that I didn't draw suspicion.

The only reason Ansgar allowed me to travel to the farm without him was because of Red. And because he'd sent along a large contingent of his best knights. He would have come himself but never went far from the king's bedside—especially lately, as the king's condition was worsening.

"Red has found a mate." I'd sensed a gradual shift in

Red's attention, and now I knew why. "I gave him the freedom to go, told him he is no longer bound to me and should live his life with his own family."

Ansgar's hands stilled.

Wind whistled through the chimney and sent sparks flying in the fireplace. I would miss Red, but my days with him had to end. Perhaps he knew that with Ansgar, I no longer needed him the same way. Perhaps my security had given him the freedom he needed to venture out on his own.

"You did the right thing," Ansgar whispered.

"I'll miss him."

His eyes brimmed with compassion. "I have a feeling he'll never stray far from you."

I sighed out my weariness as well as my relief at being home with Ansgar. Even though the castle was becoming more familiar and I was learning the customs and rules of noble life, I never felt truly at home unless I was with Ansgar. He was my home, the place I needed to be.

I allowed myself to rest against him, his solidness, warmth, and strength surrounding me. "The sacred chalice. Any news?"

He shook his head, his features creasing with frustration. "Maxim and Elinor continue to scour ancient scripts but to no avail. And Torvald and Gunnar have still not located it."

The two faithful knights had spent weeks searching each cathedral, church, and abbey in the areas around Karlstad, following one lead to the next. They sent regular messages to Ansgar to keep him apprised of their efforts. But so far, they'd faced an ongoing mystery of its disappearance.

"We must keep praying," I said earnestly, not for

myself but for the king. Already, upon my arriving back at the castle, I'd interrogated the few servants who helped me from the sleigh and learned he fared no better than when I left.

I'd also learned that no one could find a trace of Rasmus either. The day he'd been escorted from the royal castle, he'd disappeared, and no one had seen him since.

A knock sounded on the door. I pushed up, but Ansgar held me in place, pressing a kiss to my lips, one filled with all the longing from our days apart.

The knock came louder.

He broke his kiss to mumble, "Go away," then he claimed my lips again.

I started to wrap my arms around him, my body tingling with warmth, just as I knew it would.

"Your Royal Majesties." The voice from the other side of the door was grave but respectful.

Ansgar froze mid kiss. As the significance of the title of address filtered through my hazy mind, I released Ansgar and stood abruptly. As a princess and prince of the kingdom, we were called *Highness*. *Majesty* was reserved for the supreme rulers—the king and queen.

My heart kicked a protest against my chest. This could only mean one thing: The king had passed on from this life to the next.

As if coming to the same conclusion, Ansgar stood. He met my gaze solemnly, then reached for my hand.

Together we walked to the door. Ansgar opened it. The moment we made our appearance, the messenger, one of the noblemen from the Noble Council, lowered himself to one knee, as did several of his companions behind him. "Your Majesties, Queen Elisbet and King Ansgar. God save the queen. And God save the king."

Though I could feel the sorrow coursing through Ansgar, the same that spread inside of me, I could also feel something much stronger, the thread uniting us for one purpose. All along God had been working to bring us together, weaving together our destinies for this very day, this very moment.

Now, as the queen and king of Norvegia, we would walk together, side by side and hand in hand. Entwined.

Author's Note

Hi dear readers!

I hope you enjoyed getting to journey with Ansgar and Lis as they figured out their destinies! I had so much fun writing their love story and bringing the legend of the ancient sword to life.

So, you might be wondering what's next in this series. Two more of our handsome and brave Knights of Brethren get their own love stories. Can you guess which two?

If you guessed Gunnar and Torvald, then you're right! The two knights have the dangerous mission of finding the sacred chalice to save the queen from her deadly bleeding curse. Along the way, they find women who help make them into better and stronger men.

So that you don't miss out on the release dates for each of the books in this series, please visit my website at jodyhedlund.com or check out my Facebook Reader Room where I chat with readers and post news about my books.

Until next time . . .

Jody Hedlund is the best-selling author of over forty books and is the winner of numerous awards. She writes sweet historical romances with plenty of sizzle. Find out more at jodyhedlund.com.

More Sweet Medieval Romance from Jody Hedlund
Knights of Brethren

Enamored

Having been raised by her childless aunt and uncle, the king and queen, Princess Elinor finds herself the only heir to the throne of Norvegia. As she comes of age, she must choose a husband to rule beside her, but she struggles to make her selection from among a dozen noblemen during a weeklong courtship.

Entwined

After growing up on a remote farm, Lis learns she is the rightful heir to the throne of Norvegia. Even as she does her part to thwart a dangerous plot against the king, she resists pursuing her new identity and resigns herself to a simple life helping her elderly father with their farm.

Ensnared

Nursemaid to the Earl of Likness's two young daughters, Mikaela despises the earl for his cruelty to his subjects, and she longs for the day when she can make a difference in the lives of her suffering friends and family.

Enriched

Lady Karina lives in a convent and expects to become a nun someday. When her wealthy father asks her to help his textile business become more successful by marrying one of the popular Knights of Brethren, Karina complies, ever the dutiful daughter.

Enflamed

When Sylvi Prestegard discovers that her father has arranged for her to marry a wealthy nobleman known for his thieving ways, she's desperate to avoid the union. She turns to her childhood friend Espen, a Knight of Brethren, counting on his loyalty and kindness to help her escape.

Entrusted

Hoping to minimize the death and destruction of the coming war, Princess Birgitta of Swaine leads the Dark Warriors as part of her brother King Canute's efforts to take the throne of Norvegia. As she engages in a skirmish with a band of elite Knights of Brethren, she's kidnapped by Kristoffer Prestegard, a cunning warrior.

The Fairest Maidens

Beholden

Upon the death of her wealthy father, Lady Gabriella is condemned to work in Warwick's gem mine. As she struggles to survive the dangerous conditions, her kindness and beauty shine as brightly as the jewels the slaves excavate. While laboring, Gabriella plots how to avenge her father's death and stop Queen Margery's cruelty.

Beguiled

Princess Pearl flees for her life after her mother, Queen Margery, tries to have her killed during a hunting expedition. Pearl finds refuge on the Isle of Outcasts among criminals and misfits, disguising her face with a veil so no one recognizes her. She lives for the day when she can return to Warwick and rescue her sister, Ruby, from the queen's clutches.

Besotted

Queen Aurora of Mercia has spent her entire life deep in Inglewood Forest, hiding from Warwick's Queen Margery, who seeks her demise. As the time draws near for Aurora to take the throne, she happens upon a handsome woodcutter. Although friendship with outsiders is forbidden and dangerous, she cannot stay away from the charming stranger.

The Lost Princesses

Always: Prequel Novella

On the verge of dying after giving birth to twins, the queen of Mercia pleads with Lady Felicia to save her infant daughters. With the castle overrun by King Ethelwulf's invading army, Lady Felicia vows to do whatever she can to take the newborn princesses and their three-year-old sister to safety, even though it means sacrificing everything she holds dear, possibly her own life.

Evermore

Raised by a noble family, Lady Adelaide has always known she's an orphan. Little does she realize she's one of the lost princesses and the true heir to Mercia's throne . . . until a visitor arrives at her family estate, reveals her birthright as queen, and thrusts her into a quest for the throne whether she's ready or not.

Foremost

Raised in an isolated abbey, Lady Maribel desires nothing more than to become a nun and continue practicing her healing arts. She's carefree and happy with her life . . . until a visitor comes to the abbey and reveals her true identity as one of the lost princesses.

Hereafter

Forced into marriage, Emmeline has one goal—to escape. But Ethelrex takes his marriage vows seriously, including his promise to love and cherish his wife, and he has no intention of letting Emmeline get away. As the battle for the throne rages, will the prince be able to win the battle for Emmeline's heart?

The Noble Knights

The Vow

Young Rosemarie finds herself drawn to Thomas, the son of the nearby baron. But just as her feelings begin to grow, a man carrying the Plague interrupts their hunting party. While in forced isolation, Rosemarie begins to contemplate her future—could it include Thomas? Could he be the perfect man to one day rule beside her and oversee her parents' lands?

An Uncertain Choice

Due to her parents' promise at her birth, Lady Rosemarie has been prepared to become a nun on the day she turns eighteen. Then, shortly before her birthday, a friend of her father's enters the kingdom and proclaims her parents' will left a second choice—if Rosemarie can marry before the eve of her eighteenth year, she will be exempt from the ancient vow.

A Daring Sacrifice

In a reverse twist on the Robin Hood story, a young medieval maiden stands up for the rights of the mistreated, stealing from the rich to give to the poor. All the while, she fights against her cruel uncle who has taken over the land that is rightfully hers.

For Love & Honor

Lady Sabine is harboring a skin blemish, one that if revealed could cause her to be branded as a witch, put her life in danger, and damage her chances of making a good marriage. After all, what nobleman would want to marry a woman so flawed?

A Loyal Heart

When Lady Olivia's castle is besieged, she and her sister are taken captive and held for ransom by her father's enemy, Lord Pitt. Loyalty to family means everything to Olivia. She'll save her sister at any cost and do whatever her father asks—even if that means obeying his order to steal a sacred relic from her captor.

A Worthy Rebel

While fleeing an arranged betrothal to a heartless lord, Lady Isabelle becomes injured and lost. Rescued by a young peasant man, she hides her identity as a noblewoman for fear of reprisal from the peasants who are bitter and angry toward the nobility.

A complete list of my novels can be found at jodyhedlund.com.

Would you like to know when my next book is available? You can sign up for my newsletter, become my friend on Goodreads, like me on Facebook, or follow me on Twitter.

Newsletter: jodyhedlund.com
Goodreads:
goodreads.com/author/show/3358829.Jody_Hedlund
Facebook: facebook.com/AuthorJodyHedlund
Twitter: @JodyHedlund

The more reviews a book has, the more likely other readers are to find it. If you have a minute, please leave a rating or review. I appreciate all reviews, whether positive or negative.

www.ingramcontent.com/pod-product-compliance
Lightning Source LLC
Chambersburg PA
CBHW021305190726
48288CB00003B/707